## SOHO STORIES

# THE HIT TV SITCOM
# *Plus Exclusive* SEX-X-X: THE MOVIE

By Paul Chaplin

Copyright © G2 Entertainment 2022

First edition

Published by G2 Entertainment

All rights reserved. No part of this publication may be reproduced, stored in the retrieval system, or transmitted in any form by any means, electronic, mechanical, photocopying, recording or otherwise, with the prior permission of the publishers.

Every effort has been made to ensure the accuracy of the information within this publication but the publishers cannot be held responsible for any errors or omissions. Views expressed are those of the author and do not necessarily represent those of the publishers.

ISBN: 978-1-78281-389-7

Printed and bound in the UK by G2 Entertainment

| | | |
|---|---|---|
| *PREFACE* | | 6 |
| *PROLOGUE* | | 6 |
| *CHAPTER 1* | OPEN | 8 |
| *CHAPTER 2* | MODEL | 43 |
| *CHAPTER 3* | BOOTH | 71 |
| *CHAPTER 4* | VIGIL | 96 |
| *CHAPTER 5* | PINK | 120 |
| *CHAPTER 6* | SHOW | 143 |
| *CHAPTER 7* | GROTTO | 167 |

*SEX-X-X: THE MOVIE*

| | | |
|---|---|---|
| *PROLOGUE* | | 190 |
| *CHAPTER 1* | BONK KNOCK | 194 |
| *CHAPTER 2* | LOVE CANALS | 212 |
| *CHAPTER 3* | CLOG COPS | 221 |
| *CHAPTER 4* | STILL WATERS | 229 |
| *CHAPTER 5* | THE FANTASTIC LIGHT | 234 |
| *CHAPTER 6* | MASSAGE MESSAGING | 248 |
| *CHAPTER 7* | HIGH HEELED CAVALRY | 257 |
| *CHAPTER 8* | DAM AND BUST | 266 |
| *CHAPTER 9* | SMALL FAVOURS | 277 |
| *CHAPTER 10* | STAIN ON MY NAME | 288 |

## *PREFACE*

Hi readers, viewers and love boutique shoppers. If you're a *Netflix* fan, then you might have seen this sex shop soap opera. Or, this occasionally titillating traverse through these Soho Stories, may be a virginal experience for you.

I gave some account of my personal experiences in the adult industry, in the *Strange Days* biographical Chapter of *"I Want To Love But: Realising the Power of You."* (2019). Well, as much as the remnants of censorship and human decency would allow.

So, the *Soho Stories* of *Sexxx*, were drawn from life. That may not seem believable. But actual life in the adult industry was so truly bizarre, that it makes what you read here, and see on-screen, unreal only in its restrained insanity.

Writing the sitcom scripts was fun. Getting to perform them alongside such a charismatic and talented cast, was a joy. I watched the episodes back, to recapture the feel for this novelisation. They haven't really dated since. Mind you, neither has Ben.

We never got round to making *Sex-x-x: the Movie*. Which is a shame. Surely somewhere in the back cupboard of the Oscars organisation, is a little pink statue. Would have looked nice on the erotic novelties counter.

*PREFACE*

Mr Dover did, for a while, actually own the Soho love boutique, which we filmed in occasionally. The stock was a little less strange. The customers, more so.

I do hope this novelisation helps brings its readers together through the joy of Sex-x-x. In a nice way.

**Paul Chaplin**
2021

# *PROLOGUE*

A little shop, in a Soho backstreet. Decorated slightly less conservatively than an undertakers. But sharing the same red velvet curtains.

Perhaps those thousands of centuries ago, when *homo-sapiens* kind was carving the first hand axe out of stone, there was another similar place. A small cave perhaps.

Not the big cavern, where a Flintstone Michelangelo showed off his blue and red dye masterpieces. Works such as "Mammoth Hunted".[1] "Mammoth v Sabre Tooth Tiger".[2] "Dead Mammoth With Tusks".[3]

Not the one next to it. The palaeolithic *ideal caves exhibition*. With an array of useful stone utensils for doing-things-with.[4]

No, the little one. The one with the entrance where you have to kind of squeeze sideways to get in. The one where, for some instinctive - placed in your libidinous DNA by a higher power - reason, you never ever want to be seen squeezing out of.

Because, you see, it's all very well to go gawking at the sacrificial blood spattered henge rocks. In fact, it's compulsory, especially at certain phases of the moon. If you're really lucky, you get to participate. In one capacity

---

[1] titled "Ugg" in the original under-picture lettering

[2] titled "Ugg" in the original under-picture lettering

[3] titled: well you know. And yes, he was big on Mammoths.

[4] including chopping up Mammoths, yes

*PROLOGUE*

or another.

And it's perfectly socially acceptable to appreciate depictions of man and nature, red[5] in tooth and claw, in the mammoth-orium.

But what is absolutely not to be mentioned, much less openly visited, is *the little cave*.

Where they have pictures. Of women. Wearing not very much in the way of bearskins. Or anything else. With some of them even being kept warm by men. And occasionally other women.

Together with intriguing, and potentially eye-watering, uses of mammoth tusks.

Allow the sun dial to dance forward a few millenia.

To a more civilised (they have much bigger armies with really sharp bronze edged weapons), age. Togas and vine leaves, baking under a Grecian sun.

A new open-ness in social thinking (unless you happen to be at the wrong end of a bronze edged weapon). Philosophers carefully attempting to walk slower than a tortoise. Craftsmen earnestly crafting their craftiwork.[6]

And, under a sun-dappled portico, engaging in by far the favourite Mediterranean activity. An argument.

'Ah yet,' sighs Philomenos the Rhetor,[7] 'I am heavily certain that such is not the correct use of the term'.

---

[5] and blue, yes

[6] Oh *now* you want details. Sorry, too busy narrating

[7] 'or' not 'ard'

Squinting into the sunlight, Benjarstos the Bastor[8] searches for the appropriate philosophical stance in reply. 'Naff orf. It's what it says on the label innit?'

Philemonos carefully rearranges the folds of his toga around his portly frame, and points with an ink stained finger to the sign, rather uncertainly nailed to the Athenian column before him.

'There... well?' he says, with all the characteristic smugness of revealing the self-evident.

'Yer, citizen. I can read. Same as the next man. Or eunuch. So?'

As all civilised persons do, when seeking to explain matters to children, foreigners, or artisans, Philomenos articulates his next words with laboured care, and substantially higher volume.

'*Porno-Graphia*! Your sign!' indulging in another finger point. 'That is what it actually says!'

Drawing on his graduate education from the philosophical school of hard knocks, Benjarstos carefully considers his rebuttal.

'Yer well. *Prostitute-Painting*. Very honourable occupation these days, innit?'

'Indeed it is,' concedes Philomenos, in the best manner of debate. 'Oh yes. Ceramics. Shields. Warrior helmets. All rich cultural manifestations of the graphic art.'

'So,' mutters Benjarstos, casually smearing a hand

---

[8] oops

*PROLOGUE*

off his smock, 'woss your problem with this then? Bit too nouveaux eh? Janglin' your censor's nerves? Jus lookin' for an excuse to close my little portico dahn, then?'

'No, not really my good man,' replies Philomenos, with a patient sigh.

'Right then. Bugger orf, an' let me get on with my porno-graphic labours, alright?'

At that, Philomenos waddles off the portico steps and casts a last rueful glance at the scene.

'Oh I shall, I shall my good man. No need to bother the city fathers about this, I'm sure. Just, umm...'

'Yeah?' growls Benjarstos, moodily slapping a paintbrush onto his colourful palm. 'What now then?'

'Just let me know when she's dry.'

Tickle the dial of your time machine to the early twenty first century. That's the one after the one where everything was in black and white till they invented sound. And the one before the: oh you *really* don't want to know.[9]

Anyway, here in the teeming metrolopiss,[10] indulge momentarily in an arial view.

London: capital of several nations of non-anglo saxon ethnicity. A melting pot of cultures, attitudes and 56 franchise branded coffee cafes.

All of which manage somehow to be *completely different from the other ones*. Despite the menu being limited

---

[9] different book, that. With a cover looking like it's been drawn by an insane computer.
[10] spell check error

to coffee. Yet, all is justified by the mantra of consumer choice.

So now choose the invitation to swoop below the clouds, pollution[11] and watch out for the double decker buses.

You find yourself in a maze of alley-like streets. A throng of theatre-goers, tourists, and people walking past openly gay pubs while doing their best to make it obvious that they are not looking.

Choose the right alleyway, round the corner from the cut-price noodles and sushi bar, hurrying past another one of those pubs, ducking under the awning overhang of the Paradise Strip[12] and you have arrived at your destination.

Or you're hopelessly lost. Probably much the same thing, if the satnav of life's anything to go by.

Anyway, here you are. An appetite. And a little shop. With red velvet curtains in the window.

Oh. And a great big flashing neon sign saying:

*SEX-X-X.*

---

[11] mainly caused by those irritating rent-a-bicycles: little known fact

[12] topless bingo on Wednesdays

CHAPTER 1

# *OPEN*

## Part 1: The Girl I Left Behind Me

Inside, a pile of carboard boxes littered the floor like a jumble of pervy Lego. The half-filled shelves had the air of expecting company. The "Sail" signs were attributable to a certain authorship. Which will become apparent, shortly.

Ben Dover Esq, sometime adult star film producer, and present time love boutique proprietor stood proudly. The porn prince of all that he surveyed, with his steely, but often bloodshot, blue eyes. Although occasionally compared in looks to that kids' tv presenter: the one who spent his career with a hand up the rear end of Orville the Duck. Ben still rated his aesthetic appeal.

But, as Ben was willing to admit after a couple of drinks, he had to rely these days more on chat. And the image cast by a second hand, but carefully number plated Ferrari. Over forty years of experience had made him a much superior seducer and lover. Just at a slower tempo, than his youthful days, drumming with a rock band.

Ben watched Pauly, jeans bum up, head down. Rifling excitedly through boxed contents, like a baby monkey in a banana bucket.

Aah Pauly. Ben had high hopes for human society, in that they definitely did break the test tube which brought forth that lad into the world. Not a bad lad. No. Not a nasty bone in his body. A physique which, though boasting all the basic requirements of the species, was not controlled by any recognisable instruction manual. An uncombed shock of dark hair over wide brown eyes. A face which beamed the innocence of a permanently startled deer. With the dress sense of a drunken Australian surfer.

Then, did you ever see those comic pictures of the inside of a particular sort of brain. You know, where there's a string attached to a toilet seat, which then connects with a cuckoo clock, a set of toy railway carriages, and some marbles. An antique brass lever, which you push down to make the thing work. And then - it doesn't. If you could peer through Pauly's mop top with some inspecta-scope gadget, that – Ben was convinced – was what you'd see. On a good day.

It's not that Pauly was a moron, in the classic sense. His head clearly brimmed with more sparks of ideas, than a fireworks box on acid. It was rather that, like a very badly made jigsaw puzzle, the pieces couldn't fit together in any recognisable picture. Even Pauly seemed unable to see the edges.

Pauly scooped out another bubble-wrapped triumph and handed it up to Ben, who weighed it in his hand, with all the pride of a Somerset melon farmer.

'Cor, look at all this lovely kit. We'd have never got this much stock at those prices, y'know Pauly, if that wholesale warehouse hadn't burnt down.'

'Oh. Yeh,' Pauly fingered a box edge to keep in touch with his magic kingdom, 'Are you still helpin the police with their enquiries into that Ben?'

As Pauly momentarily disengaged himself from his box of delights, Ben wondered yet again at the perils of Pauly conversation.

As Ben was often kind enough to point out to strangers, there were two obviously noticeable characteristics of Pauly's diction. The first being that as his accent was so northern, you had to tread perilously close to the Scottish border before finding anyone who could readily understand it.

Then second, as a basic matter of neurological physics, Pauly's brain synapses were supposed to be working at close to light speed. Thing was, by the time any actual sentences reached the end of his oratory, even Stephen Hawking's voice synthesizer might have trouble remembering how they'd started.

No...,' Ben muttered, somewhat defensively. 'No, Pauly old son. Not anymore.'

'Oh. Right.' Pauly jiggled a box edge, considering the matter. 'Well it were daft anyway.'

'Er... yeah.' Ben straightened his shoulders. 'Course it was'.

'Yeh. I mean.' Pauly's starry smile lit up, at the thought trundling down his slow and sticky mental marble board. 'Who'd ever think it were *them* what'd done it?'

He'd been giving Pauly *that look*. For so many years,

that if he'd been whittling marks on a stick, Ben would have needed a giant redwood. So, it was more instinct than calculation which generated Ben's ritual response grimace. 'Yeah. Er... who would?'

Taking a deep breath of Soho shop air, Ben pulled Pauly away from his boxes, and spread his arms with proprietorial pride. 'So just look, and take it in. This, Pauly, this is our field of dreams.'

'Yeh.' Pauly poked a finger in the air. 'With a burnt out warehouse on it.'

'Yes, right yes. Enough on that thank you.'

Ben spread his arms wider, to embrace the vista of erotic stock display opportunity. 'Now, you know where everything goes Pauly?'

Pauly's face assumed the concentration of a novice Buddhist monk, about to perform his first barefoot fire walk. 'Oh yeh, yeh. I've been so working on it.'

Pauly took a deep and dramatic breath, as if about to give his operatic aria to a packed Albert Hall. 'Right. The D-V-Ds go on the D-V-D rack. The mag-a-zines go on the mag-a-zine rack. The an-al lubricanty goes…'

'Yes yes. Everything in its proper place and order. Thank you Pauly.'

'Only... Ben. What about this one?'

Pauly pulled a rounded, ruler long tin, packaged by a pictorial endorsement from a famous porn starlet, out of his nearest cardboard castle.

Ben considered the artefact with a practiced eye. 'Well..., it's Fleshlight. Right?'

'Like... from B & Q?'

'No. It's a ... plastic part - of a lady - that our customers can play with.'

'Oh! Any particular part?

With all the patience needed in training a urologically challenged puppy, Ben grabbed the tin. 'Yes! Look: there's a picture.'

'Oh ! Funny name then,' pondered Pauly. 'You'd think it'd be quite dark in there.'

Ben shook his head in speechless sorrow.

Pauly pulled a pair of furry handcuffs out of his cardboard wonderland. 'I think these is wrong y'know.'

'Eh?'

'Well, must be left over from them enquiries with the police.'

Ben gently took the cuffs and instructed his almost young apprentice: 'Nooo. They go in the fetish and bondage section: over there...'.

'Oh right. Lovely.'

His sense of excited discovery picking up steam, like a Thomas the Tank Engine on amphetamines, Pauly extracted a pair of boxer shorts with a prominent multi-colour 'Ben Dover' logo on them.

'And where do these go then?'

Grabbing one side, Ben hissed, 'Under my jeans, thank you very much!.

With the tired patience of a man trying to teach water not to run downhill, Ben explained. 'You know, in a boutique like this Pauly, you have to learn to discriminate between what's public, right… and what's personal.'

Pauly nodded. 'Oh. Right. Yeh got it.' Pauly announced his brilliant afterthought. 'So…not the used ones then?'

As he waggled a hand holding one end of the boxers, Katia walked in from the rear door. Katia, oh Katia. A gorgeous blue eyed busty brunette Polish girl, in a cleavage showing top, over a denim mini skirt and high heels.

Or as Ben was fond of saying, 'An Eastern European cum-strumpet with class.'
Just before Katia slapped him. Again.

Katia wiggled her bountiful way between the PVC rack and her till counter, and edged onto her stool.

'Boys and dere toys. Dis funny shop,' she commented to herself. And to an assortment of edible body parts.

Ben quickly noted the potential interpretation of his boxers-sharing pose with Pauly. He hurriedly bundled the boxers into a ball and threw them into Pauly's box.

'Hey that were a good shot Ben!' exclaimed Pauly, as he returned to his assorted erotica sorting.

'Just hope I find them again'.

Ben strode manfully over to Katia, ready to dispense more of his unique wisdom.

'You know, Katia. This is an excellent place for a girl like you, you know, from a deprived former communist isolated eastern European village, to get a wider view of life.'

Ben rubbed Katia's shoulder sensually, just as, in his mind, Pitt with Jolie. 'And the ways of the world.'

'Not to touch pliss!'

Katia, shrugged his hand off, got up hurriedly and walked over to Pauly, placing a ravishingly manicured set of fingernails on his shoulder. 'Hello Pauly. Can I be helpink yo wid dis tings?'

'Ooh lovely lass. Ta. Jenkuje bardzo.'

Katia lit up the puzzled starscape of Ben's ego with her dazzling smile, as he stepped over to Pauly's side: 'Ey Pauly. Where'd you pick that lingo up then?'

'Oh me mum. You know. She were friends with this Polish market gardener.'

'Ah yes. Your mum always had a lot of friends, didn't she?'

'Like the Pope has bibles. And it's down to 'er that we's here today in't it? I mean, all that money what she collected over the years...'

Pauly snuggled his head on the chest of his taller mentor, as they dreamed backward, to a time when it was all in black and white.

There, in their joined recollection was Pauly's mum.

Dancing around a tired wood and lino pub. Dressed in a basque, with a feather boa, fishnet stockings and stilettos. Doing the rounds with a pint glass filling with coins, as gentlemen of the borough show their appreciation in small change. And sometimes notes.

Pauly broke their reverie with a memorial sigh. 'An all invested in 'ere. Aladdin's cave for the pervy, needy, an' impatient.' Pauly puffed out a chest which would have shamed a pigeon. 'That was my idea.'

'Oh yes my son. Our field of dreams. Carpeted with gold. Cos as your old mum used to say, "where there's sex, there's money."'

Lisa swung through the glass entrance door to hear Ben's last words:

'Oh yeah?,' she snapped, in the no-nonsense tones of a Liverpudlian docker. 'An ave youse sold anythin' yet?'

Ben sighed, with the practice of a man well used to finding a hole in his trouser pocket. 'Well it's always a Mexican stand-off between pounds and passion with you innit?'

Pauly jumped a few steps over to Lisa and gave the blonde, busty forty-something a hug around her fake fur coat.

Katia noted the twenty-something suitable, clingy leopard skin dress, fishnets and stilettos, completing Lisa's striking ensemble.

'Oh, Katty,' Pauly explained excitedly. 'Have you met Lisa? This is Ben's wife.'

'Ex,' interjected Ben hurriedly

'Sort of,' wheedled Pauly.

'Former,' Ben countered.

'Nearly,' Paul pleaded.

'Terminally separated,' declared Ben, with visibly

irritated finality.

'Aww. You poor love,' trilled Lisa to Katia, 'Stuck ere between a bampot and a tosspot.'

'No Lisa. No!' Pauly reacted, with surprising force, 'That's *really* wrong.'

'Oh I'm sorry Pauly. It's just that…'

'Y' see,' Pauly continued earnestly, 'Katty's counter is ideally situated between the DVD racks and the erotic confectionery.'

Pauly beamed with the pride of achievement. 'That was my idea.'

Katia nodded. Ben and Lisa rolled their eyes at each other.

'Look, Lise. Soon as this place starts churnin' out money, your designer addictions are first in line OK?'

Lisa shrugged her fake fur shoulders. 'I've gorra *live*.'

'Yeah well. You could have a go at working or summin.'

'Din' I give up everythin' when I married you?

'Not as much as I did,' Ben shot back.

To Ben and Lisa's astonishment, Pauly grabbed a hand of each bickerer, and pulled them together. To nestle like antagonistic vipers on a hot stove.

'Oh well. I think it's nice that this place is bringing you two back together.'

Ben and Lisa stared at Pauly with wide eyed disbelief, suited to watching a short-sighted chimpanzee trying to direct traffic.

'I mean,' Pauly continued, that's what this place

"Sex-x-x" is all about in't it?'

'What,' coughed Ben, 'Having embarrassing domestics with your estranged loved one, over a cardboard box full of Belgian butt plugs?'

'No! Usin' the joy of sex-x-x to bring people together.'

As Ben and Lisa continued to stare, in the mildly horrified paralysis of watching a blind badger navigating all four lanes on a busy motorway, Pauly continued.

Y'know, maybe if we'd opened this shop before, like, you two wouldn't have had to move out.'

'Right. Well,' Ben disengaged from Lisa's unenthusiastic hand. 'Enthralling though this special retards edition of the Jeremy Kyle show is, I've got an important business meet to do. So see ya later.'

Ben stalked out with the look of a man, desperate for the bottom of the next pint glass.

Lisa looked after him. 'So where's 'e off then?'

'Important,' Pauly repeated.

'Bees-iness...' Katia added.

Lisa gave a sniff of Liverpudlian outrage. 'And you two still believe a single word that man says?'

'Which one?' Pauly asked.

Lisa leaned in to confer unsought advice. 'Tell you what Pauly.'

'Yeh Lisa love?'

'Youse two are the best ever advert for a lesbian lifestyle.'

'Well. Yaay,' Pauly hi-fived Katia. 'We like to cater to everybody in ere.'

With anger rising like steam off the Mersey, Lisa picked up a glowingly boxed dildo. 'Are these on special offer then?'

Katia proudly announced the sales pitch. 'Yiss. Ees de *Tibbles* model. De thickest plastic yo can gets. Twenty per cents de discount on dis special item.'

'Right then...'

Shoving the object into Pauly's hand, with little short of the force felt by a cruise missile hitting a terrorist bunker, Lisa shouted, 'Give it to that git when he gets back.'

Having delivered that instruction to Pauly and Katia, Lisa stalked on her stilettos to the door, adding over her fake fur clad shoulder,

'And tell 'im 'he won't be needin' no batteries where I want 'im to stick it !'

Pauly and Katia stood for a moment as the swinging exit door echoed Lisa's angrily departing heels.

'Wow!' Pauly turned excitedly, 'You better do one of your special little sticky labels for that Kats.'

'Really Pauly? Why is dat?'

'Well like Lisa just said,' Pauly explained in triumphant discovery, as Katia handed him a little pink label and marker pen.

'No batteries included - or required ! Your *very* flexible friend.' Pauly half-puffed his pigeon chest. 'And that nearly was my idea.'

\*   \*   \*

Ben and Jez sat in the warm corner of a traditional old pub, sipping pints. The lunchtime trade was middling along, with a few other customers, none of whom could be bothered to get up and put money in the lonely jukebox.

Jez Butcher was hard faced, in a black leather jacket, sporting a large neck medallion. Even while seated, he seemed to loom over Ben with quietly spoken menace. Jez was good at looming. Like he'd gone to some special gangster school for it, Ben wondered silently. Jez slurped his pint and smacked his lips.

'So you're up an' running then?'

'More or less. Yeah.'

Ben paused, considering his next words, and the safety of his gold teeth fillings, very carefully.

'Look, Jez, it'll be a while before we're turnin over any real wonga in there, y'know? I mean, it'll not be an instant score.'

Jez's hard stare seemed to harden. Then to Ben's wonderment announced, 'Oh relax me old son. We're a very modern outfit. We does instalments, y'know.'

'Cor, really?'

'Oh yeah.' Jez took a long, slow sip of his pint. 'Fingers this month. An arm the next. Kneecaps after, sort of fing.'

Jez seemed to loom a little, well, loomier, in Ben's eye. 'Ugh. Right. No pressure then.'

'None at all mate.'

*OPEN*

\*   \*   \*

Katia was arranging things behind the counter. A not unattractive man opened the entry door. Thirty-something, and dressed casually but smartly, he sidled up to a lingerie-clad mannequin doll. He reached out and fingered the lace.

'Not to touch pliss !' Katia shouted at him.

The customer came up to the counter.

'Hello love. Nice to see this open, and local.'

'Hello. Sorry about de no touch shouting, but is de retail store training.' Katia instinctively rolled her eyes. 'And de habit with someone.'

'Fair enough, love. Now then. Do you have electro-stim nipple clamps with alternate vibration modes please?'

'Just moment, sir, I ask.'

Katia opened an access door behind her, leaned in and shouted up somewhere above.

'Paul-eeee! Are we heving de electro-stim nipple clemps wid de alternate vibration modes pliss?'

Pauly's voice echoed downward in reply. 'Full or half pvc bonded?'

Katia turned back to her customer. 'Full or half de pvc bonded?'

He considered. Then replied. 'Er... Half. Please.'

Katia leaned back through the doorway and passed on the information. 'Half.'

There was a pause. The customer fingered an erotic jellies catalogue on the counter.

Pauly's voice echoed down again. 'No. Sorry.'

Katia turned back to her customer. 'No.'

'Oh... Ok then. Next time mebbye.'

The customer walked out with slow and measured steps. Katia smiled nervously behind him. She shifted her eyes sideways in her head. Then reached over and gently closed the the access door.

\* \* \*

While Ben and Jez seemed, to a not too interested observer, to be chatting relaxedly, a blonde girl crossed between their line of vision and the bar.

Ben immediately noted that her pink jumper really needed a few more stitches even to qualify as "tight" across her frontage. His testosterone temporarily fuelled, Ben challenged Jez.

'Tell me Jez, don't you ever get tired of selling pain and sufferin' for a living?'

'Well, I reckon I could arsk you if you don't get tired of peddlin smut for a living?,' Jez countered.

The girl at the sudden centre of Ben's attention, had walked over to very low table at the side of sofa. Seizing phallothropic impulses rooted deeply in Ben's brain, she bent over to put glass and bottle down, giving Ben and Jez a flash of her knickers and stocking tops.

Ben found himself transported to a domain which didn't include an answer to Jez's question in it.

Jez noted the cupid arrow flashing from the girl's bum

cheeks to Ben's transfixed attention. 'Riiiight. Smut and violence. Same effect all these years on. Same answer.'

\*   \*   \*

Katia was secretly swotting up on her accountancy exam revision, behind the counter. Pauly was arranging some fetish clothes, on their dedicated rack.

A petite goth girl swung through the shop door. She walked in her leather, lace, braids and bits of tartan, over to Pauly's designer rack.

'Wowww ! Great gear,' she enthused, in a gentle Somerset accent.

'In't it. Comes from all over. An' all sorts of designers an' all,' Pauly pointed proudly.

The customer-ette (as Pauly liked to call such) fingered a goth dress. 'Hey, this is Anton Shebardick right?'

'Definitely. An we got his shoes collection comin in later.'

'The just-past-midnight range.'

'That's the one. You could see it on the interweb of course. But until now, you couldn't reach out and actually brush it with your fingers here in the UK.'

'No, I know. Stunnin.'

'Well you, see…' Pauly got on his sex-x-x soapbox. 'A sex boutique's about more than just dvd six packs and plastic home alones.'

'Oh no. I don't do *sex*. It's messy.' The goth goddess

trailed a crimson fingernail over a lace bodice. 'I just love the clothes.'

'That's alright love,' Pauly nodded encouragingly. 'Plenty of the blokes what buy the magazines can't read either. He held out a welcoming hand. 'I'm Pauly. Welcome to sex-x-x.'

The gothess took Pauly's hand hesitantly. 'Uh - I'm Raven. But, like i said I don't do sex.'

'No, silly.' Pauly gave Raven a playful pat on the shoulder. 'I mean - that's the name of the shop: Sex-x-x. And it gets quite messy in here as well sometimes.'

The ice of misunderstanding was melted by the warmth of Pauly's harmless idiocy. They laughed together.

'So do you own this place?'

To deal with this tricky starter for ten, Pauly elected to move jerkily from one foot to the other. Putting the cruel in mind of a paraplegic Michael Jackson. 'Well, joint owner I suppose.' Step, step. 'I put in the money, like, well most of it.' Step, half-step. 'But Ben - he's my business partner - he does all the like business side.' Explanatory exhaustion setting in, Pauly subsided.

'Oh, right. Hey it's nice here. Not like them normal weird places. Can I bring me mates to come have a look round?'

Pauly's big smile lit up. 'Anytime Raven. We're part of the community, and the community should be part of us, I reckon.'

'Oh that's lovely!' Raven took a last look around,

before stepping on her gothic heels towards the exit. 'OK - be seein ya! Sex... yaay !

'That's with 3 exes Raven love!' Pauly replied. Then he addressed the fetish wear rail with pride. 'That was my idea.'

Just as Raven was removing her gothic majesty from the premises, Ben returned the other way. Politely holding the door, Ben performed a swift-necked double take at the leather and lace clad loveliness. Who ignored him.

Ben entered the premises, still high on admiration. 'Phwoof. Goth chicks not really my thing. But in a nice little school uniform, she could chalk the blackboard in my dungeon, any day.'

Pauly was quick to enquire. 'Oh... I din't know you did anythin in a dungeon. Ben?

'Well, not since I packed me bags on Lisa, no.'

As so often, following any dialogue with Pauly, Ben had to pause to collect his just-scrambled thoughts. 'Now Pauly. What we gonna do about this grand opening?'

'Well, I thought I'd get a bottle of pink champagne, and a ribbon, then –'

'No ! I mean: who's gonna be the celebrity guest opener?

'Er... Did you have anyone in mind?' Pauly asked.

'Female sky news reader?'

'Which one?'

'Any of 'em. Er.. Right. Noooo.' Ben let out a breath of disappointment.

Pauly scrunched his well-worn brow, meandering through his mental card-index (non-alphabetically ordered), of potential guest openers. 'Cheryl Cole?'

'I wish upon a thousand stars.' Ben sighed. 'But no. Not when you think about it.'

'The lady mayoress? She's a girl. Well. Woman. Er… thing.' Pauly's limited articulation skills, having all the deftness of a one wheeled rickshaw, ground to a halt. With the tumbleweed blowing by.

'Well, while this grand opening is indeed a civic occasion, I can't really see her with her rod of office in one hand, and one of our special discount dildo's in the other.'

'Yes you can.'

Ben considered for a moment. 'Yep. You're right Pauly. So... No.'

'How about Stacey?' Pauly pointed to a film poster, in pride of place above the butt-plugs shelf.

Blazoned with the words "Your Porn Princess – Stacey Saran – starring in *Who Stole Roger Rabbit*." Wrapped around a cheeky smiled beautiful blue eyed blonde. And almost wrapped around boobs which seemed ready to pop out of the poster. Boobs which a cartoonist would have worn out a lot of HB pencil in drawing. And would then have to go have a long lie down. Underneath her astonishing film frontage the quote line "Someone's stolen my Rabbit. And I'm gonna find out who."

Ben followed Pauly's finger. 'Stacey - the hottest brit pornstar in the world - Saran? And how exactly do you think you're gonna get the crown princess of Britporn down to our opening? Twitter her nicely? Pop into her DM's'

'Oh Stace's mum were best mates with my mum. You know, in the old days.'

Ben's voice ratcheted up the register of interest. 'What, Stacey's mum was a female entertainer as well?'

Ben and Pauly's necks instinctively tilted their heads, ready to enter the vintage dreamscape of Pauly's mum in full pub dance dress. Then a needle seemed to drag off the record player of their shared moment of consciousness.

'Oh no, silly. But she were a dab hand behind the bar. Anyway, I can give Stace a ring and see if she wouldn't mind helpin out.'

Ben clapped his hands in delight. 'Al-right ! Now it's coming together! This is gonna get us press, customer attention…,' Ben slid a hand around Pauly's shoulders, lustfully fingering the air in the direction of Stacey's photogenic frontage. 'And the opportunity to find out if she looks as good on my boardroom table, as she does in her posters. Hur hur.'

Just slightly spoiling Ben's moment of triumphant expectation, one of the lingerie boob mannequins fell off its stand.

'Oh dear, look,' explained Pauly, redundantly. 'That'll plastic'll need fixin.'

Ben gave Pauly a look. Again

## Part 2: Don't Show Off In Business

Ben was sequestered in what he thought of, as his ultra modern office boardroom, above the shop. Some might have offered a less generous description. Having regard to the piles of old magazines and dvd's, an assortment of awards of dubious provenance, and a stand up 3d *Ben Dover* board, complete with nineties fashion and a full head of hair.

Ben was showing off his state of the art video surveillance equipment, to a rather mind boggled Pauly. The lad had, of course, rather a head start in having a mind full of boggle.

'See this kit Pauly.' Ben tapped the boardroom table for emphasis. 'Our budget doesn't just go on smut. It goes on security as well.'

Pauly tried very hard to grasp the surveillance principles involved. 'But… why do we want to be standing here, watching us down there?

Ben gave Pauly his long-practiced slow stare of disbelief. 'No! It's not for us watching us. It's for us watching *them* !'

'Who?'

'The customers.' Ben jabbed a finger at the screen.

'Which one?' Paul scrunched his eyes up at the monitor, currently displaying a retail premises, vacant of any prospective purchasers.

'Well - anyone: tealeafs, blaggers, pervos, swaggers, rozzers, pocket liners, cover rustlers, dirty touchers, litterers, beggars and trading standards officers.'

'Ohhh,' Paul considered the towering list, just enumerated. 'You think we'll get that many in today?'

The monitor, at that poetic moment, displayed a svelte redhead, smothered in a latex catsuit, oozing through the shop door.

'Which one is she then?'

Ben rubbed his hands together. 'Well, all this expensive surveillance equipment has now... er... surveilled her, so it's my job to find out !'

Ben headed for the door, in a sudden hurry. 'You keep watchin' and you might learn a thing or two.'

In the after draft of Ben's hurried exit, Pauly pulled up a chair. Taking up a notebook and pencil, he cast his best impression of an eagle eye at the monitor activity .

'Rigggght.' Paul prepared himself to inscribe a note. 'Which one's the swagger?'

The latex lady was looking at some bondage gear.

Ben wafted in, on a breeze of what he thought of as charm. 'I see you're admiring our finest Swedish latex and leather range, madam.'

'Miss...'

Such a soft sweet voice, Ben thought. 'Oh right. Ok miss...?'

'Kitty.'

'Lovely. The eyes of a cat. The purr of a kitten. The body of a leopard.'

'Oooh - latex animal print. That's an idea.'

'Wrapped around you, it's pure genius.' Ben took a small step out of Miss Kitty's personal space, to consider the matter more fully. From redhead to latex toe. 'We can always get a special pattern made up for you.'

'Wow. Well I'll have a think about that. But for now, i do need to replace my main whip and handcuffs. They are getting rather worn.'

Ben shifted gear into full Charminator mode. 'Oh really? Him indoors got you chained to the ironing board has he? Ha ha. Well of course the best way to test riot control gear - is to have a riot isn't it Kitty- licks?'

Kitty picked up a whip and handcuffs. 'How about these?'

'Oh I'd definitely recommend that set. No marking on the wrists, and that crop leather is guaranteed for two years. Fancy a demonstration?'

Ben licked his lips as he moved to pop Kitty in the handcuffs.

Instead, Kitty grabbed his wrist and slapped one handcuff on. 'I'd love to. Would you mind?'

'Anything to please a paying customer, darling.'

Pauly was still staring at the monitor. Well, we think that's what he was staring it. He could have just been staring. The relationship between the angle of his eyes, and the world outside them, did not reliably reflect any particular relationship between the contents of his thoughts.

But now, Pauly went stiff. He dropped his pencil, in slack jawed amazement.

Down on the shop floor, Ben was heard to exclaim 'Owwww ! Jesus and all the saints in a sawmill. That *hurt!*'

Katia rushed in from the side door. She saw that Ben was handcuffed to a spanking bench, and being whipped by Kitty.

'Oww ! What the hell are you doin?,' Ben cried.

'Well I comes in when I hear de screamink,' Katia explained.

'Not you ! Hellraiser here!'

'Oh that's a good one, slave,' snarled Miss Kitty, with another lash. "Madame Hellraiser".

'You are from de hell?' Katia held a well-raised Catholic had to her mouth.

'No darling. My dungeon's a nice friendly place. Always full of people enjoying themselves.'

'Like dees?'

Kitty entertained herself to another mighty whip thwack upon her prostrate victim. 'Much harder.'

Kitty paused, to hold out a hand. 'Sorry. Getting quite carried away. Miss Kitty.' She performed a creditable curtsy 'Dominatrix to the gentry.'

'Oh. Katia Louissa Radek. Student and pervy shop assistant.'

'Ben bloody Dover. Sore arsed and sorry.'

Kitty patted his head, then uncuffed him. 'Oh my dear you're a good sport.'

Pauly rushed in. Well, as rushing as his lack of co-ordination and muscular control allowed. 'Oh my goodness ! Is anything damaged?'

'Just my pride, old son.' Ben rubbed his assaulted posterior.

'Alright, yeh.' Paul picked up the now used manacles. 'But can we get them handcuffs back in their sale packet?'

Ben shot Pauly a look which suggested – not for the first time – that the world would be a better place, if only Pauly could be shoved into some convenient and permanent receptacle.

Just as, in the periphery of Ben's vision, a choir of adult angels sang. The god of porn had decided to take a hand off his usual activity, and intervene directly into the affairs of men. And middle-aged sex shop proprietors, in particular.

Stacey Saran had just walked into the store. She was wearing a cleavage displaying sparkly gold dress, suitable for a Las Vegas adult awards show, with matching perpendicular heels.

'Hello everybody!,' Stacey trilled. Then, spying Ben, still prone from his backside encounter with Kitty, 'Ooh - what have you been up to?'

Ben's eyes widened. He looked at the poster. Then back at the living vision of Stacey Saran. Then at the Stacey poster. Then, back at Stacey. Then back at the poster. Then[13]

Finally, Ben managed 'Canaries down a coal mine!

---

[13] This could go on for quite some time. It did. At least in Ben's overexcited head.

That's you! That's her. It is - isn't it?'

Displaying complete disregard for Ben's porn celebrity meltdown, Pauly sauntered over to greet Stacey. 'Ello Stacey love. Ey its lovely to see ya.'

They had a friendly hug.

'Awww, you too gorgeous,' twinkled Stacey. 'How's this place going?'

'Be like open day in heaven when you do the big ceremony,' said Pauly, with a surprising turn of wit. 'Hey pudding butt - fancy a cup of tea while we're getting ready?'

'OK plonk pants,' replied Stacey.

Ben mouthed to Pauly 'Pudding butt?'

'Oh, only from behind.' Again, completely oblivious to the rapid and conflicting displays of emotions crossing Ben's face, Pauly continued. 'Go on, I'll leave you two to make the introductions while I get the kettle on.'

With that, Pauly popped out to the back room.

Finding his feet at last, Ben snapped smoothly into Charminator mode. All systems pink. Ready to eradicate any resistance. 'Well hello, dolly.'

Stacey giggled. 'They have actually made a dolly out of me.' She paused for consideration. 'Well...' Stacey looked down, or it may have been across, 'A *bit* of me anyway.'

'I'm sure it's a lovely bit as well. My name's Ben Dover and I'm the owner of this delightful boutique, and –'

At that inexcusably inconvenient moment, a customer

decided to walk in. A man of average description, in average clothes. That kind of normality stood out in the shop. Mr Customer walked over to Katia's position. 'Scuse me darlin. 'ave you got that *Who Stole Roger Rabbit*, with Stacey what'shername in?'

Ben butted in. He pointed to the Stacey poster. Then at Stacey herself, holding his arms open, with a big smile.

The customer looked up, then across, and shook his head. 'I'm just after the dvd thanks. Oh, And the Stacey *boobs with a lube*.

Katia nodded. With quiet competence, she collected the products, popped them in a bag and rang the till.

As the customer was handing over his money, Ben felt compelled to intervene. 'Just a minute, mate - that's the real thing - standing just there innit?'

The customer took a longer look this time. At the poster. 'Yeah, maybe.' Then back at Stacey. 'But I can't take 'er home in a plastic bag can I?'

Katia handed him the bag

'Thanks love.'

With that underwhelming crescendo, the customer headed out. He nodded to Stacey. 'Afternoon love.'

Stacey gave her shoulders a little shrug, causing something of an avalanche below the neck line, and gave him a warm smile.

Pauly came back, nursing Stacey's new brewed cup of tea. 'Here you go Stace. Two sugars like you like it.'

'Thanks !' said Stacey, as she gave Pauly a big smile, and took a hot sip.

Coincidences are strange things. They only ever seem to happen together.

At that moment, the swinging shop door was propelled open, by Jez making his entrance.

'Oh no,' Ben remarked.

'Alright Dover?'

Strangely, Stacey spat a mouthful of tea back into her mug. Well mainly into her mug. Pauly rubbed her back, 'Are you alright Stacey love?'

Ben took a manly step forward, with the determined intent to get Jez out of the shop before... Well, before anything, really.

'Jez. Look.' Ben adopted his fair but firm negotiator voice. 'We've had our chat, right? There's a lot going on here today. So, you know, like I can see you round the pub at the end of the week, like...'

Drawn to the Ben and Jez floorshow, Pauly elbowed Stacey playfully. 'Eh Stace... In't that your new boy- toy you were tellin me about?'

Stacey tried to shush him. In vain, as Pauly grabbed her reluctant hand, and shoved it in the direction of Jez's meaty palm.

Ben's smut antennae bristled with new intelligence. 'Hang on!' Just a minute Jez. You're doin dvd bonus tracks with Stacey here?'

'Yeah... What if?' Jez menaced.

Stacey looked up at the tower of terror with a warm, adoring smile.

'Well...,' Ben continued. Now getting into the

confident stride of a marathon runner, twenty feet away from the finishing line. 'Don't think Mrs Butcher'd be too maritally blissed about that now would she? I mean, I'm all in in favour of open and monetarily compensating relationships. But, others tend to have a more Jeremy Kyle view of the world don't they?'

Jez drew up his full six and a lot foot frame, and clenched his one available oversized fist. 'Are you fretenin' me Dover?'

Ben adopted a face, and tone, of cherubic innocence. 'Gawd, no, no no! Just helpfully pointing out that any... erm... attachment between you and this curious establishment might well, in all the potentially misunderstood circumstances, lead a certain type of obsessively jealous person, to draw some Stacey-centric conclusions.'

'Well, I keep all Stace's clippings from the gossip pages when she's spotted around town with her little guy friends,' Paul chipped in.

'Aww do ya? That's so sweet.' Stacey gave Pauly a kiss on the cheek.

Ben rolled his eyes, and inclined his head at Jez to communicate, most effectively *see - told ya*.

Jez took the unsubtle hint. 'Right. Well. Er...' He seemed suddenly to deflate from Godzilla in a leather suit jacket, with flashy medallion, to a sullen teenager, dumped by his first date. 'Be seein yer around then. Erm.' Jez unhanded the porn princess, and backed away from Stacey space

Just forget abaht fings. Er... forget abaht everythin'.

'Jez walked out, shoulders high. But slightly less tall.

Ben rubbed his hands, with the joy of finding an unexpected gift at the bottom of his cereal box. 'Well that's a turn up for the books innit? Ha ha. So, Stace, you got your speech, being an actress and all?'

'Yeah. Got it all mesmerised. Just like for a film.'

'Ok - have a go.'

Stacey took a deep breath and stepped, regally, into the centre of the shop. 'I declare this sex shop open. And may everyone who gets some sex from here be very happy!'

Pauly and Katia applauded.

That boobs and lace mannequin fell off its stand.

'Well, it's been a great day!' Ben enthused. 'But we'll have to get that plastic fixed.'

Stacey, thrust her hands over her boobs, in protection against her shock and embarrassment. 'Oi! Rotten cheek!

Pauly indicated Stacey's extended frontage. 'Aw no Stacey love. He din't mean pinky and perky.'

'Oh, alright then.' Stacey brightened. 'Shall we go outside and do this thing?'

Ben smiled, possibly translating Stacey's last words into his own Dover language. 'And I thought you'd never ask. The stage, my sweet lovely, is yours.'

Ben motioned towards the doorway, as Prince Charming must have shown Cinderella onward to the coach.

Pauly made whimpering noises of panic. He desperately pulled Ben to one side, to give an urgent whisper. 'Ben... I didn't have time to put the red carpet down. We've only got a ribbon over the pavement.'

Ben considered the issue. 'Well, just make sure she doesn't stand in anyfin, an we'll be ok.'

With that, Ben shepherded the opening party through the door and out into the thronging crowds.

OK. There weren't any crowds. Just a man walking a dog. Another man, not walking one. A gay couple, sharing a pretzel. And someone selling chestnuts, guaranteed to keep you up all night.[14]

\*   \*   \*

Later, after all the excitement has died down,[15] Pauly is sitting behind Katia's counter. He's drawing with big bumper pen on pairs of white cotton stretch boxer shorts.

Katia is standing watching, in puzzlement.

Pauly holds one pair up for Katia to see. It has *Sex-x-x* written on it.

'Hmmm. I not really sure about it Pauly.'

'No it's alright Kats. I got it all worked out. I's goin' one better than Ben on this.'

'Oh yiss? How is dat?'

Pauly stands up. He is wearing a pair over his trousers.

'I'm wearin them on the *outside*. Ya see? *Proper* advertisin' all day long.' Pauly lights up his last big smile of the day. 'That was my idea.'

---

[14] There always seems to be one of those, at any street gathering.

[15] OK, so there wasn't all that much. Except for the Alsatian biting the chestnut man. Which was quite good.

CHAPTER 2

# *MODEL*

## Part 1: Downstairs Upstairs

The Sexxx boutique windows blazoned its wares to the passers by of Soho streets. Once upon a time, in the days of 1976, the just-starting Sex Pistols had played a gig in the pub opposite. With about the same audience reaction.

Nowadays, Johnny Rotten happily discusses his love of classical music, and advertises on TV, having had his teeth done. Is the micro world of Sex-x-x really that strange in comparison?

Inside, Pauly was helping Katia to bundle up magazines into sets of four. And putting them in plastic bags. Occasional prospective customers were drifting in and out.

Ben, self-cast in the role overseer, gave encouragement. 'That's it sexmates. Get them mags bundled and bagged and that's discounted dinglin' all the way to the cash register.'

'Oh. Right Ben.' Pauly held up an Angling magazine. 'But is ones like this s'posed to be in this lot?'

Ben was slightly taken back by the piscinary article, but rallied magnificently. 'Well... I mean, how'd we know they don't like a bit of watersports, innit?'

'Yeh. But s'not exactly like nudey girly stuff it it?'

'Depends what you're doing with your tackle me old

son, know what I mean? Hur hur...'

'Oh... Right...,' Pauly nodded. It was obviously going to take a while for Pauly to take this gem of Dover wisdom into his head, and carry it to the correct shelf.

'Yeah. Er...'. Ben paused, in preparation of his next salvo of smut wisdom, as he became distracted by a movement in the shop. 'Oi!!! Just a minute !!!'

The baggers paused in their bagging, to look up.

A man in a long leather coat ran out of the door, slamming it behind him.

Ben screeched 'Oi! Bloody shoplifters!'

He dashed for the door, and ran out. His hue and cry could be heard from inside. 'Oi you ! Come back 'ere !'

Pauly paused, a four pack held in his hand. 'Oh deary me no.'

Katia nodded. 'I know Pauly. It is terrible dis problem.'

'It is that, Katia.' Pauly nodded, sadly. 'He forgot his bonus sample.' The Pauly smile lit up. ''That was my idea.'

Katia gave a sympathetic smile at poor Pauly. 'No Pauly. See, dat guy, he don't wanna pay for nothing.'

'Is this some special membership scheme that Ben's running?'

Katia looked Pauly square in the face, hoping that attention from some part of his brain would respond. 'No. Is like in my country. Everybody is to stealing everyting.'

'So... That keeps the prices down then?'

*MODEL*

'Pauly.' Katia sighed. 'You don't really know too much about de people do you?'

Pauly's face rippled in puzzlement and concentration. 'I don't know. I don't think about it much. I mean, I know you're every good with folk.' Pauly's smile displaced the frown ripples. 'But that's maybe 'cos you're always smiling at them.'

'How you mean?'

Pauly indicated his head at Katia's bulging top.

Katia shook her head. 'Yeah well. Dat's something get more in way of conversation, you know.'

'Still though. It's nice that people make eye contact. Sort of...'

'So how comes it is dat you don't spend all de day looking like all other peoples, Pauly?'

'Well it's like this shop window in't it? All the really good stuff's inside.'

Katia lit up a pleased, but embarrassed smile, and put her hand on Pauly's arm.

The shop door swung open to admit one Ben Dover, all flustered and in a temper.

'Bloody little tearaway. I just about had 'im at the corner of Sheep's Alley.'

'Right...,' Pauly nodded.

'Then this twonkin taxi jams up against the curve and off he's gone like a virgin after a wild night out.' Ben emphasised with a sweep of the palm of his hand.

'Oh. That's a right shame. ' Pauly paused. 'So you

didn't get to give him his right change then?'

'What sodding change?'

'Well. I thought you was doin customer service. You know?'

'Oh gawd. Katia love. Can you explain it to him?' Ben rubbed Katia's shoulder. 'And the wicked ways of the world.'

Katia shrugged his hand off. 'Not to touch pliss!'

Ben climbed on his oratorical soapbox. 'That bloke, Pauly was a tealeaf. A blagger. A n'er do well. A bandit. A... Shoplifter. Geddit?'

Katia nodded, emphatically. Pauly became lost in the intricate and confused alleyways of Pauly thinking.

'So - why dint he just ask?'

'Ask for what?!'

'Well I'm sure there's some free samples we could of given him. I mean, I always find some old throw outs for the Big Issue fella on the corner of Chutney Lane, don't I Kats?'

Katia nodded. 'He does.'

Miss Kitty chose that moment to make her entrance. 'Morning slaves. How's business?'

'Hey Miss Kitty. Well our field of dreams is not exactly gonna keep us in clover, with this sort of lark.'

'Having trouble with your vinyl goods stand again?,' Kitty asked.

'No,' Katia replied with her best serious voice. 'Is de shoplifting.'

'Oh dear, I see,' Kitty nodded.

'Yeah, well...' Ben hit the starter button his charm engine, and sidled over to Miss Kitty's personal space. 'So, er, how do you deal with matters of security at your bijou establishment?'

Quick as a flasher on a nudist beach, Kitty pulled a whip out of her boot and firmly pushed it against Ben's cheek. 'You *really* want to find out?'

'No it's all right Kitts.' Pauly began that dislocated jig of his, like a marathon runner, stuck to the spot. 'I know I know I know! We need us a security guard. You know. In a cap and everything. And we'll get the shoplifters to pay for him.' Pauly's pigeon chest swelled with pride. 'That was my idea.'

Ben's blue eyes opened wide. 'Saints and miracles on a Sunday. Common sense from Pauly-land.'

'Yaay. I'll get on it Ben.' Pauly pointed to Kitty's riding crop. 'Only... I think we'll go without the whip stuff.'

'Why so?,' asked Kitty.

'We'll never get them boots in his size.'

Ben's hand made contact with his forehead, in a familiar slapping motion.

The quiet pub was fairly empty of drinkers. Which accounted for its quietness.

Jez was sitting at table, talking with Liza. There was a lot of body language going on. Although perhaps, like people trying to remember the words of a very old song. One they'd never really understood the lyrics to, anyway.

'So that's basically it Jez. I've not got two sardines to

rub together,' Liza urged.

'Nor even the tin to keep 'em in. Yeah, I get it.'

Liza leant forward, in her overtight leopard skin dress. 'So look, I mean, come on. Ben must be coinin it in smutland, and you'll be gettin your cut.'

'Ah well…,' Jez cleared his throat and stroked his goatee, as he tried to tiptoe round those particularly poisonous tulips. 'Er... Not necessarily there.'

'Come again?'

'Well, as the drunken rabbi says: many a slip twixt cut and dick.'

Yeah, whatever.' Pursing her very red lipstick landscape, and sitting back -which allowed the stressed leopard print to regain some composure - Liza allowed Jez some breathing space. 'Don't tell me then.'

Sipping her drink, Liza looked for another way to pounce. 'Look Jez. We go back a long way, yeah?'

'True enough. Last time we had a dance they was playin Oasis'.

Liza warmly matched Jez's smile of remembrance. 'So, like, I mean. There must be something you can help with.'

'Depends what you're up - or down - for.' Jez wiggled his eyebrows.

'Yeah well after the last few years pretty much anything feels like 'up'.'

'Awww. You invitin' me up are ya?' Jez placed a meaty paw on Liza's wrist.

'Aww gerroff,' Liza said, but without making any

effort to remove the hand. 'You know what I mean.' Liza arranged her lips so that a "come get me" speech bubble seemed to emerge from them. In neon lights.

Jez smacked his own lips. Whether from the last sip of his drink, or carnal wanderings around his consciousness, was tricky to tell. And you didn't ask Jez that sort of question. Not within his hearing anyway. 'Alright doll. Leave it with me. I'll give ya a bell, alright?'

'Aah, you're a diamond babe.' Liza snugged a hand over some of Jez's.

'Nar. When it comes to diamonds, I'm more of a transport facility. Cash and carry, know what I mean?'

Liza nodded, as of she had a clue what Jez was talking about. Which had always been safer than actually asking.

'Cheers,' Jez proposed.

They clinked glasses.

The quietness of Soho's newest love boutique, was disturbed by two policewomen entering, truncheons held firmly at the ready.

'Oh the long legs of the law. Hur hur,' Ben observed.

The police officers stood, uniformed and severe, in the centre of the store.

Ben continued his complaining citizen harangue. 'Well, good you could spare the time from filling in forms about parking meter harassment, but your main suspect fled the scene quite some time ago.'

'I'm sorry sir, we don't know what you're talking about,' said the first officer.

Ben turned to Katia and Pauly. 'You didn't call the robbery in then?,' he quizzed, in ritual tones of disbelief.

'Nope,' said Pauly. Which for him, was a stunningly fast and eloquent retort.

The second officer chimed in. 'Well sir. It's unfortunate if you've had an incident. But we're here about reports of contraband stock being provisioned by these premises.'

Kitty failed to stifle a snorted laugh. 'Dodgy dvd's, eh, Dover? Whose really been a naughty boy then?'

Ben allowed his outrage to bubble over. 'Oh gerroff. As if. Look, er, ladies of the law. You're welcome to poke your night sticks in any part of these premises. And all you'll find is good solid smut and very reasonable prices. Tell 'em Pauly.'

'Oh right. Well I dunno really,' Pauly commented.

Aided by years of exposure to almost addictive quantities of vodka, Ben's facial arteries bulged in crimson symphony. 'What?!!!!'

'Well we do go quite a mark up on leather goods don't we?' observed Pauly.

The first officer spoke with gravestone etched severity. 'Right sir. While we do a search, we'll ask you to accept civil restraint.'

'Assume the position please, sir,' ordered the second officer.

Together, they thrust Ben into his namesake position on the centre counter. Ben's face brushed up against a spectacularly discounted dildo display.

'What the? Oh no come on. Look, leave it out alright?'

## MODEL

One officer snapped the regulation handcuffs shut.

'Owww! That's tight!' Ben complained.

'Hey that's my act,' Kitty observed.

Ben sent up a signal flare of desperation. 'Pauly! Kati! Do something for god's sake.'

Katia nimbly moved to her counter. She popped an iPod in a speaker player, and hit play. The store suddenly flooded with dance music.

Struggling round from his handcuff handicapped position, Ben's mouth fell open. As the two officers went into a strip routine. Off came the police jackets. Down slipped the A-line serge skirts. To reveal bra-busting flesh, suspenders and stockings. The hats stayed on.

Ben burst out in smiles. 'Right you two. Soon as I get out of these I'm gonna hug you and kill you. Not necessarily in that order.'

Katia and Pauly let loose party poppers.

'Happy shop opening!' Pauly enthused.

Katia joined in with a little jump of her own. 'Yaay!'

Pauly provided vital extra information. 'We were gonna do it last week. But they only had a King Kong and a Towie lookalike available.'

'Bananas and fake tan. Nice combination,' observed Miss Kitty.

As the routine ended, and the performers gathered in their discarded uniforms, Ben drew breath. 'Ok, while this was a lovely thought for a shop opening present; next time please just get me a cardiogram, set to music. Then I can truly re-live the experience of needing panty padded boxer shorts.'

The second officer let Ben out of the handcuffs. Kitty handed the first officer a card.

She read it out. "Miss Kitty. Dominatrix of dark passions. Strictly by appointment. Est 2009."

'I could use a feisty pair like you down the dungeon, if you fancy it,' Kitty offered.

The passion police nodded at each other.

'Sounds interestin,' yeah,' said the taller one.

Pauly clapped his hands with joy. 'Yaay. See that's what Sex-x-x is all about. Bringing people together.'

'Come on then cop-rocks,' Kitty purred. 'Let's go get a dommy drink and chat about it.' Kitty took the officers by the arms and led them out. 'See you slaves!'

Pauly waved. 'Bye Kitty. Bye Officer-ettes.'

Katia joined in. 'Bye. Djenkuje!'

Ben rubbed his wrists, checked his pulse, and took a commanding position, next to the erotic novelties stand.

'Right then. Pauly: remember that thing upstairs we were talking about?'

'The leaky loo?'

'Er, no. The *other* thing. '

Pauly looked blank. OK. More blank than usual.

'Yep,' Ben sighed. 'The definition of teamwork in this place. Just do it your self. Right.'

Ben paused, presumably assembling his thoughts into the correct order of vulgarity, indecency and invitation. 'Er, Katia…'

'Tak. Er... yes?'

'You know we've got that separate stairway round the side of the shop.'

Paul butted in to assist. 'Well we will have when I've cleared the discount toy boxes.'

Katia's well-honed Dover instincts warned her that what was coming next was probably something she did not want to hear. 'Ahu...?'

'Right. Well there's that song, stairway to heaven.' Ben held out his grand showman's arms. 'And you, Katia, could be that place of paradise.'

'What you mean?'

'Show her the sign Pauly,' Ben invited.

Pauly reached under his counter and pulled out a sign. Carefully inscribed on a sheet of A4 card, it announced: 'Russian Model'. Pauly had helpfully placed a Russian flag sticker on the corner.

Katia made the Catholic sign of the cross, with her fingers, to ward off the unspeakable evil revealed to her. 'Please say dis ees da joking!'

'No Kati. It's a nice idea,' Pauly insisted.

'See, Polish princess. Even Pauly thinks so. Can't see your problem. Lovely little earner for ya.'

'Yeh,' Paul explained. 'I mean they just come and do their little photographs. I mean, some of them might want to do watercolours.'

'Yeah, see..'. Ben halted his approval, as he realised what Pauly had just said. 'What?!!!'

Paul continued with his enthusing explanation.

'Russian... Model. Though I can't really see how the Russian bit helps. Must be an art thingy.'

Katia had by now moved from outrage, to wetting herself with suppressed laughter.

Ben now felt himself stuck in the Pauly poured cement of embarrassment. 'Uh. Doh. Look. Pauly...'

'Yeh.'

'Will you *please* go do something *useful*, and collect me motor from Den's garage.'

'Yep no probs.' Paul headed for the side door. 'I'll get your coat.' Pauly popped out.

Ben, frowning and drowning, turned to Katia. "Get my? ...Doh.'

Ben let the sign drop on the counter. 'Anyway, we'll have a look at this another time.'

Katia walked off.

Ben held up the Russian Model sign, gazed at it, longingly, and sighed. 'And in my field of dreams, there's dosve-bloody-danya to another few dodgy dollars.'

Ben threw the sign away. He knelt his elbows on the counter, and slumped his chin into his hands. His face assumed the look of a six year old who's just been told that all the amusement park rides have closed early.

## Part 2: Pet a Thief

The car mechanic workshop was not exactly the cathedral to hi tech, which might you might expect with, say, a BMW sign over the door. Car parts hung from every available nook and crevice. Mismatched tyres propped each other up. The air had a smell of engine lubricant, which was past its sell by date.

In pride, or disgrace of place, stood a rather old red Ferrari.

Pauly was having a word with Mike, the mechanic. Or rather, mechanic Mike was directing some choice words at Pauly. Mike was fingering the dancing horse emblemed keys fob.

'So… it's not an easy job then ?'

'Pauly, mate, some of the parts for this one are so old, you have to order them in black and white.'

Pauly nodded. That didn't mean he understood a word mechanic Mike was saying. That was just Pauly's instinctive response to anything he didn't comprehend. Which was, let's face it, just about everything life had to offer. 'Right, sounds complicated.'

At which point, the dark goddess of fate took a hand, and allowed Liza to walk in.

'Oh hello Liza love,' Pauly greeted. He hopped over and gave her a hug, to her usual surprise.

'Oh Pauly. Er… Hi.' Disengaging from Pauly's panda hug, Liza moved on with the business of her day. 'Mike, any news on the mini?'

'Oh I was gonna get onto it after this Lize.' Mechanic Mike indicated the red Italian stallion.

'Way past the sell by date, completely unreliable, and loads of parts are knackered,' Pauly announced. Showing , remarkably, that he had actually been listening.

'Yeah. I know who you mean,' Liza shot back.

Pauly's face re-established its usual look of puzzlement.

'Well you know Pauly,' Liza continued, oozing innocent compassion for the downtrodden, 'if you want to run along, I can take care of his little red devil for you.'

'Oh - really Liza love? That's smashin. Thanks'

Mechanic Mike intervened, in much the same way, and with the same effect, as the second mate on the Titanic. 'Er... Pauly. Are you sure you want me to give these keys to Liza here?'

Liza jutted her neck. 'Oi. Nose out you.'

'That's alright,' Paul chirruped. 'As me mum used to say - 'never give anyone the key to your heart…'. Pauly paused. 'Make do with a swipe card'. He began his wandering steps towards the garage doors. 'Bye then.'

Stunned by Pauly's quote, Mechanic Mike and Liza stared at each other in disbelief for a second.

Then Liza gathered her feral senses. She stepped over to Mike, and grabbed the Ferrari keys. Triumphantly, she clenched them in her scarlet nail fingered hands.

'He he. Gone in 60 seconds. Vroom bloody vroom, Mr D!'

The warehouse was cavernously full of wares. Shelves stacked high with top class smut, as Ben was fond of saying.

He was walking along an aisle between shelf stacks of dvds, with the manager, Julia. What ran through Ben's head, and unfortunately would slither off his tongue about luscious Julia – at least when she was out of earshot - is unprintable in any country with a vestige of decency laws.

We can say, on this side of the vulgarity line, that Julia was a blonde thirty-something executive. Dressed in a pinstripe skirt suit, with a hint of cleavage showing through to top of her buttoned blouse. He blue eyes were looking through horn rim spectacles, perched on the edge of her cute nose, at a clipboard, with typed notes on. As Ben, in a more printable moment of recollection had remarked, 'Like an executive angel, guarding the stairway to heaven.'

Trying to swipe away such thoughts, Ben focused his attention on the hard realities of porn commerce. 'So like I said Julia, i can't see that Swedish erotica stuff moving much.'

Julia put a pen stroke through a clipboard entry. 'Hmm that's a shame.'

Ever succumbing to temptation, Ben added, 'Now, if I could interest *you* in a dramatic role, saturated with executive romance, passion and er... passion. Then we'd have to redirect bus routes to my shop frontage, just to cope with the demand.'

'Knock it off Ben,' Julia snorted. 'You do realise don't you that your corny eighties porn chat up lines are about as enticing, as a rat holding out a hand grenade?'

'Yeah alright, alright. Can't blame a professional perv for tryin. Look tell you what. From the catalogue, that *Dirty in Dagenham* series looks a goer. Can we get boxed up with them please?'

Julia looked at her clipboard, and sighed. 'Oh right. Well that would have to be on the top stack, huh?'

She shouted out, 'Darren! Shelves!' her words echoing off thousands of vinyl covers, and a high strip light ceiling.

'Oh, I saw your little shelf stacker wandering off for his lunch break when I came in,' Ben offered, helpfully.

'Typical.' Julia tapped her pen on the clipboard in frustration. 'Muscles of an Expendable, brain the size of a smartie, and the work ethic of a dead gerbil.'

'Oh dear, Ben oozed. 'Story of your life innit Jules? Can just never get a real man to support you properly.' Ben paused. 'I'll get the ladder.'

Ben took a few strides, and grabbed a wheely ladder. With a show of compassionate effort, he positioned it, ready for the climb up. He motioned with his hand, in the manner of Prince Charming's degenerate cousin.

Julia looked at the ladder. She remembered her executive training, sighed, and handed Ben her clipboard.

'Room at the top for a career minded executive girl. Huh!'

Julia climbed up. She spoke to the air, while looking

up the ladder.

'I mean, that's the thing, right? They say it's equal opportunities, no glass ceiling. But as a woman, you still end up doing twice the work for half the pay. And then you have to justify...'

Now safely mounted on the ladder top platform, Julia trailed off, as she realised that Ben was not listening, but staring open-mouthed at her legs and stocking tops.

'Yeah. Life's a school of hard knocks,' Julia continued. 'Plenty of bumps along the way, huh Ben?'

Lost in the thigh-high wonderland of his imagination, Ben muttered 'uh - uh.. Yeah...'

'Well here's another one' Julia said, through angrily gritted teeth.

She grabbed a carton of dvds and dropped it, right on Ben.

'Owwww! That hurt!

'Well you know: pride - and perving - come before a fall.' Julia dusted her hands. 'See you at the sales desk. And it's cash only. So make your wallet do some work, Dover.'

Pauly was walking along a Soho street. He turned into an alleyway. Perhaps he had a very acute sense of direction, place and movement. But probably not.

Lost in his own landscape, and not for the first time, Pauly walked into someone.

The man bumped, wearing a long leather coat cried out, 'Oh no! Don't call the cops: Pleeeeeeease!' All in a broad Brummy accent.

'No, it's alright,' Pauly said. 'It were my fault. Not looking where i was goin.'

'Uh, oh. Aren't you, like, after me. For earlier?' came the worried voice.

'Ohhhh! The shop! With the door... Running. Thing. Of course.' Pauly seemed to remember.

'Yeah. Look, I can explain, I mean –'

'It's lucky I caught up with *you*.'

The overcoated man cowered, as Pauly fiddled in his coat pocket.

'I know. I mean I'm sorry. It's just that there's this –' the overcoated man babbled.

'You didn't get the free sample popper.' Pauly held up little popper bottle.

'You what?'

Pauly pressed the little bottle into Mr Overcoat's hand.

'There, look. Gotcha sorted now. So we need say no more about it.'

He stared at bottle. 'Uh - aren't you gonna get me nicked?'

Pauly laughed. 'Well - it's not exactly a hangin offence to neglect to collect your giveaway goodie, is it?'

'But...' the man decided he had to come clean to Pauly. Which was not proving easy. ' I-am-a-shoplifter.'

Pauly paused in what we will have to describe as, thought. 'Are you any good at it?'

'Well, it comes and goes. Good days, bad days kind of thing.'

'Well, uh, why do you do it?'

'Uh.. It's cheaper than *buying* things.'

Pauly gestured his head at the popper bottle.

'Well, mostly.'

'So you must know all the nicky-nacky tricks then?' Pauly asked.

'Well. I do alright I suppose.'

'There you are then, perfect. Look, Ben - the excitable rather out of breath man - that chased you this morning. Ben's been saying that we need a security guard. So how about it? I mean, you're not working at the minute are ya?'

The overcoated man took a step back in shock. 'Sorry, you're inviting me to become security for *his* shop?'

'Well, our shop really. Like partners in crime. Yeh.' Caught up in his tumbling flow of ideas, Paul went on. 'Well, as me mum used to say *set a thief to catch a thief.*'

The man considered. 'Yeah. Makes sense I s'pose.'

'Yaay. Right then,' Pauly put his round Toby's shoulder, 'let's come on back to the shop and sort out the details.

As they walked off down the alleyway, Pauly kept up his stream of consciousness. 'I mean, we've got plenty of uniforms. Like, we've got a sort of Star Trek one that we could jivy up a bit.'

The man took a look round his shoulder, indicating that perhaps he was not taking the wisest steps in Soho.

Pauly continued. 'Oh and a Whip! Yeh.'

Pauly stopped for a moment. 'Bring your own boots though.'

Katia was minding the shop alone. There was an upside to this. Ben wasn't there. The downside, was having to deal with actual customers. Katia did sometimes wonder if perhaps she shouldn't have signed on at Selfridges. Or any other normal retail outlet. Like an undertakers.

The problem was that commerce in this environment seemed to happen in a language all of its own. When people asked if you had a dress in size 8, there on the woman's floor of Top Shop, that was definitely what they meant. In here, it probably wasn't.

On cue, a male customer entered, and wandered over. 'Mornin Miss. Have you got anything to help stop sex?'

'Well, yiss. We has de delay cream, which is make de much longer wid it.'

'No no. I mean for stopping doing sex.'

There it went, Katia thought. 'Sorry. I is not sure what you means wid dis'.

'Well, look. Like, if i go into a shop with cigarettes, they'll normally have nicotine patches and that as well.'

'Er... Yiss?' Katia tried to be helpful. 'So you is wanting to stop de smoking?'

'Already trying that. So it's the same idea, right? You selling something to stop sex.'

'But dis ees de sex shop.' Katia waved her arm around. 'For de being more de sexy. De clothes, de dvd's, de magazine, de –'

'Yes yes i get all that Miss. But I don't want to do *more*. I want to stop doing it. You see?'

'Right...' The penny finally dropped in Katia's confused slot. 'So you is wanting de help wid to stop doing de sex at all.'

'Exactly.' The customer folded his arms.

'Well you better wait till Mr Ben, de owner gets back.'

'So... Can he help?'

'Has always worked wid me.'

The customer nodded. OK, I'll come back later then shall I?' The customer exited, with apparent satisfaction.

Katia reflected, as she looked around the shop. 'You know,' she spoke to the assembled menagerie of sexual paraphernalia. Ees not de bad idea.'

Pauly walked in with overcoat man.

'Here we are again. Let me introduce you to Katia.'

In the street outside, Ben was struggling with a cardboard box full of dvd's from Julia's warehouse. He stared in open mouthed amazement at Pauly and his guest, walking into shop.

Ben's face contorted in rage. He muttered to himself, 'why you little...'

Ben broke into a run, still holding the box.

Pauly was performing introductions, in the middle of the shop floor.

'Toby, meet Katia Radek. She's Polish. From Poland. Say dobjy den.'

Toby greeted her, with a tinge of embarrassment. 'Oh. Roight. Hi.'

'Hallo,' Katia replied graciously.

Ben ran in with his box. He threw it to the floor and rugby tackled Toby to the ground. Ben went down on his back, with Toby landing on top of him. He grabbed tight hold of Toby, breathing heavily.

'Right sunshine! This is a python death grip. And you're nicked! Ben paused for breath. 'You rotten slimin skivin soddin tealeaf!'

Pauly and Katia were staring at the floor bound duo.

'Er... Ben...' Pauly urged.

'S'alright Pauly. I got the law on my side.'

Toby struggled a bit.

Ben tried to tighten his python grip. 'Knock it off.'

Pauly tried further intervention. 'But that's Toby, he's...'

'Yeah you'll share the credit for the collar, don't worry. Katty love. Grab some of them handcuffs!'

'OK'. Katia went to get some handcuffs, still stuck to their carboard backing, from a display.

Ben addressed his catch. 'And we won't be needing the key for a long time, you...'

Pauly tried again. 'We won't be needing the handcuffs either Ben.'

'What?'

Pauly explained his explanation. 'This is Toby. Our new security guard.'

Toby wriggled to face Ben. 'Hello.'

'Yeah,' Pauly continues. 'We had a chat. It was all just a misunderstanding. He just left his free sample.'

'Roight,' Toby confirmed. 'But Pauly here sorted that for me.'

Toby brought out the little popper bottle and shook it.

Ben had a little think. Then sighed. 'Well. I suppose it makes about as much twisted sense as anything else round here.'

Ben held out his hand to Toby. 'Welcome to our field of dreams. You can tell it's mine and Pauly's from the "all nutjobs welcome" sign on the plastic fence.'

'Yeh,' Pauly happily agreed. 'We call it Sex-x-x. That was my idea.'

Toby decided to go with the flow, as Ben released his by now very tired arms. 'Roight. Thanks.' Toby shook Ben's hand. 'Toby Jackson.'

'Er...,' he continued. 'Pauly was saying something about a uniform.'

Ben shot Pauly a look.

Some time later, Pauly, Katia, Ben and Toby were chatting. It seemed that Ben was warming to the idea of his new security staff. Katia was glad of the company too, even though she was finding Toby's broad Brummy accent a little difficult to understand. Pauly was happy to see the joy of Sex-x-x bringing people together, in a nice way.

Two more uniformed policewomen walked in.

'Afternoon. Who's the owner please?', asked Officer One.

'Oh, there must have been a report,' Pauly said. 'It's Ben here.'

Ben sidled over to the two officers.

'Oh right, yeah. Suck me once, shame on you. Suck me twice, shame on me. Hur hur.'

The officers look at each other.

Ben leered over them. He fingered the upper chest of Officer 1. 'Bustier for body armour, eh? Nudge nudge.'

Then, Ben leant to the waist of Officer 2, and ran his hand up her leg. 'And stockings or naughty little hold ups, hey?'

The Officer shuddered. 'Sir. Are you aware of the penalties for assaulting a police officer in the execution of her duty?'

'Phoooar. Norralf!'

Pauly stepped forward, with unusually co-ordinated urgency. 'Ben. I din't arrange these. They're proper 999's. You know. With forms.'

Ben hurriedly took a step back. Jesus Christ! Flatfoots in heels!' He held out his arms in abject apology. 'Look, I'm sorry, right…'

'Yes officer-ettes,' Pauly chipped in. 'Just a little misunderstanding. We was doing some security training. Our security guard...' Pauly indicated Toby.

'Hello,' Toby offered.

'…and someone got the wrong end of the stick. Er.. Truncheon,' Paul continued. 'So there's no crime to investigate here, officers.'

The police persons looked at each other.

Paul continued his continuing. 'And look, sorry for taking your valuable time. Have some free samples.'

Pauly grabbed a couple of durex size plastic packets. He handed one each to the officers.

'Er ok. Thanks,' said Officer One. 'What are they?'

'Well,' Pauly happily explained. 'You pop it on your finger and it gives the other person, or person-ette, a buzz.'

Ben, recovering his aplomb, added 'Yeah. Could come in handy in your line of work.'

The two officers – or officerettes - looked at each other and shake their heads.

'Right sir,' Officer Two intoned. 'We'll be off.'

'Try not to make any more false reports,' Officer One added.

They exited.

A hushed sigh of relief filled the shop.

Drawing breath, Ben leant heavily on counter.

'Phew. What a day.'

Drawing back his self-control, Ben began organising. 'First job Toby. Go make us all a cuppa, eh? Kitchen's out back.'

'Alroight Ben,' Toby complied.

Ben had a stretch, and rekindled his courage. 'Right then. Katia. The beautiful Katia.'

Ben put his hand on Katia's shoulder. She shrugged it off. 'Not to touch pliss.'

'Okey dokey,' Ben stepped out of her personal space. 'Well. Have you given any more thought, I wonder to that Russian modelling idea. I mean, look, it's easy work, love.

Think of the extra money you'd be making.'

Katia took a deep intake of breath. Paused for patience. Then decided she wouldn't bother. 'OK, I say it nicely. Which bit of shove your dick-head down toilet do you not understand?'

Katia's voice ascended further the spiral of outrage. 'I Polish girl. So? I am a stupid? I have nothing in my life for to do that i must become good time girl in your crappy attic to make my way? Nye. Nye. Nye!!!'

She waved a negatory finger, for emphasis. 'I have a pride to myself. I have dignity. I am a strong woman!'

'And to be fair Ben,' Paul popped in, 'she's not actually Russian.'

Katia rolled her eyes in disbelief.

Ben sighed, in surrender of loss to the inevitable. 'Alright then.'

He turned to his partner. 'Pauly...'

'Yes Ben?'

'Go find us a proper Soviet slapper, there's a good lad.'

Pauly relapsed into puzzlement.

Ben slumped on the counter, dejected. 'Oh well. There's gold beneath this field of dreams somewhere. Just gotta keep diggin. '

Suddenly, Ben brightened with a thought. 'Hey Pauly, is the motor gonna be finished today?

'Oh - I don't think so. But I left the keys with Liza anyway. She said she'd look after alright.'

Ben's face turned both white and mottled red,

simultaneously. 'You... !'

He stomped a circle of disbelief. 'My pride. My fire engine red joy. About the only thing in my life that - little mechanical difficulties aside - is actually a source of genuine pleasure and excitement.'

Ben screamed his crescendo of frustrated outrage. 'And-you-gave -the-keys-to-my-Ferrari- to... Her!!!!!'

You could, at that point, have heard a silk suspender belt drop in the shop.

Ben went to grab his coat. 'Right. Suicide is painless. But life on the other hand is full of little Paulys. I shall remove myself to the pub. Where me and a rat's arse are going to become very close acquaintants by the end of the night.'

He paused at the door. 'And please do not extend the offer of employment to any more shoplifters. Good soddin night.'

Ben walked out.

The remainder of the Sex-x-x crew exchanged looks.

\*  \*  \*

It is night time.

Toby gives a little victory punch after he has just thrown something. 'Roight in. Top gear!

'Yaay,' Pauly congratulates. 'Good one.' Pauly pauses. 'OK. Focus.'

If we popped into the shop at that moment, we would see that they are throwing dildos, still attached to their cardboard presentation backing, into a toy basketball hoop. Which is wedged between the arms of a blow up dolly, stood upright on a presentation stand.

Pauly throws. It goes in the hoop. 'Yaay! Michael Jordan stand back!'

'Yow's good at this.'

'Aww. It's just practice.'

And the tossing continues on, as the neon Sex-x-x sign blazons outside.

CHAPTER 3

# *BOOTH*

## Part 1: See the Light

Behind the frontage of the Sex-x-x shop, strange happenings were, well, happening. Given the nature of the trade conducted behind those windows, and the razzle of neon lighting, that was perhaps to be expected. But there have to be limits, even in smutland. Getting any kind of agreement as to what those limits actually were: well there was a problem.

Gothic princess Raven, was showing Pauly how new age cosmic energy can work. Her chosen experimental object was 12 inch pink rabbit dildo, on a counter. Bent over the stimulation stimulator, Raven was holding her hands a few inches away from it. With focus.

'You see, Pauly. As the cosmic energy flows in, through and around, it grows warm,' Raven uttered, in her energy trance.

Pauly touched the dildo. 'Cor yeah. I can feel that. Wow.'

'Gawd, will you give that new age codswallop a rest please,' Ben interjected from behind his counter.

'But Raven's energy's workin,' Pauly protested.

'Oh as if,' Ben countered.

'It's alright Pauly. When you're *old*_age like Ben, it's difficult to accept new ideas,' Raven giggled.

'What, like you actually *buying* something, stead of usin' this place like some rocky horror shop,' Ben said.

'But Ben – look!' Pauly exclaimed.

Pauly handed Ben the dildo. Ben felt that it was kind of thrumming. Ben's hand even shook a little. 'Well run rabbit run.'

'Convinced now, grandad?' jibed Raven.

'Werl, this could just be a way...'

'Yes...?'

'To cost us all those repeat sales on replacement batteries,' Ben shot back. 'So how about you sod off back to Hogwarts and take Harry Pornter there with you.'

Ben tossed the rabbit on the counter. 'I'm leavin' this field of dreams, now infested by crop circles, to stretch my horizons on big boobs monthly.'

Ben picked a magazine off the stand, and stomped off.

A middle aged female customer passed Ben, on her way into smut energy land.

'Customer Katia!' Pauly shouted.

Katia entered from the back of the store. 'OK. Morning Pauly.'

They gave each other a cheek peck.

'Hello Raven,' Katia smiled at the goth princess. 'Is doing good?'

'Apart from the living dead. Yeah thanks.' Raven blew a kiss as she gothed out of the door.

The lady customer had made a swift and decisive selection of products. She brought her pink basket over to

Katia's till counter.

'Good morning. Nice things you are choosing there,' Katia greeted politely. Katia paused for effect, before adding, 'I.D. please.'

'Sorry?'

'Please to see I.D.'

'Well, I haven't got any really,' the lady customer's face turned to puzzlement.

'Oh. Well I am sorry but you see from de sign dat you must to be over de eighteen to make purchase from dees shop.'

'Well, do I *look* under eighteen to you?', the lady asked, with obvious intimation of growing impatience.

Pauly whispered to Katia. In a voice clearly audible to the lady customer. 'Remember your training, Katty. Polite but firm. That was my idea.'

Katia stood her Pauly-instructed ground. 'Sorry, is must be to show eighteen. Yiss.'

'How in the name of Ann Summers can I *not* look over eighteen Miss?' said the lady, her tone rising.

'Er... You could be good at pretending,' offered Pauly.

The lady turned to her new tormentor. 'Who are you?'

'Owner. Well, co-owner. Well, partner sort of but without it being all official.' Pauly concluded his business affairs briefing.

'Right. So *you* don't know who you are. *She* can't tell the difference between a minor and a pensioner. And all *I* wanted was a basket of erotic novelties for the weekend.'

'Oh. We never ask customers the reason for their purchase,' Paul stated. 'We just look for their satisfaction.'

'Well I suppose the only way I can get *that*, is by asking if you sell straight jackets in your bondage section over there.'

'Yes indeed we do. And only the finest,' Pauly proudly confirmed.

'Good.' The irate lady slammed her basket down. 'Because you both need one. Cheerio.'

Her patience strained beyond constraint, the lady customer stomped off.

'Oh Pauly. I sorry,' Katia said.

'Not at all Katty. Polite but firm. You done it.'

Pauly looked in the ex-customer's basket. 'Don't think she were really interested in bondage gear anyway.'

Meanwhile in another corner of Soho, down some steps, and through a stern oak doorway, lay a dungeon. One of the finest in London, according to *Whip!* magazine. With a genuine flagstone floor, flaring torches and fascinating – if ultimately painful – impedimenta of the torturer's art through the ages.

Miss Kitty, dressed in her finest dominatrix garb, was looking after a client. A small, rotund man, wearing pvc boxer shorts, and a studded leather collar. His arms were spreadeagled in chains and handcuffs, all attached to a metal frame.

Kitty wacked him most forcefully, with her whip.

'That's "Yes Mistress Kitty I am a bad boy". Say it !'

'Yes Mistress Kitty I am a naughty boy'.

Kitty thwacked him again. Harder.

'Not "naughty" you limp arse. "Bad'! Bad bad bad!'

Kitty punctuated each repetition with a severe thwack.

The client howled and writhed against the chains. Suddenly, they gave way. He catapulted, face-forward, onto the forbidding floor.

'Owwww! By dose!!!'

Miss Kitty pulled her feet out of the way of a sudden spray of nasal blood. 'Oh- Oh, my whipping boots!'

She leant down to his level. 'I'm so so sorry. Are you OK?'

'I dink I broke by dose.'

'Uh. Oh. Nooo. There'd be more blood than that. Trust me. I'd know. Look, is there anything I can do?'

The client staggered to his scuffed knees, with a bit of dried blood sticking in his nose. 'You doh dat sign dat ses 'Strictly do refuds' ?'

'Mmm hmm.'

'Dow id in de bid wid dat frame.' He paused for a nose wipe. 'Ad gib be by fuffin bunney bad.'

'OK OK. Soreee.'

Kitty muttered to herself, 'God. You get some knocks in dungeon life, doncha.'

In Ben's boardroom, he was edging to the end of the pier of patience, in explaining something to Pauly. This was, to be fair, not a novel experience.

There had been endless little difficulties of ordinary life, which had needed explaining to Pauly. Who seemed to have the same difficulty understanding them, as when you see the equations filled blackboard of a famous nuclear physicist on a documentary channel. Things like: you press the button, wait for the little man, and then you can cross this crossing: the black and white lines thing. Or, you lift the toilet seat up first. All those complicated things.

'So you see how that works, now Pauly?' Ben tried.

'Right,' Pauly nodded. 'So he pays to go stand inside the plastic box with the girly.'

'No!' Ben rubbed his brow in eternal frustration. 'No, look. God give me the strength of ten saints.'

Ben grabbed Pauly by the shoulders, to position him. 'You be the customer guy, OK.'

'Mr Pervy,' nodded Pauly.

'Mr Pervy. Yes.'

'What's his first name, so I can get in character.'

'Pain in the arse probably.' Ben steadied Pauly's shoulders. 'Look. Forget that. Right. Now. There's a plastic window between you - and me - the girly. O-K ?'

Ben mimed a window.

Pauly scrunched up his over-concentrating face. 'Between...'

'Right. And so I go all sexy, right.' Ben mimed a girly tease dance.

'Yeh, I get that bit.'

Ben rolled his eyes. 'And then the light goes off, until

you put more money in the slot.'

'Right.' Pauly considered. 'Well, do I get a torch then?'

'What in the name of Satan's trousers do you need a *torch* for?' Ben gasped.

'To see the slot I put the money in.'

Ben tried to speak. But no more. Having finally fallen off the pier, Ben went red faced. He pulled Pauly up by the front of his jumper, and shook him like a tambourine accompaniment: 'The-light-is-on-the-girl-side-of-the-booth.'

Ben ran his eyes and head along an imaginary line between them. Pauly followed with his head and eyes.

'That's genius!' Pauly jumped on the spot, tried to hi-five Ben, and missed. 'I'll go find a curtain.'

Ben looked at Pauly, holding his hands up questioningly.

In mute reply, Pauly mimed pulling a curtain drawstring, and winked.

On the thriving retail floor below, Katia was arranging a counter display.

A middle aged man, in a grey suit, wandered in. 'Hey love'. He produced his police warrant card to Katia. 'Inspector Trent. Is Mr Dover around?'

Ben entered from the back, with Pauly following.

'Yes, he is as a matter of fact. Take a tea break Katty. And what's Kill Bill doing here?'

'Oh, checking up on my investment. You know,' Trent said.

'Oh yay,' enthused Pauly. 'Did you enter our business card draw for the free bottle of nude champagne? Pauly did his quote marks: "Guaranteed to get your clothes off by the end of the bottle." That was my idea.'

Trent observed Pauly, with astonishment. 'Is he nibblin my trouser leg or what?' he asked Ben.

'No no it's alright Trent,' Ben sighed. 'You know what Pauly's like.'

Ben put a hand on Pauly's shoulder. 'Look Pauly. Great idea about the booth curtains. Pop down Haberdashers Lane and see what you can do, eh?'

'Yeh. Lovely. On it!' Pauly clapped his hands. 'Nice to meet you Inspector Bill.'

Pauly wandered out.

'Is he...?' Trent muttered to Ben, as he mimed a screw loose in head.

'Only on his mother's side.' Trent nodded, as Ben continued. 'Never knew his dad of course.'

'Anyway. A peep show eh,' Trent narrowed his eyes, knowingly. 'That'll be a nice extra earner.'

'Yeah. Well we'll see, right?' said Ben, defensively.

'Sure. Just don't forget that the forces of law and order in these parts need proper funding, alright?' Trent tapped the side of his nose.

'Yeah. The only thing free in this life is eternal rest. I know. Now bugger

off and go nick some innocent sod will ya?'

Trent nodded. 'Did that this mornin. Lunch break now. See ya.' Trent sauntered out.

Ben's mobile chirped.

He looked at the name indicator, and sighed. 'Yes Liza.' He listened to rather loud speech, coming from the other end of the technological miracle.

'Yep. Broke. Ferrari worth more for scrap than the remortgage to pay for repairs.'

He listened again. 'Have you heard of 'work'. Yeah. Might be a novelty for ya, at your age. Bye.' Ben hung up.

'Any tea going Katty?'

Just then Katia entered, with 2 mugs.

'You little eastern European angel.' Ben slid his hand onto Katia's shoulders. 'Now why couldn't I have divorced someone like you?'

Katia shoved his arm off. 'Not to touch pliss.'

Saving that part of the day, Dom entered. 'Look but don't touch eh?'

Ben came to shake Dom's hand. 'Dom mate, how's tricks?'

Dom was of average build, with slightly long hair, and a smart suit. If asked to state his occupation on an official form, the entry would have read something like: selling people things that they don't necessarily need, and being quite good at persuading them they do. He and Ben had found fellow spirits, even before Ben's entry into his marital, then post-marital state, with Liza.

'Well, you know how it is,' Dom said. 'Never complain. Never explain.'

'Yeah. Well, if only your sister would take that mature attitude to life.'

'Oh, Liza still givin ya bother is she?' Dom consoled.

'Does the measles give you spots?' Ben nodded. 'I know she's family like.'

'Huh. At least *you* can actually divorce her.' Dom nodded back. 'I been stuck with her every christmas, since she was old enough to complain about her barbie dolls.'

A good looking twenty-something boy and girl couple wandered in. The boy was dressed casually, but smartly. The girl looked like she'd just left a lap dancing club, on her lunchbreak.

They wandered over to the dvd racks.

'Is it there? Is it?' the girl asked excitedly.

'Er... can't see it babe,' the boy replied.

Ben came over to them. 'Hello there. Any assistance required?'

'Er hi. Well, this is my girlfriend, Cindy Behr.'

'Hello,' Cindy said.

'I'm Jamie, and we're lookin to see how sales of her latest dvd are doin.'

Dom sidled up. 'Would that be the scintillating Cindy from *The Secret Garden*. With you as Fairy Bluebell?'

'Yaay! That's the one,' Cindy confirmed. 'You know, where I go all giddy with those three garden monsters and...'

'Yes, well, best not spoil the plot eh?' Ben interrupted.

'So how's that gem movin Ben?' Dom asked.

'Well, it's shiftin pretty well actually. Obscene rituals in an English country garden. Whoever came up with that one either needs psychiatric help...'

'Or a serious sales campaign,' Dom suggested. 'Hey Cindy. Is anyone looking after your PR?'

'My what?', she asked.

'Your publicity,' Dom clarified.

'Well... the two footballers I shagged got in the paper, the other month.'

'You said it was just one,' Jamie questioned.

'He got tired at half time.'

'Oh.'

Dom took a hand. 'Well look Miss Bluebell. I'm sure I can help boost your sales figures.' He mimed a little hip hop jig. 'You got da boobs. I got da attitude.'

'Why do all salesmen have to sound like a DJ these days?' Ben enquired.

'It's all a matter of style, crocodile,' answered Dom. 'Look here's my card you two. Give me a bell.'

Dom's phone swooshed. 'Oh. Next text from the west. Gotta run mate.'

'OK. Catch ya later for a quick one,' Ben said.

'As the stripper said to the F1 driver. Yep. Deal.' Dom gave a quick wave as he scooted for the door.

Ben turned to the couple. 'Tell ya what love. Sign a few of these and we'll do a special promotion all week.'

'Yaay!' Cindy gave a big smile. 'What do you want me to write?'

Ben sighed. 'Give her some help with that advanced level mastermind question would ya mate. Ta'

Pauly came in. Walking with all the enthusiastic speed his

uncoordinated limbs would allow.

'Ah the curtain snatcher returns,' Ben observed.

'Yeh. I got some bargain crushed red velvet,' Pauly confirmed. 'Comin' Tuesday.'

Ben nodded, vacantly. 'Made my day that has.'

Ben clapped his hands. 'Right you two...gather round.

Paul and Katia grouped up.

'Now,' Ben declared, 'I have a mission for you, should you choose to accept it.'

'Yaay,' Pauly enthused. 'Like that mission impossible thing. You can be the spy girl Katty.'

Katia rolled her eyes.

Ben tried to stride over the Pauly interruption gap. 'Well, it should be mission moronically simple. But I'm confident you'll find a way to make it difficult.'

Katia folded her arms. 'Just tell us what is you is want.'

'Right. Pop down Paradiso strip club, right, and find us some likely ladies to come ply their trade in the peep show booth.'

Pauly burst out laughing. 'Oh well that *is* an easy one yeh.' He laughed some more. 'Just wait till I tell 'em about the curtains.'

Ben and Katia tried to look in some other direction, which didn't have Pauly standing there, miming a curtain drawstring.

## Part 2: The Sound of Silence

From the outside, the Paradiso lap dance club was a simple pile of bricks- obviously in the shape of a building – and with a more obvious neon sign outside.

Inside Pauly and and Katia were sitting at a table, watching various dancers go by. Pauly had managed to acquire a drink with a rather large dayglo paper umbrella on a stick, poking out of it. That didn't seem to be calming Pauly's nerves.

'Y'know Katty. I'm not sure if any of these'll be alright,' he ventured.

'Why not? There is many so pretty ones here.'

'Yeh,' Pauly did a sizing movement with his arm. 'But they're all so *tall*. I mean, how they going to fit into Ben's little booth?'

'Is probably quite big box you know.'

'O...K.' Now, Pauly got done to the meat of the matter. 'What am I going to *say* to them?'

Katia straightened her shoulders and counted off on her fingers. 'Well. Just tell to them the truth. Be straight about what you is wanting and what you think about it and anything you feels about it.'

It might have been a trick of the UV lights. Pauly's face seemed to turn a very strange colour indeed. 'But they're *women*.'

Ben was minding the shop, with Toby at till.

'Leaving you next to actual money like that Toby,'

Ben pointed to the till. 'Still makes me nervous.

'Fair enough. I mean I feel the same about waiting to get my actual wages from *you* at the end of the week.'

Paige Ashley entered, carrying a large fold up canvas bag. 'Hello!'

'Do you need a hand with that?' Ben offered.

'Well you can *carry* it for me. Applause jokes are a bit wearing this time of the morning.'

'Here you go,' Toby offered. He manfully took hold of the canvas, and stripped it off, to reveal a portable massage bed. With a little pushing and fiddling, he managed to get it erected, in the centre of the shop.

'Well, you've been a long time comin,' Ben said. 'And I never used to say that on set. Ahem. I thenk yo.'

'Oh it's funny you say that,' Paige replied. 'You know what my favourite line from all our adult movie scenes was?'

'Can I guess?' Toby asked.

'Go on,' Ben said.

'The *last* one.'

'Serves you right for filming in Hungary,' Ben shot back.

Now here, some backstory is essential. Though perhaps not useful. Ben, as we know, had been a one man pornstar, in his day. Well, obviously not just one man, as that would hardly have been filmed entertainment. Except for a very specialised market. So: Ben and his hand held video camera, and special guest stars.

Which had in fact included Paige, when she was

taking her first steps, as it were, in pornoland. They had both gone on to bigger, if not better things. Co-starring in big budget, award winning adult movies. Paige herself had matured from a stick thin brunette to a curvy, busty ash blonde. Bearing her piecing blue eyes through the transition. And baring everything else.

'Anyway, what's this kit all about?' Ben continued.

Paige waved a hand to Toby. 'Toby, could you...'

Toby hopped onboard.

'I thought you was supposed to be getting away from all that,' Ben observed.

'Yes,' Paige nodded. 'Unlike the inside of your head, I actually am able to move on.'

Toby lay on his back and leant up with his elbows.

Paige pulled out little electro pads, attached to wires. 'This is the latest thing in all over body health massage. The little electrical currents in these,' she indicated the pads, 'flow around the body, clearing blocked pathways and enabling the chi to circulate, bringing a feeling of health and vitality.'

'Is that with or without the little nurse's uniform, hur hur,' Ben offered.

'Oh - with please,' suggested Toby.

'Never work with children and animals,' Paige sighed. 'Right...' Paige pushed Toby flat on the bed. 'Flame on.'

Paige started applying the pads. 'Don't worry, it works through clothes. And in moments, you'll start to relax and feel the healing energy.'

'Frying tonight. Mind the bolts on his neck,' Ben jeered.

Paige jabbed a pad in Ben's direction.

He backed off. 'Alright nurse Frankenstein. I'll go make the cuppas.'

Pauly and Katia were still at their table. But now, they had been joined by three girls, all cracking up with laughter.

'So I said to her, is it always like this on Wednesdays, and she says: only if you forget the jelly,' Pauly concluded.

The dancers cracked up again.

'Aww you're amazin Pauly,' Trina said.

'Wish I had a boyfriend like you,' Dixie sighed.

'We've all got your card for the booth thing. So we'll pop by tomorrow after our shifts, yeah?' offered Ronita.

'Yaay OK Trina, Dixie and Ronita,' Pauly smiled.

'We'd love to stay Pauly, but we better get money-boogy-ing, OK babe,' Trina smiled back.

'Yeah. Just put the drinks on our tab honey. Mwah!' smooched Dixie.

The girls left to play their scantily dressed trade.

'Aww. They were nice,' Pauly commented.

'Yeah. They will all do good in de booth I think,' Katia nodded.

A hand, its fingers covered with rings, slinked over Pauly's shoulder. 'Fancy a dance honey?' cooed a seductive, yet familiar voice.

'Liza!' Katia exclaimed.

'Where?' Pauly asked.

Katia motioned with her head to the hand.

Pauly performed a slow turn, to find himself looking up into Liza's lap dance dress cleavage and face.

'I can do the waltz,' Pauly gulped. 'But I'm not so good at this hop-hip stuff.'

Ben, Toby and Paige were standing around the massage table, chatting.

A potential customer entered. Bearing a quite heavily build, he walked up to the massage table. 'What's this one all about then?'

'It's the latest addition to any home dungeon sir,' Ben helped out. 'Just stick it into your ac/dc and you'll never have to self- stimulate again.'

Paige elbowed Ben in the ribs. 'Take no notice sir. This is Paige's Pleasure. A vitality enhancing gentle electro massage service, which - I have to say - will definitely aid fulfilment in the use of any articles in this shop, or life in general.'

'Massage? Hmmm. But, I mean, out here?' queried the customer.

'Sorry?' Paige's eyes narrowed.

'In the middle of the shop. Or do we go out back, like behind beaded curtains?' the customer clarified.

Ben sniggered.

Paige took a sharp breath. 'I believe that the environment for this apparatus is giving rise to a slight misunderstanding there sir.'

'Oh OK,' the customer nodded, slowly. 'So do you

do home visits then?'

'With appropriate clients, yes,' Paige replied.

'Oh definitely appropriate.' The customer held up an index finger, for emphasis. 'I've got a PVC French maid's outfit, if you're alright in that.'

Paige held out her palm in a gesture of firm and unmistakeable dismissal. 'Next please.'

'Oh. Fair enough.' The customer slouched out.

'Minding my own business and all that,' Ben noted. 'But do you think you need to work on your customer service skills a bit?'

'Yeah. You're right.' Paige turned to face him, her blue eyes blazing. 'I should fit you a flamin' ball gag.'

Pauly was walking, with Katia, up the stairway from the Paradiso basement bar.

'I'm a bit puzzled Katty.'

'Well, Liza she is still good looking woman. Why not to make the money. Better than to rely on Ben for it.'

'Oh no I understand that. I mean, if she's got them dresses she might as well wear 'em.' Pauly stopped. 'No, it's just that...'

Pauly pulled out of his pocket a g-string with telephone number written in lipstick on it. He showed it to Katia.

She giggled, perhaps a bit tipsy. 'Oooh…is belong to Trina, Dixie or Ronita?'

'I don't know,' Pauly said. 'Just found it in my jacket pocket.' He stared at the apparel, then cried out, 'Oh! I geddit!'

'Aha...' Katia encouraged.

'Yeh,' Pauly nodded. 'It's like your name written on your blazer label at school.'

'Kind of...' Katia went with him.

'Yeh. I just give the number a ring when I get back to the shop, an I can get her address.'

'That's my boy,' Katia applauded.

'An pop them in the post to her.'

'OK Pauly,' Katia sighed. 'Well, let's just hope ees not de number for Liza.'

'Oh no no. It'd never be,' Pauly exclaimed, holding the elasticated article aloft. 'Not on ones this size.'

Ben and Dom were chatting over a pint, in a friendly Soho pub.

'So wotcha reckon then Dom. A suitable investment for your expanding portfolio?'

Dom sucked through his teeth. 'Hmmm. Not sure, you know.' Dom stood. 'Hey - let's do a trial of concept test, alright?'

A sexy denim skirted, tight topped girl, was seated at the bar, together with her boyfriend.

Dom walked over, with Ben in tow. Dom rested his pint on the bar. 'Scuse me mate. Is this your girlfriend?'

'Fiancé...' The girl held out a ring-adorned finger.

'Nice.' Dom turned to the young man. 'But, listen, I can get you a few more carats for that mate if you're interested.'

'Well... er... maybe,' her affianced said.

'Now suppose you imagine your lovely lady here wearing a few less clothes,' Dom suggested.

The boyfriend looked at his fiancé. 'Ok.'

'And doing a nice naughty teasy sexy dance,' Dom continued.

'Yer... ?' the boyfriend replied.

Dom turned to the girl. 'And for you babe, well you're safe in a booth. There's a plastic screen between you and him.'

'Right. Bit weird. But sounds OK yeah,' the girl considered.

'Right then mate,' Dom clapped his hands. 'Dolly in a box. All yours for 3 quid a minute. You likee?'

'Er...' the guy clarified. 'Can I hear her when she's talkin?'

'Nope.' Dom tapped the bar. 'Soundproof as a BT phone line.'

'Yep. I'm in,' nodded the boyfriend.

The girl gave her boyfriend's arm a shove, and pouted, 'Oi'.

'They you are!' Ben rubbed his hands. 'Market research proof. Watcha reckon then?'

'Thanks you two,' Dom politely wrapped up. 'Whatever they're havin, on me, doll,' he said to the Bar Girl.

The couple nodded and raised their glasses.

Dom took Ben aside. 'Not sure about it as an erotic venture Bro.' Dom picked up his pint. 'But I can see its potential in reducing domestic violence.' Dom supped. 'Cheers.'

Ben nodded, gloomily.

Back in the land of dreams, Paul, Katia and Toby were looking at the booth, which had been delivered. Resembling an oversized telephone box. Painted a garish – or inviting – pink, depending upon your tastes.

'Have you had a go yet Toby?' Pauly asked.

'No. Well I mean there was nothink to look at was there?'

'Go on then Katty. Let's try it out,' Pauly suggested.

Katia giggled. She opened door and stepped inside the pink booth.

'Do a little dance,' Pauly encouraged. 'And just imagine the curtains.'

Pauly got Toby a chair to sit on. 'Right And then you put the peep tokens in... er...' Pauly surveyed the sides of the booth, in mounting desperation.

Ben entered. He marched up to Pauly, grabbed the coin tokens, and showed where the slot is. 'Right here. OK?'

The booth lights turned. A music beat started. Katia stood there, uncertainly.

Pauly mimed sexy dancing to Katia, 'Go on Katty.'

Katia began to do a very creditable boogie.

'Phooar,' Ben enthused. 'Now, you see what I mean. Might as well get them tokens made out of solid gold!'

Ben shimmied up to the glass and pressed his hands

against it.

Katia stopped dancing, opened the door and leant out. The music stopped. 'Not to touch pliss.'

Miss Kitty entered the shop, trailing her whip. 'Yeah. I'm always warning slaves about getting finger-marks on the equipment.'

'Hello Kitty love. What do you reckon to the new booth?' Pauly asked.

'Yeah,' Ben chorused. 'When you've brushed the cobwebs off your whip, *this* is the way to make a crust in the erotic trade.'

'Oh well,' Kitty replied. 'You know what they say. For every solution there's a problem.'

Kitty angled her head to the door.

Albert Bonsor, a forty-something council inspector entered.

'Oh gawd,' Ben muttered.

Ben and his emporium had experienced quite a few run-ins with Councillor Bonsor. In Ben's view, Bonsor took an unrestrained and exquisite pleasure in stopping people enjoying anything to do with sex. With the same intensity, as people experimenting in all the different ways to do it.

'Good afternoon,' Bonsor waggled his ever-present clipboard. 'Yes. I had heard that you was intending to install this mechanical display device. Contrary I must say to Regulation thirty paragraph g of the Revised Licencing Brackets Soho Premises Brackets Regulations.

And possibly paragraph k.'

Ben climbed a mammoth set of steps onto his speechifying soapbox. 'Look, what *is* the problem? It's not as if any actual sex is gonna be going on with a two inch thick plastic wall in the way. It's all look, don't touch, right? I mean for god's sake there must be twenty lap dance clubs within a thong's throw of this doorway!'

Ben threw out his arms. 'What is it with this ethical do-gooder, poke your nose into everything pleasurable attitude, that your corrupt councillors have got about every bloody thing we try and do to bring exciting, legal, erotic business into this benighted area?'

'You haven't got a music licence.' Bonsor pen-tapped his pad, in bureaucratically stifling satisfaction.

A silenced pause filled the four walls of the shop.

Finally, Ben recovered. 'So how am I supposed to run a naughty naked dance booth without the sound of bloody music?'

'It's alright, Ben,' Pauly said, reassuringly. 'Look, Kitty, you know how you were saying about that slavey what had that nasal distress from an equipment failure.'

'Yeah?' Kitty nodded.

'Well,' Pauly smiled. 'How about using this? I mean you don't need music to make 'em scream do ya?'

'You know Pauly,' Kitty waved her whip, in enthusiasm. 'I think you've got something there.'

'Yaay! 'Is that alright Albert?, Pauly enquired of the man with the demon clip-board.

Kitty sidled over to Councillor Bonsor, and slipped

him a card. 'Course it is. Special rates for public officials.'

Albert's manner softened. 'Right. Well. I have given out the regulation information. So. Er...' Albert shoved his clip-board under his arm. 'I shall attend elsewhere.' He left, not quite as he entered.

Pauly did a little jig of joy. 'Yaay. Well that's all sorted. Tobes, you can sort out delivery to Kitty's can't ya.'

'Yeah sure Pauly,' Toby confirmed.

'Right. Er... Ben.' Pauly took Ben by the elbow. 'I think we better have a chat about Liza.'

'Oh gawd,' Ben muttered. 'Is this gonna make a rotten day better or worse?'

'Both, I think.' Pauly ushered Ban through the door to the next room, at the back of the shop.

After a pause, Katia and Toby heard only a Ben shriek from next door: 'She what!!!'

\*     \*     \*

It is night, in the smutland of dreams.

Toby is stood at counter filling tubes of lube with sand.

'Toby,' Katia warned. 'I not sure. But are you supposed to being doing that?'

Toby holds up the bottle he has been messing with. He reads: "Extra glide. Non stick. Pleasure enhancing." He gives the lube tube a shake. 'Keeps 'em coming back for more, I s'pose.'

Katia shrugs. 'Oh. Dat's de one way to looks at it.' Katia leans forward. 'Just please not to do with de anal lube.'

'Why not babe?'

Katia gives a wry smile. 'Could to really spoil my weekend. '

On the other side of a neon sign blaring Sex-x-x, the sleepless world of Soho goes about its night time business.

CHAPTER 4

# *VIGIL*

## Part 1: Dangerous

A Soho alley. A neon blazed shop frontage. We might expect events inside to have a little raciness. Perhaps edginess. We might more realistically expect plastic wrapped fantasies. Exciting only to those who have the right skill set. Or lack of one.

Inside today, Ben was explaining his latest money-making enterprise to Pauly, Katia and Toby. You'll remember that Ben had been a star, well at least a long-standing twinkle, in the adult films universe. When he'd first started, you actually had to put a video cassette in a bulky player, next to your TV. Which only had four channels.

Quality, in those far-off days of the nineties, had taken a second – and third – place, to availability. Your average film set was a living room sofa, after any domestic animal life had been popped in the kitchen. At least in the legally illegal productions. The actresses had tended to be models. Who were more successful at spending half an hour juggling Ben and his bulky equipment, than getting on Page 3.

Which brings us necessarily to explain that last part to readers of a younger disposition. From the 1970's through to the 1990's, page 3 of the Sun newspaper, used to carry a full page picture of a topless girl. Boobs only on view, and no more. In bikini bottoms or frilly knickers, and a smile. Sometimes she would hold an item relevant to the day's happenings. A shamrock on St Patrick's day. A jockey cap on Grand National day. A voting ballot in election day. You get the very sophisticated idea.

In olden days a glimpse of stocking was looked at as something shocking. So the song went, in 1934. Almost a century later, the wheel of public opinion had turned. And smiles placed over naked bosoms, in newspapers available in the supermarket, had become outlawed. Pictures of ISIS executions, American mall massacres, and leading politicians were deemed acceptable. A titty twinkle was not.

Now, while Ben was technically aware of these ebbs and flows of social standards, the core part of his mental outlook remained firmly fixed on that suburban sofa. From the days spent in search of sets for his video enterprises, an idea had rolled down the marble pathways of his mind, and ended up in the out-tray.

Ben was addressing his faithful. 'So then you see, we just put the 'closed' sign up at the door, switch on the camera, and: bang bang porn scene in the can, at not very much expense whatsoever.'

Ben slid his hand on Katia's shoulder. 'Our field of dreams - as a film set. With a *very* candid camera. Hur hur.'

Katia, yet again, again, shrugged his hand off. 'Not

to touch pliss.'

'Yeah. I geddit,' Toby considered. 'Neat.'

Paul was not so convinced. 'But Ben, you know what you say about the expense. Pauly waved his arms at the shop floor. 'How about the loss of business while we're closed? All them customers.

Ben looked around empty shop. '*All* them? It's about as busy as the inside of Joey Essex's brain.'

At which point, a collection of brain cells, carried in the head of a male customer, entered smutland. The customer approached Katia's counter. He removed a quite large pair of pvc knickers, attached to a pump, out of a bag. Then placed them firmly on the counter.

'Excuse me, but there's a problem with this item,' the customer said.

'Tea break time,' Ben muttered to himself. He sloped off through the back door.

'Morning sir,' Katia smiled. 'And what ees dis problems pliss?'

'Well, you can see a quite distinct hole. See?' The customer pointed his index finger at the distinct orifice.

'Scuse me,' Pauly noted, 'but that model's supposed to have a hole in it.'

The customer turned the item around to show a distinct tear hole in the side. 'Not *there*.'

Pauly considered the problem. 'Oh. Oh yeah. Well, have you been using the item per specifications?'

'Oh come on. I mean it's not like this comes with an instruction manual.'

'No well certainly not sir.'

'See?'

'The manual's 50p extra,' Pauly informed. And then helpfully, 'I can get you one.'

This barrage of accurate, but useless information, was not assisting the customer to remain calm and cool. 'Oh right. So I get a dodgy item, I come to complain and refund, and I'm now supposed to pay 50p extra for the privilege?'

'It'll cost you a lot more than that if you carry on using it like a demented gerbil.' Toby butted in, doing his little mime of an overactive rodent.

The customer actually paused, to consider the matter. 'Fair point.'

In the meantime, Katia had gone to get a replacement. 'Bag...'

'Tag...' Toby ripped off the price tag.

'And there you are sir,' triumphed Pauly, over this model of customer service work.

'Oh - OK. Well thanks then.' The customer took his newly bagged item and exited.

'See, we got it goin' like a clockwork orange now.' Pauly applauded. Then he stopped, and threw his hands up in horror. 'Oh! He forgot his manual!'

'OK, I'll go look for him.,' Toby volunteered. Toby grabbed the manual from the counter, and briskly followed off after the customer.

Ben wandered back in. 'All sorted then?'

'Yah. We got it smooth as sixpence here, now,' Pauly advised.

Ben saw Liza push through the shop door, in an obvious state of high stress. 'You'd be well advised to keep a tight grip on any loose change, just now son.'

Liza marched up to Ben's personal space. 'This place. It does its trade in obscenity, right?'

'Well not exactly Liza,' Pauly clarified. 'You see, strictly speaking, under the Obscenery Publications Act 1959, there has to be a tendency to deprave and corrupt and...

Liza fingered Ben in the chest. 'Depravity. And corruption. Right here in one snivelling, grassin, cowardly tossrag.'

Ben rolled his eyes. 'Look woman. I spent near on twenty years not knowing what you're goin' on about. And it's about the only thing you got any better at.' Ben paused for breath. 'What?!!!'

Now, Liza's finger was poking at Ben's face. 'You got me sacked, you rotten little turnip. From my dancin' job.'

'Now why would I do that strange thing?'

'Because you don't want me to have my independence. You like me bein' destitute, hanging around for any crumbs off of your filthy table. You just want me to be miserable!'

Ben sighed. 'Well you don't need any help with that last one. Let's face it - you're a one woman clinical depression ward.'

'So you admit it, you rotten sod. I just try to drive away - and what do you do? Stick a twisted knife in my tyres.'

Pauly took Liza by the arm, gently. 'I think the problem's more on the driver's seat there Lize love.'

'Eh? Wotcha mean?'

'Well, me and Katia was talkin to some of the girls. And they was sayin. Well...'

Katia took up the story. 'That is is quite the embarass to have de elderly lady working wid dem.'

'Elderly!!! I am not bloody elderly!!!'

'No right, Lisa love,' Pauly nodded. 'I mean. Life begins at forty an' everythin'.'

'Yeah?'

'Yeh. It's just that after...'

Ben butted in, before Lisa took another step in Pauly's explanatory minefield. 'Look, love of my life. What they're tryin to say, as I heard it, is that the younger girls din't want the compctition. From a more experienced, more sophisticated entertainer.' Ben nudged Pauly in the ribs. 'Right Pauly?'

'Oh yeh,' Pauly came in on que. 'Definitely more experienced.' Pauly's feet did a little embarrassed shuffle. 'Er... so they like petitioned the manager to... well...'

'Leave me in queer street,' Liza's voice rose to a glass-smashing pitch. 'Bitches the lot of them. I'd be ashamed to call any of them my daughter.'

Ben had to restrain a cough. 'So maybe an apology in order then, sweetheart?'

Liza's hands jutted from her hips. 'Oh I am terribly sorry for tellin a few home truths. So how about one from you.' Lisa's torso now jutted forward. 'Have you actually sold anythin' yet?'

Ben rolled his eyes, the other way, and sighed.

'Well when you do, it's me first dibs. Just you remember that. After all, I have very *mature* needs.' Liza's finger went into full-on pointing mode again. 'Like the taxi fare to a new job interview!'

Liza stormed out.

After: well more in the middle of, a decent period of shocked silence, Pauly patted Ben's arm. 'Hey Ben. I saw a job ad in the Soho Gazette, this mornin. Undertaker's assistant. No previous experience necessary. Shall I... ?'

'Better not son.' Ben let out a deeply held breath. 'She'd only end up arguin' with the customers.' He rolled his eyes in penance. 'And their relatives.'

Toby returned, slightly breathless.

'Did you get on alright?' Pauly asked.

'Well: there's good news and bad news on that,' Toby replied.

'I bet there isn't,' Ben observed.

'On the good side,' Toby continued, 'although none of the people I stopped from behind was our customer, I did get us a nice invitation to a display of erotic paintings.'

'Told ya.'

'Framed ones?' asked Pauly. 'I like them.'

'Oh, Pauly Picasso. The conaisseur of Soho. Right then. The bad side Toby?

Toby slapped a flyer on the counter.

It had a picture of the front of the Sex-x-x shop on it.

It read: "Anti-smut vigil. Reclaim the night. Stop this evil trade now."

Ben picked the leaflet up. His face grew desolate and haunted. 'Oh well that's just great. Yeah. I mean, unleash the gates of hell and let assorted mad loony demons in pink doc martens spit at our shop windows.'

Pauly stared at the leaflet. 'What "evil trade"?'

'I think they means us,' Toby said.

'Oh no no,' Pauly objected. 'Me mum would never stand for that would she Ben? I mean, all them years she collected her tips...

Pauly snuggled his head on the chest of his taller mentor, as they dreamed backward, to a time when it was all in black and white.

There, in their joined recollection was Pauly's mum.

Dancing around a tired wood and lino pub. Dressed in a basque, with a feather boa, fishnet stockings and stilettos. Doing the rounds with a pint glass filling with coins, as gentlemen of the borough show their appreciation in small change. And sometimes notes.

'And she always said to me, "Pauly - if you can't do do something good, do nothing." *She* gave me that idea. And I've lived by it all me life.'

Ben ran the words through his head, trying to make sense of Paulyness. He gave up.

'Well doing nothing is not exactly a survival tactic at this point is it? Options? People? Come on - executive decision making.'

Toby put his hand up.

'Yes Toby.'

'Move.'

'No Toby. Katia?'

'We have a saying in Poland.' Katia paused. 'When you is standing in something dat is really de smelly...'

'Yes...' Ben encouraged.

'Make to sure it is only de one foot.'

'Sound strategic advice for the mono-pedal retarded. Thank you Katia.'

Raven entered, carrying a pile of the same feminist leaflet. 'Hey guys, have you seen this? Looks like Gotham city has declared war on the bat cave.'

'I don't think we stock any bat-erotica do we? I mean I suppose the jumbo love beads could make a kind of batarang...' Pauly mimed the motion, 'and...'

'Yes Raven,' Ben interrupted. 'We are about to be publicly vilified by an army of feral feminists as the most hated store in Soho.'

'Well, there have been complaints about Burger Melts, in Popple Street.

'Quite right! As a vegan I object to the whole idea. Doing that to innocent animals. Disgusting.'

'Thank you Gothic Ghandi,' Ben nodded, irritably. 'Although we are rather more focussed in this discussion on the matter of sex.'

'No that's alright. I mean - love's love right?'

'Oh,' Pauly contributed his contribution, 'you wanna

try that down-the-steps shop in Brewer Street 'Down and Dirty'.

'Pauly. You know that if someone lifted the khazi lid, positioned your flies and gave you standing room, you'd still miss on the floor?'

'Hey. You said you wouldn't mention that.' Pauly reassured Raven. 'I've been getting better. It's just a matter of concentration.'

'Ann Summers give me strength. Look: problem - solution - gap in the middle big as Katia's cleavage and needing to be filled.'

'Pliss not to...'

'Not literally! Not today anyway.'


Stacey Lacey, a ravishing brunette aspiring porn star entered. She was wearing (nearly) a tiny denim cop top, possibly tinier denim mini skirt, and heels clearly borrowed from a lap dancing wardrobe.

'Hello. I'm here for the audition.'

Pauly looked up from the leaflet. He was using his finger to focus completely on the printed words. 'Oh, not right now love, thanks. Bit busy. '

Ben shimmied over to Stacey, turning the calor gas cooker of his charm onto full burn. 'No that's alright. Always got time for talent er...'

'Stacey,' she held out a hand in greeting. 'I've not done anal yet. But if its for the right movie...'

'Well, we can talk about that,' Ben smoothed. 'I mean as an actress, it is always important to keep expanding your horizons.'

Yet another new love boutique entry entered, in the shape of a svelte blonde, with green goddess eyes, wearing a quite transparent shirt, tight jeans and boots.

'Hey up Ben, another one look,' Pauly pointed out.

'Are you in charge here?' the new visitor enquired of Pauly.

Ben shimmied over. You'll have noticed he does this whenever opportunity knocks. Or gently taps, even.

'That would be me, my little vixen. Well I must say you've come dressed for the part. A feisty little cum-strumpet, with a touch of executive arse-class.'

'Excuse me?'

'No, that's alright honey drips. I can see talent from a mile away.'

'Oh *really*?' The lady moved into Ben's personal space. 'And can you sense an opportunity for living extremely dangerously?' The lady kept on walking, Ben found himself mesmerised, pedalling backwards. 'Burning your lecherous fingers with fire. With your back right against the wall and finding there's nowhere to go but hell?'

'Cor! You betcha,' yelped Ben, with his back to an erotic novelties counter.

The lady whipped a vigil leaflet out of her jeans back pocket and shoved it, like a guided missile, at Ben's chest. 'Well today's your lucky day then, you filthy miserable disgusting excuse for a human being!'

Ben fumbled at the leaflet. 'What the... ?'

'Yes! I'm Nadine Moss, leader of the Save Soho Night

## VIGIL

vigil.' Nadine raised a hand of warning. 'And you just take a good look around this cesspit of female degradation Mr Creep Dover...'

'Have I missed something?' Pauly looked around the shop, the puzzlement etched on his face.

'Because... what?' Nadine trailed off, losing concentration, under the ferocious pressure of Pauly's idiotic facial expression.

Ben took the opportunity to jump in. 'Now look here Adolf Titler! What do you think gives you the right to come... comin' it in here, like some deranged blonde Nazi lesbian rottweiler?'

'I am not a lesbian!' Nadine retorted in shock.

Stacey, who had been watching with intensity, sidled a few sinuous steps over to Nadine. 'Well. That's alright love. I mean, I'm not really either, but I'm sure we can still do a good and filthy girl girl scene together.'

Nadine lost it. She instinctively raised her hand. Then realised she couldn't apply physical force sister Stacey. So she gave Ben's cheek a good slap instead.

'And I came here to reason with you!' Nadine howled. 'But you're all just disgusting degraded, degenerate...'

'Oh are we doing 'd' words? Er... doorknobs?' Pauly jumped in.

'Right! Tonight! This valley of vileness shall close forever!' Nadine threw a pile of vigil leaflets in the air, and stomped out.

'Ooh that was really good!' Stacey cooed. 'What's my part like?'

'Not doorknobs then?' asked Pauly, having the feeling he'd lost at scrabble to a 6 year old again.

With the leaflets still scattering down, Ben took urgent control of the situation. Picking up up one of the leaflets, he read: "Action Meeting. Friends Hall, Dolphin Street, 2pm." Ben clapped his hand. 'Right. Pauly, Katia, gather round. We have a time and a place and I have a plan.'

'A cunning plan?' Pauly asked.

'No. We don't do those in this shop. Your mission, should you choose to accept it, is to infiltrate this meeting, learn what is planned, and find a way to stop it.'

'Oh Kats, you'd better write that all down,' Pauly noted. 'Then... er swallow it. That's right in't it?'

'Why do I have the feeling this is gonna turn into mission cockup,' ben sighed. 'But, when you've got your balls in the bonfire, as they say, all you can do is pray for rain. Right - off you go!'

Pauly and Katia headed out., with urgency. Well Katia did. Pauly got a little lost around the bondage wear rail, and Katia had to help him to the actual door.

Ben turned to Stacey, who smooched, seductively, 'We could go somewhere a bit more private and talk about me getting the part in your film?'

Ben sighed, with resignation. 'Tell you what love. You find your intimate spot...'

'Yaay,' Stacey giggled.

'And I'm off down the pub.'

'Oh.'

## Part 2: Past Relief

Friends Hall was a red brick witness to a century of Soho life. Originally a meeting place for good citizens to meet, read improving pamphlets, and pray. It had always welcomed non-conformists, dissidents, and people needing a warm space for a few hours. Karl Marx himself, was supposed to have addressed meetings there. But there hadn't been many buyers for his drab and dismal watercolours.

Once, people had gathered together to discuss street action for suffragettes, struggling for the vote. To plan protest against Oswald Moseley's fascist blackshirts. To vilify the Vietnam warmongers.

Now, the shrill protest was against plastic wrapped erotic entertainment. An assorted crowd of feminists and students, occupied the wooden seats. Anti-porn placards were ranged round the room.

Over to one side, Jessie, a pixie faced brunette, was nodding, as Nadine talked to her. Pauly and Katia were seated anonymously, amongst the middle of the crowd. Pauly was wearing a big badge shouting "End Free Porn".

'Pauly - where did you get that from?' Katia whispered.

'It's good innit?' Pauly pulled his jumper to look at his trophy. 'Jessie gave it me. Nice girl over there.' Pauly pointed out Jessie. 'I dunno what Ben's so worried about. They's right about this aren't they?' He fingered the badge.

Katia knitted her brow. 'End free porn. Yiss. I don't think they is think same about dis as yo Pauly darlink.'

'Well some of it can be a bit overpriced, I know,' Pauly went on. 'I mean the American stuff...'

Katia shushed him, as Nadine climbed the stairs onto a little stage, and clapped her hands.

'Right. Thank you all for coming,' Nadine announced, confidently. 'It's great to see such a good turnout in this worthy cause.' She started warming up the audience. 'Protecting our streets from this filth. Reclaiming the night from evil perverts feasting on the lifeblood of women.

'Vampires?' Pauly whispered to Katia.

Katia shushed him.

'Did someone say vampires?' Nadine echoed. 'Yes Yes! Exactly. Parasites. Demons of depravity.'

'Hey that's a good title that,' Pauly whispered to Katia. 'Make a note Kats.'

'And tonight. We few shall be joined by many more. As we march on the temple

of degradation to women. We-shall-reclaim-the-night!'

The audience applauded. Then broke into chants of "Save-the-night".

Katia turned her head to see Pauly joining in.

There was shuffling, as the audience stood and got into little chatting groups. Jessie skittled up to Pauly, with her cute pixie steps.

'Wasn't that great Pauly?' Jessie enthused. 'Inspirational!'

'Defintely. Yeh,' Pauly nodded. 'We made notes.'

'I mean. Nadine. Standing there.' Jessie threw an arm out to the stage. 'Like a biblical angel, bright and fierce, brandishing her sword of truth!'

'Angel. Angel? Oh yeahhhhh !' Pauly started doing a little step, step jig, as his Pauly brain lurched into manoeuvres which would baffle any competent neurologist. 'Ooh. Um, Katia do you want to do a milkshake or something with Jess?' Pauly pushed them together, gently. 'I'll have to – uh - well; see you later.'

'At the shop?' Jessie asked, with a bright elfin smile.

'Yes love. Definitely.'

Pauly hurried off. Jessie and Katia exchanged puzzled glances.

Inside Nadine's temple of degradation to women, Toby was minding things.

Ben entered. 'Has that Stacey girl left then?'

'It's OK,' Toby replied. 'Don't think she stole anything.'

'Just my heart. Oh well. '

Paige pushed through the shop door. Without her portable massage bed, and wearing a cute tartan dress and heels. 'Hello nice day everyone.'

'Hello no it damn well isn't Paige,' Ben said, cross and frustrated.

'Ooh no what's the matter? Lost a blonde and found a brunette? He he'

'Well, funny as how you mention that. Anyway.' Ben

motioned a hand towards the vigil leaflets.

Paige had a read. 'Cooo. I might go join that.'

'What! You rotten turncoat!'

'Oh no silly,' Paige smiled. 'I mean they've obviously got a rather angled outlook on life. Just wanting to stop fun. But where there's strife, there's stress. And I have just the thing to help anyone with that.'

'And I thought I was the sharp one. You're like a feral car salesman in tights.'

Paige performed a quick stocking top flash. 'Hold ups darling. Like name, like nature.'

A female customer walked in. She was blonde and petite, and wearing a long beige mac.

'Hello. Have you got anything special for the disabled?'

'Ben's business sense?' Paige offered.

'Thank you, Rough Spice,' Ben pushed past her. 'Certainly madam. Is it for someone special may I ask?'

'Well, I'd more call it someone particular. You are Ben Dover, the owner of this place?'

'Long and proud of it, yes.'

The customer whipped out rape spray canister and rape alarm. 'Then this is for you, gangster pervert! Rape Alarm! Mace mace mace!'

She pulled the rape alarm, then sprayed Ben right in the face. He fell over.

'Sorry Miss,' the assailant said to Paige, then ran out.

Ben was still writhing on the floor. While Paige was helpfully giggling.

'Toby stop her!' Ben cried.

'But she ain't nicked anyfin'.

Paige bent down to the hapless smut store proprietor. 'Aww poor Benny. Having your heart and your pride stolen in the same day. Come here.'

Paige stopped the alarm and helped Ben up.

Ben groggily raised to his feet, and brushed himself down. "You see? You bloody see? All this talk of peace and love and helpin the oppressed. And all along they're just a bunch of feminist terrorists with crap haircuts. All we do here is offer harmless fun. And what's their agenda? To kill. To maim...'

Paige held up the rape spray bottle, and eyed the label. 'To spray artificially salted water at middle aged shop owners.'

'What? Gimme that here.'

Ben looked at the bottle label. 'Right. Well, that could still put a child's eye out. Mind you...' Ben fingered the rape alarm. 'Could do with keeping this handy.'

'For police evidence!' Toby enthused.

'In case Liza comes round.'

Pauly entered carrying plastic bag. 'Have they started yet?

Ben sighed. 'Well, did you have to just negotiate your way through a cordon of fascist feminists brandishing home made rape alarms?'

Pauly looked around, in concern. 'Where?'

'No Pauly. World War Three in leggings and flat shoes hasn't started yet.'

Katia and Jessie came in.

Pauly waved at Jessie. 'Oh. Sorry I had to slope off. Just I had an idea...'

Ben smoothed (again, again, again) over to pixie Jessie. 'Oh ho ho. Well what have we got here Kats, another audition hopeful? I must say they are getting cuter. So, sexy, what shakes your beautiful curls out of bed?'

'I'm here to see Pauly. Is this the shop?'

'Yeh.' Pauly went over to take her hand. 'And strictly no free porn here Jess love. Just like your badge says.'

'Hang on,' Ben objected sternly. 'I send you undercover to foil a fiendish plot of feral feminists.' He pointed at Jessie. 'And you bloody get off with one!'

'No, it's just that Jess gave me an idea, and...'

'Oh I'll bet she did. No! Not one more word from you. You Judas of Soho.' Ben turned his back on the pair of them.

Suddenly, sounds of shouting could be heard outside the shop. There were lights waving outside the windows.

'Doh! Poisonous love beads,' Ben murmured. 'They've damn well started!'

Nadine entered. She was wearing a tshirt with the vigil logo on it, under a leather jacket, with her hair up. With skin tight jeans and ankle boots, the very model of an anti-porn protester.

'What's the matter Nadine?' Ben taunted. 'Failed the interview for a Nazi concentration camp guard?'

'Well actually. They *did* stick pornographers in prison. So they had that going for them.'

'And interestin uniforms,' Pauly offered. 'I mean you're all blondie blue eyed and everything, so you'd quite suit.'

Nadine opened her mouth to speak. But her mind just couldn't find a way to occupy the same mental universe as Pauly.

Then, she noticed Jessie. 'Jessie - what are you doing here? Consorting with these hopeless smut skunks!'

'Er... no love,' Pauly objected. 'The customers have all gone. See?' Pauly motioned to the empty shop.

'Jessie!' Nadine took her by the arm. 'I insist you explain yourself. You're a feminist sister of the night. Why are you consorting with this retarded porn peddler?

Pauly and Jessie shrank together, under Nadine's withering torrent.

'Well I could just as well ask why Pauly here is cavorting with one of your jackboot jillies, you mad ranting period pain,' Ben hit back.

'Shutup when you're not even fit to be shit on a shoe! I'll discipline my campaigners any way I want. So you keep your disgusting dick breath diatribes to yourself.'

Katia nudged Paige to look at Pauly and Jess. 'It is like de porno version of Romeo and de Julieta.'

'Yeah!' Ben shot back. 'Well a bit of dick breath might do you some good, though there's nowhere in Soho you'd find some poor sod demented enough to stick anyfin inside of you!'

Pauly put his hand up. 'Er... actually I think you're not right about that one Ben.'

Pauly fished in his carrier bag. 'See, when Jessie said about the Angel, well it got me thinkin. So I went did me homework, well streetwork, really. And... oh sorry. Do you want a mint?'

'What?' Nadine asked, utterly confused.

'For the dick breath.'

Nadine gripped a first. 'I'm gonna kill him, I swear, I'm gonna...'

'Form a queue, love,' Ben interrupted. 'Pauly. What exactly is it that's filling the vast empty space between your depopulated brain cells, and trying to emerge via your generally useless oral orifice?

Pauly brought a dvd out of his bag. It had an unmistakable picture of Nadine on the cover. Wearing a very similar leather jacket. But without the t shirt. Or anything else.

'Well, I mean, I never thought I'd meet her in real life. But here she is: Angel Floss! The inslip angel between the sheets.' Pauly waggled the dvd case. 'But only in this really rare Hungarian footage.'

'Coo let's have a look.' Paige pushed next to Pauly's outstretched hand.

Nadine made a grab for the dvd. 'No!'

Paige grabbed back, and while the two of them had a mini tug of war, Paige looked at the back cover. 'He he he. Well I must say, I'd never have recognised you, Flossy - er... Nadine. Not from this angle!'

Ben, Katia and Toby all gathered round to look.

'It's OK,' Pauly said. 'I've got copies. See, I thought that as Nadine's here, we could do a proper nice window display. You know, special offer. I can get some angel wings from the G-A-Y shop down the street.' Pauly mimed angel wings. 'Would look dead sexy and classy,' he reassured a horrified Nadine.

'This is just blackmail!'

'Naa.' Ben tapped the dvd case. 'More like pornmail. Hur hur.'

Jessie detached from Pauly and took a couple of pixie steps forward, blazing with anger. 'Nadine Moss! You're worse than these people. At least they aren't pretending.'

'I was young. Just a student. I don't even speak Hungarian!'

'No... It's all subtitles,' Pauly said.

Ben stepped forward and took Nadine by the shoulders. "So how about it then Miss Floss-Moss? Nice little autograph. Get a big screen in and play the best bits for discerning customers... and protesters.'

Nadine lit a cigarette, with trembling fingers. She inhaled, deeply. 'Right. Well. I am not going to allow a single minor indiscretion...'

Pauly rattled the carrier bag 'And Volume 2 and the Bangin Best of...'

'Well...' Nadine rallied. 'The movement should not get itself compromised by individuals... this is about feminist politics, not personalities. So er...

Ben pointed to the door. 'Shall we?'

Night had fallen over the streets of Soho. The vigilists were still chanting, and thrusting their placards. A scene reminiscent of that old black and white Frankenstein movie. Where the peasants have marched up the castle with fire torches and pitchforks.

Nadine stood in the entrance, and clapped her hands.

'Listen! Listen to me everyone. Tonight had been a great success. We have struck a blow at the black heart of the male fantasy monster. Now we should all disperse and meet at the Cock and Spaniel, Goodge Street, per plan.'

Ben nudged her in the ribs. 'And...'

'We've made our point and... I'm sure these law abiding rate payers...'

'Do we?' Pauly asked Ben.

Ben rolled his eyes.

'Will henceforth take our well intentioned concerns to heart. Well done.'

Pauly took a little step forward. 'And thank you all for coming. There's free samples still for anyone that wants.'

Paul looks at Jessie and remembered. 'And say No! to free porn. Yaay!

Pauly raised his fist in a power salute. Jessie copied him. Ben and Nadine hid their faces in their hands.

The crowd roared with satisfaction, then began to disperse.

'Tell you what Nadine,' Ben said. 'Whatever else,

your a damn good actress.' he sighed, and looked her full in the face. 'I'd offer you a part in my porno, but...'

'Worried that I might say yes?'

'Only in the degenerate dreams of an old filth merchant.'

'Come on all you lost lovers,' Paige cheered. 'Let's all get rat arsed on vodkas and shisha's at Rafis.'

'Paige,' Katia asked. 'Why is dis part of de rat in drinking?'

'Aww. You'll get it by about the 3$^{rd}$ glass sweetheart. Come on.'

They headed off down the street. Ben looked at Nadine. They headed off in the other direction. Pauly looked at Jessie. They slipped their hands together, then walked after Paige and Katia.

\*   \*   \*

Now the Soho streets are quiet. Well, apart from the usual nocturnal noises.

In the shop, Toby is in alone.

He is writing "Have fun with a Feminist" on protest placards. To which he has stuck pictures of Nadine's dvd cover.

He holds one up and smirks.

The night continues quietly. As for the day: we'll have to see.

CHAPTER 5

# *PINK*

## Part 1: All Sorts

As plumbed somewhat in the Prologue, there is no depth to which the erotic imagination will not plunge. In its efforts to stimulate the hights of ecstasy. Is there a right and wrong, a moral centre to this kaleidoscope of sexuality?

Other ages have thought so, and imposed prison and other punishments to mark where the prohibition line is drawn. In modern mores, among consenting adults, anything goes. Yet still, for those within the fervent of liberated eroticism, boundaries still abound.

Is it all just a matter of taste, in the appetites of the taster? Is the objective impulsion of commerce itself, the arbiter? Perhaps the ironic truth is that, in an era where nothing is forbidden, anything goes: but.

Ben, Pauly, Katia and Toby were experimenting with a new love toy. A bum, with anatomically correct orifice. The realism quotient of the object and experience, was a matter for the user.

'So, then you apply the special lubricanty,' Pauly said, rather like a demented sports commentator, 'which we's doin' as a complementary sample for the first ones. Let's have a good smear there on Katia's finger.' Pauly pushed an open lube tube at Katia.

'Nooo! I not putting any parts of me into dat thing,' she recoiled.

'Yesss,' Ben put in. 'Rather reminds of of what I said on my date last night.'

'The Mongolian,' Pauly nodded.

'Come again?' Toby puzzled.

'Barbecue!' Ben said. 'Pauly means I took her for an unusual dining experience. Look, can we get on?'

'Right, well OK I'll get sticky,' Pauly offered. 'Ey, it's kind of like being a vet this in't it?'

'Nooo!' his love boutique colleagues shouted, in repulsed unison.

'Right. Goin for anal entry.' Pauly did his space shuttle moment, with finger poised.

'Oh well,' Ben shrugged. 'You're both virgins and over the age of consent.'

Pauly now had his finger well-inserted into... Well, inserted. 'Owah! I can feel me circulation going. That's right tight arse that is.'

'What ees dis model called? De Ben Dover? 'Katia giggled.

'Oh your sparkling wit must be in great demand amidst the cabbage patches and coal mines of your homeland,' Ben replied. 'Hey up. Shop.' Ben motioned to the door.

Katia and Toby move to their places. Pauly had, meanwhile, become glued to the spot by his insertion. The averagely male customer wandered up to Pauly and the love toy.

'Oh. Is that new?' he asked.

Pauly gasped. 'Yeh. I think that's why she's so - uh. Could you lend me a hand please?'

The customer took a firm grip of Pauly's wrist. Applying some leverage with his foot against the display counter, he pulled. The love toy sprang off the counter, with Pauly's finger still well-inserted in it, smacking Ben in the face.

Katia and Toby tried to hide their about-to-explode sniggers.

'Ey Pauly,' Toby said. 'Oi think you've got that arse about face.'

'Enough you two!' Ben warned. 'Not in front of the customers. Remember your Sex-x-x etiquette please.'

'Oh, that's no problem. Good to see it in action,' the customer said.

'But that's not...' Ben began to protest, then thought better of it. 'Right. How may we be of assistance sir?'

The customer paused. He subjected Pauly's finger companion to a detailed stare of scrutiny. 'Well. That's nice.' Then he stood back. 'But have you got any other body parts.'

Ben struggled to keep his features even. 'Such as?'

'I like ankles... Feet?'

'Shall I put that Hannibal Lecter poster up in the window?' Toby chipped in.

'What my young assistant means is, such anatomical extracts would appear to offer rather less in the way of erotic interaction than...'

'Melinda,' Pauly offered.

'The operating parts of Melinda here,' Ben waved.

'No no. This is Melinda,' Pauly corrected. 'I don't know what the rest of her's called.

'Hands? Elbows?' persisted the customer.

Ben struggled to contain a sigh. 'Look I'll tell you what sir. If you'd like to take a card here, and give us a call when the new stock arrives next week.'

'Then we'll see if we can give you a hand! Yaay,' Pauly offered up some Pauly wit. The customer ignored him.

'Or a shoulder blade.'

'Well. Thank you for calling.' Ben folded his arms as unwelcoming as possible. 'And do view our splendid collection of straight jackets - there in the bondage section - on your way out, sir.'

'OK. Thanks. ' The customer slowly wandered out.

Ben looked around the walls of the store in wonderment. 'Never think you've seen it all, eh?' His eyes fell on Pauly, still well-inserted, and waving helplessly. 'You can put that down now.'

A while later, Ben opened the door to his boardroom. 'What are you doing here?' he asked.

Katia was sat behind Ben's desk, with study books on accountancy, a calculator, pencil and paper.

'I ees study for my accountancy exam.'

'Well, despite what you might think I am not going

to make any jokes about double entry.' Ben paused for effect. 'It's far too serious a subject for that.'

Katia sighed. 'Yiss, is why I do here when's quiet. So I can get some de serious space for study.'

'So - what you botherin with that for?' Ben picked up a pencil, and tapped out his following points, on the desk. ' Two plus two equals four. Always count your change. Never let your wife see your bank statement. School of life my girl.'

'Yiss well I is wanting somethink more de life dan in de service of your perverting people,' Katia waved a dismissive hand.

'Customers Katia. That's *business*.'

'I knows what you tink. Dat is women has smaller de brain dan a man so is why is make hard de head with study.'

'Well, I could have put it better myself, but yes, that's the gist.'

'You maybe have bigger de brain. But smaller de mind means you is never understand,' Katia replied, a bit miffed at Ben's palaeolithic brand of blatant sexism.

'That's fair enough. Any man who claims to understand the mind of a woman is playing Russian roulette with all pistol chambers loaded.' Ben threw the pencil back on the desk. 'Just sharpen me pencil when you've finished, alright?

Ben walked out. Katia gave an irritated flick of her head, as if a pervy porn fly had just stopped buzzing.

Toby was minding the counter. Essentially safeguarding the store treasures from invisible shoplifters.

Ben entered, to see Pauly struggling through the door, with large cardboard box. 'Good to see ya gettin the hump. Oh go on then.' Ben went to give Pauly a hand. 'Where'd you get these from then?' Ben peered at the box. 'Not Julia's regular stock.'

'Yeh,' Pauly perked his smile. 'I used my own initiatti-tive on this one. Bit pricey, but the mark up... Yaay. That was my idea.'

They struggled together with the laden box, succeeding in propping it on the centre counter.

Katia entered, and watched.

'Right,' Ben rubbed his hands together, 'lets see what new roses are blooming in our field of dreams, then.'

'Three guesses?' Pauly suggested.

'Go on then. Toby?'

'Er... has it got anal in it?'

'Yepo deffo,' Pauly nodded.

'It will to be somebody else has to put all dat on de shelves,' Katia chipped in.

'Yeh. I will,' Pauly volunteered.

'Not exactly content-related,' Ben noted, 'but relevant. Right: multiple, group action?'

'Oh yeh,' Pauly clenched his hands in excitement. 'Come on then?

'Uh well I can fink of lots of things,' offered Toby.

'Well. Not all at once,' Ben replied. 'But yes. We are in pretty wide open genre territory here.'

'That's it!' Pauly threw his arms in the air. 'See - genius. That's why you're my partner.'

Ben just shook his head in puzzlement.

Pauly lettered the words with his finger in the air. 'W-I-D-E O-P-E-N. See ?' Pauly pulled a dvd out.

Ben picked it up. He put his glasses on. He read: "Wide open: when six virile backpacker hunks find themselves stuck in the outback, they explode wide open, as..."

Ben dropped the dvd on the counter like a scorpion. 'No!!! Elton John on a deckchair!'

'What's matter boss?' asked Toby.

'These! These... filth!' Ben pointed in horror at the dvd's. 'Obscene. Disgusting.'

'I thought is what we is heres for,' Katia commented.

'No! Not this... these. I can't. What would me mum say?'

'Well, same as mine I s'pose,' ventured Pauly. 'Where there's ass there's brass.'

'Look,' Ben drew breath to speechify. 'The dear lord above, or whatever is your higher power - a gerbil in your case Pauly - did indeed create the arse, and all that shimmers with it, as the finest expression of natural beauty in the universe.' Ben jabbed his finger at Katia then Toby to illustrate his next point. 'Hers! Not his!'

'Pliss not to...' Katia objected.

Ben sighed. 'Yes, I know. So you can put that rancid box away Pauly.'

'Oh, no problem. I were goin to do that anyway,'

*PINK*

Pauly said.

'See?' Ben waved his hands. 'Reasonable people, reasoning together, can do reasonable things.'

'Yeh. 'Cos I have to make room for all the other stuff that' comin.'

'What stuff?!'

'Well, there's the vids, mags, special toys. All brilliant. An' we can do a special section of the shop called 'Pink'.'

'Or, just call it 'moron', after its creator,' Ben snarled.

'Why then?'

'You just don't geddit do ya?'

'You think Pink's not a good name?' Pauly queried.

'Love beads on a barbecue give me strength.' A troubled vein began to pulse in Ben's forehead. 'No it's not the name. It's the whole gay trade game. They-don't-mix.'

'Eh? But they all get on fine down at Halo's nightclub. Specially on Tuesdays.'

'No! Of course *they* get on. Ben sighed with utter frustration. 'Look. Do you understand that you can't put sharks and dolphins in the same fish tank.'

'I think you can boss,' Toby pointed out. 'Saw it on BBC2. Dolphins can, loike, nut the sharks and...'

'Right right OK. Bad example. Pauly, *please* understand before I handcuff this wrist to a razorblade. You just can't mix gay stuff and straight stuff. It just doesn't work.'

'So how comes we sells all dose lesbian dvd and things?' Katia asked.

"Cos they're women! Doing stuff with other women. For the telly tubbying pleasure of men.'

'Yeh. Exactly,' Pauly put in. So it's - like - men who watch - well the backpacking hunks. In't it?'

'Oh please, please. The god of porn. If you are up there. And your right hand isn't busy this moment.' Ben raised his eyes in imprecation to the store ceiling. 'Just please smite this painful person down before I have to shove a cardiac patient off his bed.' Ben fixed Pauly with a hard stare. 'Pauly. Listen. Carefully.'

'Yeh.'

'They-are-not-the-same-kind-of-men!!!'

Now, there was silence.

'Yeh. You're right. I know,' Pauly said.

Ben relaxed. 'Right...'

'They spend more money.'

Possibly saving Ben from imminent cardiac arrest, Paige came in. 'Helloo.'

'A sign from porngod. Thank you.' Ben turned to her. 'Right Paige - you tell 'em.'

'What?'

'That straight and gay materials cannot happily co-exist in a retail smut environment.'

'Don't see why not,' Paige said. 'I mean, I get all sorts on my massage table.'

'Oh god not you as well. So alright then: what do you do with the gay ones following on after *straight* users of your service, eh? Tell me that?'

'Give them an extra towel.'

Ben turned his back on the bunch of them. 'Right. I'm off down the pub. To drink myself either back to sanity or into total amnesia. At this point don't really care which.'

'Ooh, before you go, I wanted to chat to you about me putting a little card in your shop window,' Paige cooed.

'Sounds lovely Paigy.' Pauly said.

'A card? Saying what exactly?' Ben queried.

'Well, advertising my little massage business. And some swingers parties I'm doing. Maybe you'd be interested?'

Ben scoffed. 'Groups of fat forties chunking their chubby wives around like refillable sausage rolls at a bad disco. No thanks.'

'Oi! My parties are not like that at all!'

'What are they Paigy?' Pauly asked.

'Sumptuous evenings of sophisticated sensual exchanges, satisfying new experiences and pushing the boundaries of human sexuality."

'Yaay!' Pauly applauded. 'So what happens then?

'People shag other people's wives,' observed Ben, morosely.

'But I've not got one.' Pauly objected.

'Or girlfriends. See?' offered Paige, with an unsubtle hint.

'So... oh! Like the Jeremy Kyle show!'

'Yayssss... well kind of I suppose...' Paige conceded.

'Oh well that's fine,' Pauly said. 'I've got a shell suit and trainers.'

'Er... no Pauly,' Toby offered. 'I think you've got to wear loike a smart suit and put a mask on.'

Pauly mimed putting a mask on. 'Like... Shrek?'

'Yeh that'll work fine for you Pauly,' Ben muttered. 'Till it comes off.' Ben buttoned his jacket. 'Pub.' He stalked out.

'Can it be any character, really?' Pauly asked.

'Don't worry about it darling,' Paige smoothed. 'I'll explain later.'

A while later, round a Soho corner, Ben was at a pub table with Jez. There seemed to be a dark and drizzly cloud of bad feeling, hovering over the table.

'Your round then,' Jez growled. 'Since you missed the last payment.'

'You know Jez, you're basically a chartered accountant, with a serious anger management problem,' Ben took a sip. 'You should get it together with my Katia. You could talk double entry while sharpening your flick knife.'

## Part 2: Pride

Toby was minding shop, on the evening shift. He liked it. The shades of night tended to bring in customers who were more interesting than the average pervy nutter: as Toby liked to say.

On cue to that line of thought, a female customer entered. She was actually quite attractive, in a forty-something bohemian kind of way.

'Evening madam.'

'Oh hi. I'm looking for something suitable for use on a sunbed.'

Toby snapped his fingers. 'Just the thing here!'

He reached under the counter, and brought out a leather blindfold on a little hanger. 'New in yesterday,' he offered.

'No. I've got the infra-red goggles. It's something, more, to keep me occupied.'

Toby thought. Then reached under his counter, and pulled out: 'Chocolate body paint. You know. Do patterns and suchloike.'

'Look,' the customer sighed. 'I just want a heat resistant sexual aid.'

Toby wandered over to a rack, and brought back a glass dildo. 'Here you are. Instructions say to pop it in the microwave, and it'll do to you what ready-brek never managed.'

'You haven't listened to a word I've been saying, have you?'

'Well...' Toby considered. 'Some of 'em.'

The customer looked at dildo Toby was holding. 'Alright.' she sighed. 'How much?'

'I'd say about one in foive.'

The now irate customer grabbed the toy, checked the price, then threw a £20 note on the counter. Shaking her head, she walked off and out.

Toby picked up the banknote, and gave it a flick with his fingers. 'Oh! A tip! See - just treat 'em roight and they show their appreciation.'

The frontage of a secret London mansion house was swathed in light. Spotlights dipped in arcs, while coloured neons cosseted corners. Well, obviously the building wasn't secret. By day, it functioned as premises for interior decorators, and fine art boutiques. But inside, tonight, was a chamber of secrets.

There, through the double door, and up the marble staircase, the swingers party was in full swing. Wall to wall girls in basques, stockings and masks. Guys in smart suits, bowties and more masks. Some latex clad lovelies, in riots of red, green, pink and blue, were peacocking.

Katia, more modestly, was wearing a shimmery evening dress, with a silver mask. Pauly had his own concept of sophistication on show. A dinner jacket, a t-shirt with a bow tie printed on it, black jeans and plimsols. He'd not gone with the Shrek mask. Sensible boy. Instead, Pauly was wearing a dark knight Batman mask, with little ears, on a stick. Paige too, had a mask on a stick. A little green pvc number, to match her figure hugging, well outrageously squeezing, tiny pvc dress.

They were all watching Miss Kitty doing a burlesque number, on a little stage.

'Ooh you look lovely Katia!' Paige oozed.

'Tenk yo. But i is not takink dis mask off. Or anyting de else.'

'No that's fair enough,' Paige brushed Katia's arm. ' The rules here are really simple. Only do what you want to. And do *anything* you want to.'

That got Pauly excited. 'Does that mean I can slurp my drink?'

'You can get as lip smacking as you want sweetie.' Paigy thrust her almost pvc covered frontage within touching distance of Pauly's tongue. 'Well. It's swinger's night. I'm here. You're here. So... Fancy it Mr Mask?'

'Yeh. Yeh. Definitely. I am so up for this.'

'Whay hayy! Yaay!' Paige excited herself.

Pauly grabbed Paige's glass and slurped a long drink from it. 'Oh yeah. Slurrrp. Yum yum.'

'But that's not...' Paige faltered.

A little group of nearby swingers watched the scene, with amused interest.

Katia giggled over her drink. 'Only rule Paige is do *anything* you want to, hmmm?'

'Hmmm. Can't argue with that,' Paige replied. She thrust her drink into Pauly's hand, grabbed Katia and gave her a full mouth kiss.

Pauly stared, open mouthed. Then furiously started

slurping both his drink and Paige's drink, while the kissing continued.

The onlookers nodded, satisfied.

Meanwhile, a mask throw away, the empty show floor of lap dance club was hosting an interesting sales pitch.

Dom walked Ben onto the pole stage, and looked around. 'So, watcha reckon then? Cut above as a venue, right?'

'Yer,' Ben nodded. 'Fair enough. But I mean, Soho's already got it's fair share of lap dance clubs right Dom? I mean, what's the major mojo with this one?'

'Aha. You look at this and see a clip joint.'

'Well, yeah. I mean, it's not exactly a halal butchers is it?'

'But in my entrepreneurs eye,' Dom sparkled 'I see something very different.'

'Like?'

'A comedy club.'

'Well, again. Clip joint, laugh joint. The monopoly board's pretty chocca with both round ere, no?'

'Aha my friend. With *both*: not. People love a caged bird that sings, right? So how about a pole bird that jokes.'

Ben stared at Dom. 'You wanna run...'

'Topless comedy nights. Jiggle the booty - suck in the laughing gas. Can't fail, right?'

Ben stomped off the pole stage. 'Thank god you're only my *former* brother in law.'

'Wassa problem?'

'Well can *you* laugh and play tiddly winks together? It'd be like that game where you gotta rub your stomach and pat your head at the same time.'

Dom jumped down to Ben's level. 'But... Topless comediennes. Never been done before. The real alternative to alternative comedy.'

'No, look mate,' Ben shook his head. 'I've seen plenty of boob jobs to crack a smile about. But never a laughter track to go with 'em. I don't wanna get too 'Dragon's Den' about it, brov. But on this one, "I'm out".'

'Fair do's. I'll put my thinking lap on.' Dom put his arm round Ben's shoulder as they walked out. 'In the meantime, you know what you said about halal entertainment? Funny that, cos...'

The swingers party lounge was still swinging. Couples, and more canoodling. Exhibitionists exhibiting. Voyeurs, well, voying.

Pauly was still holding onto Paige's glass, and his, plus his mask. Rather uncomfortably.

Liza appeared in basque, stockings and face mask. She had, by the hand, a tall, well built and handsome mid-forties man.

Pauly's other person recognition system having been cobbled together in the back of a garage somewhere, failed to recognise her.

'Ooh. It's always the quiet ones you have to watch isn't it?' she said.

'And the noisy ones,' Pauly chatted. 'Like those over

there look.'

'Are you all on your own, handsome swinger-linger?'

Pauly looked around. 'Not really.'

'So… You wanna play some musical shares?'

Pauly looked puzzled.

Katia and Paige reappeared. Katia looked a little flustered. One strap of her dress was hanging off her shoulder.

'Awww Liza! Stop it,' Paige giggled.

'Where?' Pauly swung round in surprise.

Paige pointed to Liza, who slipped her mask off.

'Swinger surprise!'

'Oh!' Pauly's reacted. 'I'm that sorry Liza love. I didn't recognise you with your clothes off. Ey are you alright Kats: you look a bit hot 'n bothered.'

'Yiss yiss. Is fine. Everyting. Paige was just showing me...'

'A *very* groovy time,' Paige smooched.

'Er... De curtains and nice de toilets.'

'Ooh yeah I bet,' Pauly nodded. 'I mean they are lovely the curtains in here. Very classically.'

Paige turned to Liza. 'And who's this hunky dunk then?'

'Oh. May I introduce Jake Drummond.'

'Hey guys,' Jake held up a hand in greeting. 'How's it hangin. Well actually with you two, I can see fine.'

Katia shrank back a little.

'Oh don't worry, girls,' Jake continued. 'I'm gay as an Amsterdam nightclub.'

'Ok dat is de nice and to meet yo.'

'Damn!' Paige muttered.

'Say, Pauly. Liza was telling me you're in the sex business?' Jake asked.

'Well Jake. I see it as more of a vocation. You know, bringing people together.'

'Just like this place,' Paige offered. 'Only in plastic covers.'

'That's cool man,' Jake nodded. 'Don't wanna talk shop on a fine night like tonight, but I do run Europe's largest gay networking and distribution trade. So maybe there's something we could do together Pauly?'

Pauly shuffled from one foot to the other. 'Er... Well. I was really sort of looking for a girlfriend more.'

'Don't worry Pauly,' Paige put in. 'If you could just put contact lenses in that mask, you'd see you've already got one. Jake: no problem, I'll bring you down the shop and you can meet Pauly when sober, and with luck, Ben when drunk.'

'Sounds cool. So, hey guys, me and Liza are just gonna wander over to crimson corner there and swing some champagne.'

'Sorry Jak. I tought you are de gay?' Katia puzzled.

Liza chuckled. 'He is love. I'm not. See ya!'

Jake and Liza walked off with their arms round each other.

'Ok, now even I'm confused, Paige said. 'Fancy another slurp Pauly?' she purred.

'Yeh. Lots.'

The morning after. Sex-x-x was a full house. With Ben, Toby, Katia, and Pauly all there. In various states of post-party experience. Raven entered.

'Morning Raven love,' Pauly greeted.

'Hello Pauly. Hey, I heard you had a pretty rock goth night last night, hey?' Raven asked.

'Yeh it was brilliant.' Pauly announced. 'It were a swingers do, so I got to slurp from all these different cups.'

'Just a minute, Ben sought urgent clarification. 'What: *you* did?'

'Not so surprise Ben,' Katia derailed Ben's mental express train. 'Pauly mean it like de words he say. Not what de Dover brain is theenk.'

'O-k,' Ben replied. 'Bemused puzzlement replaces surprise for breakfast. What about you then?' Ben's arm instinctively snaked towards Katia.

'How many times I have say not to touch pliss?'

Raven chuckled. 'Er... Quite a few more if I heard about you right at the old swingalong.'

Katia tried to 'shhhush' Raven.

'She never.' Ben said.

'I didn't nothink,' Katia defended.

'Oh yes you did. He he,' Raven giggled back.

Pauly put his hand up. 'Oh if we're doing pantomime, can I be Buttons?

Paige entered, with Jake in tow. 'If I can be puss in boots. Hello hungover people. Ouch, it just hurt to say that.'

'Oh, that were a lovely dress you had last night Paigy.'

'Aww, thanks,' Paige smooched.

'Yeh. Lots of people were admirin it when you left it on the stair rail.'

Paige got stern. 'Pauly: do you know what 'secrets' are?'

'Yeh.'

'Go on then. What are they?'

Pauly drew himself up. 'Secrets. The new intimate apparel range by Le Plaisir of Belgium.' He closed his eyes and pointed. 'Third rail down, second shelf along.'

Ben moved the away from the conversation between a stern beauty and well-informed lingerie retailer. 'Anyway... Hello and you must be Jake.'

'You got it. Pleasure to meet. And after a hard night's play, a good morning's business I hope.'

'Well let's see. Pauly says you run the largest distribution and networking operation in Europe?'

'Your man got that right. And we're always looking for tie-ins. Now with your store's location and profile, you'd be great.'

'Ok, so we tie in and... ?' Ben asked.

'Increase your net after costs on this sector, ooh, thirty, forty percent.'

Ben turned to Pauly. 'Now see *this* is my kind of man.'

'Told ya! Yaay! So I'll get that box out then and start the angel wings display?'

'Whaddya mean?' Ben puzzled.

'Jak is der king of der Europe gay network,' Katia clarified.

'Yeah dude,' Jake nodded. 'I mean forget the old school - boy shags girl stuff. That's pennies. We're talking about pink *pounds*. That's the buzz: "gay pays".'

Ben's jaw sagged. 'And that would mean that you're... And I just said you're my kind... And...' Ben slid his hand over his face. 'Angel wings.'

Pauly nodded and mouthed: 'g-a-y.'

Now there was a pause. A stretching silence. Ben drummed his fingertips on the counter.

'Right' Ben clapped his hands. 'Nice big display Pauly. Toby - go get them wings. Katia: order in plenty of pink pricing labels.'

Paige took Ben aside. 'Ben. You *really* ok with this?'

'Oh god. I'm going to hell anyway when this is all over,' Ben winked. 'May as well go arse first. So, Jake, Katia'll show you up to my office and we can finalise some details, yeh?'

'Cool. Let's get Amsterdamming.'

Katia walked Jake out.

Jez chose that moment to make his entrance.

'Hell and Amsterdamnation,' Ben muttered. 'Hey Jez.'

Jez rubbed his hands. 'You know, morning's always a *good* time for collections. Gives the rest of the day for people to worry 'bout it. Heh heh.'

*PINK*

'Oh hello Jez,' Pauly greeted. 'Yeh. We got lots on today. Just gettin our g-a-y store section sorted. Yaay. You'll be the first one in Soho to be collectin' off of the gay trade. Lovely!'

Jez shuddered. 'Come again sideways?'

'Oh yes,' Ben spotted his opportunity. 'I mean, you'll be the talk of the street on this one, won't you Jez. *The* hard man of this parish, tippin his wink off of, well, lots of other *very* hard men.'

'And they are all over 18. Definitely. Look, says so on't cover.' Pauly thrust a gay dvd cover in Jez's face.

He recoiled. 'No! It's a bloody disgrace to the street. You lot turnin George Michael. I'm not 'avin anyfin to do wiv it.'

'Oh fair enough. You not comin to the grand opening then? ' Ben slapped Jez playfully on the shoulder. 'We're just tartin up the back passage now.'

'Eeugh!' Jez stepped back in horror. 'You lot. Worse than a bent copper. At least you know they're *straight*. Right' Jez tugged on his leather coat, 'I'm off down the strip joint to freaten some *normal* people.'

Jez stomped out.

'Right… hair of the dog, Raven? Paige offered. 'Or bitch in my case. He he.'

'Yaay sure babe.'

'Ooh. I'll just… Er… Grab Katia to come with us. Come on.'

Paige and Raven headed out the back of the shop.

Ben scratched his head. 'You know: I kind of feel like

I should of come along last night.' He sighed. 'But I'm very glad I didn't.'

'Ah well,' Pauly put in. 'I always find that fantasy's not so good as reality, when it actually happens. I mean, that's why we've got Sex-x-x in't it?'

'Just go where the wind of small change carries you. That's all you can do, eh Pauly?'

Ben gave a rueful smile. He picked up a straight dvd. Then a gay dvd. He weighed each in the palm of a hand. Then he carried both out with him to the back, where Jake was waiting in his boardroom.

\*     \*     \*

In the night time solace of an empty Sex-x-x shop, Toby is alone.

But idle hands make play for Toby work. He is busy wrapping together bundles of gay and straight dvd's. With a bumper pen sticker: *Best of both worlds: surprise pack*.

Toby holds a pack up to the neon window light. He casts a knowing smile at the fragility of our world.

CHAPTER 6

# *SHOW*

## Part 1: Footwork

It's a seeming law of nature that things just want to get, well, bigger. Not perhaps a tiger, tiger burning bright, with its perfect symmetry. But natural for those of a more homo sapiens disposition. Especially *homo sexualis*.

Ben had definitely always thought size was important. Not merely his own immodest dimensions, but in any twin objects of his amorous affections. To quote him in reflective mood 'I you can get a 'and round one Pauly, it ain't worth handling.' You can see Pauly's puzzled reaction to that drop of Dover wisdom, from here.

Just as he used to engage in teenage fantasies of his sportswomen and girl popstars swelling to life off his bedroom posters, the dreams of a middle aged love boutique owner stretched to chains. Sex-x-x emporia in every high street and out of town mall in Britain, and beyond. In Ben's world view, small was definitely not beautiful. Not that he would have turned down an opportunity with a sexy dwarfette, in stockings.

Anyway, on this day, Pauly, Toby and Katia were on the relatively modest shop floor.

Pauly was playing with a battery powered item. 'Variable speed, look.'

'Always a good feature that,' Toby nodded.

'*Very* powerful vibro. Don't need to ask twice with this one,' Pauly declared.

'What's it called?' Toby asked.

Ben entered and snatched the tool off Pauly. 'My home improvement sander - slash - stripper. Give it 'ere.' Ben grabbed the home tool. 'That's why I'm glad you don't smoke, Pauly.'

'Lungs?' Pauly's hands illustrated anatomically over his chest.

'Cos you couldn't tell the lit end from the other.'

Liza stormed in, holding a set of A4 size court forms. 'Showin off your DIY tackle huh? Well at least you've *got* a home to improve.'

'No,' Ben countered. 'It's a one bedroom knock up maisonette with shared shed. *You* got the *home* remember?'

'And all the bleedin bills to go with it! I'd be better off with a cardboard box and a Big Issue tube station sales pitch. At least then I'd have enough money at the end of the day to buy a large drink and a small bit of self-respect.'

'Look, for the last time woman. This is my place of business,' Ben snapped. 'Not the set for a Dear Deidre picture column.'

'Oh no it's alright. I din't come 'ere expecting sympathy,' Liza said, sharply.

'Nah. You visit cancer wards for that, doncha?'

'You rotten... No, right. This is *it*.' Liza slammed the

# SHOW

forms on the counter.

Ben looked over at them. 'Miss Soho entry forms? Nah. I'm sure they held that final in 1982.'

Liza wagged a very cross finger at him. 'I'll tell you what this is Mr Bent-Dover. Final demand. Court ordered. You pay what you owe by mid-day. Or you can stick some nails in that drill thing and crucify yourself to the counter there.'

Liza started stalking out, then performed a heel turn, the dreaded finger going up again. 'Mid-day pay. Or shop closin' pain. Your choice, dog brain.'

Liza left, with a slam of the door.

'Does she always rhyme when she's angry?' Pauly asked, softly.

'Yeh. Sounds like cookin stunt,' Ben replied.

Katia asked Toby, 'Pliss?'

'No, Toby. Don't.' Ben pulled himself together. 'I'm gonna go buy a Big Issue and cheer myself up.'

Ben left, muttering to himself.

A female customer walked in. She was slim and petite, wearing a mac and heels.

'Morning madam. How can we assists?'

The customer nodded politely. 'My best friend's husband's passed on. So I'm looking for something to give her a little solace at bed time.'

'But diss ees not de church. Eet is, well…'

'Yes I know that dear,' the customer stopped her. 'But while we all might say a prayer for the soul of the dear departed, the needs of the body still have their urges, you know.'

Pauly popped over to assist. 'If I may. Condolenceries and everything.'

'Thank you.'

'Yeh. We have a smashing range of stuff all in black. Even the box.'

'Sorry, why black?' the customer asked.

'Well... the funeral. Respecting tradition.' Pauly put his hands together in prayer and did a little bow.

'Hang on!' the customer reacted in shock. 'You don't think the grieving widow is gonna be deploying one of your dildos by the graveside is she?'

'Course not. No. Obviously,' Pauly agreed.

'Right.'

'She'll probably pop behind a pew. Or a confessional box, if its Catholicy. Or whichever.'

The customer turned her back on Pauly. She spoke quickly to Katia. 'Just give me something nice and discreet, love, thanks.'

Katia quickly bagged a dildo box, took a £20 note, and handed over change. 'So sorry. Tenk yo.'

The customer began to walk out. She paused in front of Pauly, and stared for a moment. 'Most gravediggers are retarded you know.' She stared some more. 'You should sign up.' Then, the customer exited.

Katia blew out a breath. 'Dat was bit embarass.'

'I know. Never really got religiousy stuff.'

'Well, do yo belief in de life after death?'

## SHOW

'Er... I'm not sure you can tell the difference from this end.'

Ben was at the usual pub table with Dom, having a drink.

'Look mate, it's just Liza's way, right,' Dom consoled him. 'I mean, it was the same when we was kids.'

'How'd you mean?' Ben asked.

'Well, say there was a toy she wanted. She'd scream and stamp her foot, unless you'd give it to her.' Dom banged his hand on the table, for emphasis.

'Sounds familiar. She's the same with my hard earned business income. So?'

'I was, even then, square and firm. I just said, very clearly, "no Liza".'

'And she gave in to that?' Ben asked, his eyebrows raising.

'Oh yeh. Just firmness. Lettin' her head see your determination not to give in.'

'Riiight. Got it.' Ben nodded. 'Not ruthless. Just tough. Yeh. Cheers.'

Dom nodded, and sipped his drink. 'Mind you, soon as I turned my back she'd snap the damn thing in two.'

Ben got up and sighed. 'You know Dom. Gettin drunk with you's not the pleasure it used to be.'

Pauly, Katia and Toby were minding the shop. Obviously it didn't actually take
all three of them for that: but what else do you do when Soho streets are full of rainy skies.

A petite blonde girl rushed in, wearing very high heels, a tiny denim mini, and a crop top. She seemed very agitated. 'Where is it?'

She rushed over to magazine stand. There, she started pulling mags off the stand and throwing them to floor. 'No! No! Disgusting. Never!'

Toby ambled over. 'Scuse me Miss. Could you not mash the mags loike that please.'

'Ey,' Pauly chipped in. 'The feministy women have done their protest already you know, love."

'I'm not a feminist! I'm a model.'

'So why's you goin at our "Deep Inside" issue like a rottweiler after a baby, then?' Toby asked.

'Cos I shun't be in these. I never signed up. Flamin photographer. Telescopic lens. Huh!'

Pauly grabbed a fallen mag and leafed through. 'So, which one's you?'

Tina stopped him at a page.

Toby came to Pauly's shoulder, for a look. Pauly turned it sideways, then back again. 'Well. To be fair love. It's not exactly a face shot, is it?'

'Exactly! It's disgustin. What if me boyfriend.. ?'

'Er...,' Pauly considered. 'I suppose it depends, like. Positions. Things... But I can't see anyone really recognising you from... these.'

'Not even in that skirt,' Toby said.

'What's wrong with my skirt?'

'Well,' Toby pointed gently. 'It's just a good thing you're not plannin on bein' a shoplifter.'

## SHOW

'Ugh! Look, what are you goin to *do* about this? Hey?'

'Um,' Pauly's brain actually began a dynamic approaching common sense. 'What's your name?'

'Tina Guy. G-U-Y.'

'Right. Well we could write a little sticky label and put in that it's not you.'

'Would I get paid for that?' Tina asked.

'Well yeh, if you sign it,' Pauly replied.

'Oh. Alright then.'

Pauly went to counter and pulled out a roll of sticky labels. 'OK Tina love. Off you go off, there's a nice pub round the corner, do your dabs on these and bring 'em back. And Toby'll get stickin.'

'Does it have to be joined up writin?' Tina looked worried.

'Not if you can't manage it love,' Pauly reassured her.

'OK. Later then. Thanks.' Tina exited, with her pile of magazines and sticky labels.

'See?' Pauly glowed. 'It's like that sign sayin' "do not throw stones at this sign". Saw that on Facebook.'

'But Pauly dat is joke, not?' Katia objected.

'Oh, is it? I though it were governmental,' Pauly said.

'Same thing?' Toby offered his view.

Plans are strange things. Imagine planning history. Like, start with the Romans in Britain, and ask how that ends up with a priapic Tudor and six wives. There's no way you'd get there. And that's the past. Which is all laid out there in black and white, with engravings. So: what do we ever expect plans for the future to work out... er... per plan?

"No plan survives first contact with the enemy." So said German general Von Moltke. The one who started the first world war 40 years early. Which martial dictum Ben would have modified, to note despairingly, that no plan survives attempted explanation to a Pauly.

In the corporate majesty of Ben's boardroom over the shop, Ben was pacing around Pauly's placid seating position.

'So, you get how important this one is Pauly?'

'Well, yeh. That was my idea.'

'No. *Your* idea was to set up a trestle table next to Leicester Square tube

'With lots of leaf-lets,' Pauly pointed out.

'Leaflets, yes. But as a mobile store concept it did lack a little something.'

'Like?' puzzled Pauly.

'Common sense. And the opportunity *not* to get arrested.'

'So... what we're doin instead is...' Pauly frowned with the same concentration as a two year old trying to figure out which building block gets put on top of 'B'.

'Just picture it Pauly. The premier exhibition hall in London. Filled with adult paraphernalia of every description. And there – the jewel in the erotic crown - our own Sex-x-x booth, brimming with our best bargains. A mecca for porn punters of every description.'

'With leaf-lets.'

'Yes, yes. Many as you like.'

'Right!' Pauly stood and tugged his Invincibles t-shirt with determination. 'I am fully seized of this commercial opportunit-ary and I shall strive to ensure its fru-ition.'

'Eh?'

'Saw it on Dragon's Den,' Pauly nodded with pride.

'Yeh. Well I don't think any of the grumpy Scotch bloke, the patronising woman, or the other faceless ones'll be lining up to back this venture. So it's up to us, alright?'

Pauly ticked his fingers: 'Booth. Venue. Leaflets.' He gave a triumphant smile. 'Like licking ice cream off the side of your cone. How hard can it be?'

'I hate to say it,' Ben acknowledged, 'but that's actually quite a catchy strap line for one of your handouts.'

'Yaay. And that *was* my idea.'

Ben and Pauly walked in to find Toby arguing with Terry Barnet. His identity was spelled out in an identity lanyard, hanging from his bull-like neck.

Barnet was a mid-forties stocky, aggressive bailiff, in a cheap suit and thin tie, and partly balding. He was holding a clipboard with official forms pinned to it. And jabbing with a pen at Toby. 'Let me pass, I say!'

'I told you, you can't have nothin,' Toby said, standing his ground.

'Well you get your boss in here then and you'll find out that I can do just that, right son?'

'Hold up,' Ben waded in. 'What's this bit of Jeremy Kyle all about then?'

Barnet straightened up and declared his status. 'I am officially here. As bailiff. On official business.'

'Yes?' Ben said.

'As per Court Order. To seize goods or stock or business chattels to the value stated in satisfaction of debt due.'

'What?' Ben stepped back, in amazement.

Pauly was peering over Barnet's shoulder at the form.

'Oh, yeh. I can explain.'

'Hmm?' Ben ventured.

'Yeh. It definitely looks official. There's forms with boxes and stamps all over it as well. Yeh.'

'Oh you're just a one man citizen's advice bureau Pauly aren't ya?' Ben said.

'Er... What's a chattel though?' Pauly asked. 'Is that, like, farm animals, you know "oxen and chattels"? Only we don't have any here. There's a shop three streets down from here that specialises through...'

'Chattels is moveable property,' Barnet declared. He waved his clipboard. 'Like all this you see around here. Nothink to do wiv animals. He paused, and scratched his head. 'Although it can be.'

'It's bloody Liza innit?' Ben swore. 'Gawd I knew it! She wun't kick a man when he's down. Oh no. She'd wait till he was hanging by his fingertips off a cliff edge, then stamp.'

'Well, yes,' Barnet confirmed. 'The Claimant is Ms Liza Baker, says 'ere.'

'Knew it,' Ben nodded, sourly. 'And that's it then is it? This verdant field of dreams to rack and ruin, because the British courts of justice allow a woman, powered only by hate and vodka, to fill their forms in when she's got PMT.'

'I wun't know about that,' Barnet shook his head. 'I'm just here to collect. Goods or stock or business chattels...'

'Are you sure though?' Pauly piped in.

'Eh?'

'Well, you see,' Pauly continued, 'I mean you look like a very official sort of person.'

'I am. Got me licence. And a badge.'

'Right. So is it gonna go alright if you have to wander around with boxes of the Best of Big Butts videos, Spank Me Backwards magazine, and Giant Thumper butt plugs.' Pauly turned his gaze round the boutique. 'Cos that's all the chattels we've got round 'ere.'

Barnet also looked around, taking in his surroundings.

'Oh, yes, captain,' Ben joined in. 'Unless you fancy winning a caption competition as High Holborn's most perverted debt catcher, I'd have another think.'

A silenced pause filled the shop.

'You got any *normal* stuff,' Barnet asked, slowly.

'Erotic chocolate?' Pauly offered.

'Pineapple and mango flavoured condoms,' was Ben's offer.

'Mango! What for?' Barnet's voice strangled.

'Oh - well, you see...' Pauly began to explain.

'What the world outside these windows, and what

Pauly here, would call normal, don't exactly fit in the same dictionary,' Ben clarified.

Barnet paused again. he drew in a long breath. 'O-K. I fink I shall tick the box for nil stock, here.'

'A wise, and possibly career saving decision,' Ben clapped Barnet on the shoulder.

'You're welcome to some free samples though,' Pauly offered.

'Er... No. No. Thanks all the same. Right.' Barnet tapped his clipboard. 'Gotta go turf a single mum out of her bedsit.'

'Yer. Go on. That'll cheer you up,' Ben said.

'Yeh.'

Barnett exited with what bailific dignity he could muster.

Miss Kitty brushed past him, as she strode in.

'Final demands. Screaming fits. Bailiffs. What next?' Ben asked.

'Slamming the toilet door,' Pauly said.

'What?'

'Well when women's cross they always go in the toilet and slam the door don't they?' Pauly clarified.

'Hmmm,' Kitty said. 'I generally make sure there's a slave's head in the way, though.'

'Aah, Kitty. And we were just discussing loony heeled women,' Ben said, feeling cheerless.

'Yeh. Well these boots were made for walking all over you. But not today.' Miss Kitty clapped her pvc gloved hands. 'I've got a foot fetish party on this afternoon. Anyone want to come.'

'Yaay, sounds fun. Yes. Thank you,' Pauly said. 'Kats?'

'Yiss, I suppose. OK.'

Ben shook his head. 'No thanks dungeon diva. The mood I'm in right now, I'd probably bite.'

Pauly shuffled a bit and raised his hand. 'Er… question Miss Kitty.'

'Yes darling Pauly?'

'Do we just bring our own feet or…'

Everyone just stared at Pauly in astonished silence. That's OK. It was probably about the seventeenth time that week.

## Part 2: Ideal

In his boardroom, Ben was regaling Julia with his vision of Sex-x-x at an exhibition.

Pacing, Ben pronounced: 'So you see, Julia. This is pushing Sex-x-x into the big league. Where it rightfully belongs.'

'We're certainly happy to support your venture. It's a win-win scenario for our product lines, and your retail presence.'

Ben sat on the corner of the desk. He smarmed his charm. 'Hmmm. You like to win, don't ya Julia?'

'Well in business, it *is* the only point in taking part.'

'So, what counts as a victory in personal life?'

'Leaving this room without feeling you've spent the entire conversation trying to work out whether I'm wearing stockings or tights.''

'OK, you caught me.' Ben did his charming smile. 'I'm happy to do the shortcut, you know.'

Julia winked, and flashed some stocking top.

Ben fell off the desk.

Still seated on the floor, he cried out 'Mother Mary on a nudist beach! What was that for?'

'Call it executive encouragement. You get that booth thronging with customers for us, and you never know.'

'I thought it was all un-PC to use female wiles in the boardroom?' Ben protested, weakly.

'Not at all. Maximise your assets. That's just good business sense.' Julia fixed Ben with the sort of stare that wolves use on bones. 'But, from where you're sitting right now, if your line of sight deviates one centimetre below my top button, you'll be presenting your booth from a wheelchair.'

Ben hurriedly got up and dusted himself down. 'OK, fair enough. You do love keeping a man off balance, doncha Julia?'

'Always in business, sweetie. But only sometimes in pleasure.'

Miss Kitty's dungeon was thronging with, well, a throng. Half a dozen girls in various states of dress and undress, were lounging on chairs and sofas. Their bare feet were entertaining male customers.

Touching, tonguing, licking, kissing. The girls' feet were receiving lavish lustful care and attention.

Kitty was dressed in best dominatrix style. Pauly and Katia were looking around. With fascination (him), and bewilderment (her: well a little fascinated as well).

'All going good so far,' Kitty commented. 'What do you think?'

Katia shrugged. 'Sorry but I not understandink dis. Is de sex or what?'

'Oh darling,' Kitty purred. 'Sex is all in the mind. Or in this case, the feet of these bipedal lovelies. The punters just want to look, touch, stroke.'

'And lick, look...' Pauly pointed out.

They looked

'Oh! Dat is not de nice,' Katia shuddered.

Kitty smiled. 'That's Tony toe-sucker. He's good though. He never tickles.'

'Er... I'm not volunteering,' Pauly put in. 'But, how d'you know you're not getting a mouthful of someone else's toe tonguing?'

'Foot bowls darling. A little rose petal water after each session and the pinkies are good as new.'

'Oh that's dead hygenicky that. Yeh. Cool,' Pauly nodded. 'Fancy a go Kats?'

'I rather be touch by de Ben Dover in a dark room wid no window and no de doors.'

'Oh. Fair enough. You don't mind if I go for the toe-tal experience ey? Eh?' Pauly brought a plimsol covered foot off the floor, and wiggled it. With all the fluidity of a premier ballerina, who had just broken her ankle.

'Oh ha ha that's good, yes, very funny,' Kitty observed, without laughing. 'We don't get many jokes in my dungeon. Go on then, have fun.'

Ben and Dom were back at their usual pub table.

'So you'll back it then? The exhibition booth? Julia's right up for it,' Ben encouraged.

'Bet she's not.'

'No... Business. Full steam ahead. Working on the other one,' Ben winked.

'Aah. So you reckon that showing her the dynamic entrepreneur is gonna push her passion buttons?'

'Definitely. Heart follows head with that one,' Ben nodded, knowingly.

'You should be so lucky.'

'Eh?' Ben took a sip of his pint. Only then realising Dom's interpretation of the words just uttered.

Toby was minding the store. He liked his alone time. Just him, the empty store, the cash register: only a few seconds run to the door, and... No.

A middle aged male customer came in, at that fortunate moment. 'Hey there. Interesting place this. Got a wide selection. Very wide.'

'We try to cater for all tastes, yeh,' Toby nodded.

'Right. How about something a bit canine?'

'You what? I mean, pardon?' Toby's face went white.

'Well, my German Shepherd, see. Manfred. He does get a bit frisky. As they do, you know.'

Toby slightly shook his head. 'Not really, but I s'pose so.'

'Now we can't have Manfred running around the neighbourhood chasing every little bitch he can scent a whiff of, you see?'

'Kinda like me boss. Yeh.' Toby tried to brighten the cloud of madness he felt descending over him.

'Oh, right. Anyway, it occurs that something in the erotic distraction department might well keep Manfred occupied. Harmlessly, you know.'

Toby pushed his cap back. 'Roight, hang on there. You want me to sell you a sex toy... For an Alsatian *dog*?'

'German Shepherd... It'd need to be resistant to a fair amount of chewing.'

'Look,' Toby folded his arms. 'We're not a vets. I mean, don't they have something...'

'Did ask. But they pointed me rather more in your direction.'

'Oh roight. Pass the nutter,' Toby muttered to himself.

'Excuse me?'

'Oh nothin. Sorry. Look, this is gonna need looking into by one of our exotic specialists. How about if I take a number or email and I'll buzz ya when he's worked something out.'

'Oh would you. Very kind. Terribly.'

The eager canine-centric customer scribbled a number on a bit of paper and handed it to Toby.

'Roight. So we'll be in touch then,' Toby nodded.

'Excellent. I shall tell Manfred to get his doggy hopes up. Bye now.'

The customer exited.

Toby finally breathed out, screwed up the paper and aimed a good shot into the bin.

'It's not the weirdos I moind,' he announced to the empty store. 'It's the other ones.'

The girls and their customers were still contentedly foot fetishing, down in Miss Kitty's dungeon.

Kitty and Katia were standing on a little stone viewing platform.

'You've known Pauly a while haven't ya Katia?'

'Yiss. I supposing.'

'Do you ever think there's something a bit... not right

there?' Kitty puzzled.

'Well wid company he keep, it not surprise.'

'No. Still...' Kitty forcefully inclines her head in the general direction of Pauly.

Who was reclined on a chaise longue, while having *his* feet tickled by a dungeon-ette (as Pauly called them), dressed as a schoolgirl. Pauly was giggling.

Kitty sighed. 'I must re-check the member's rulebook. Really...'

Still in the pub, Ben and Dom had relocated to the bar.

Inspector Trent sidled over. 'Alright Benjy? Hear you're branchin out into the exhibition business.

'You know, they talk about rats *leavin* a sinking ship. Ben sipped his pint. 'They don't mention them pestering you at the cocktail bar, then charging protection money for the life jackets.'

'Now then, now then.' Trent wagged his finger. Just takin a healthy interest in the affairs of business proprietors on my patch.'

'Yeh. Well if you was checkin your missus' affairs you'd need a whole new notebook wun't ya.'

Trent took half a step towards Ben. 'Look son. This isn't the Sweeney and you're not in an interview room. So you can cut the hardman blagger jibes and just get down to it, alright?'

'Alright then Inspector Toad. My shop is on your patch. Fair enough.'

'Right.'

'But the exhibition isn't. Got it? In that district, they got proper policemen. You know? Who help old ladies across the road, tell you the right time, and only use the evidence they've actually got, stead of fabricating it on used toilet paper.'

Ben got off his bar stool. 'It's out of your league, Trent. So get your nose outta my drink.'

'Alright Dover. This time. But your card is marked. Remember that.'

Trent stomped off.

'Hey, that was a bit heavy,' sighed Dom.

'Oh no worries mate.' Ben eased back on his stool. 'He couldn't find his truncheon with both 'ands, that one.'

The echoey vastness of Earls Court exhibition hall. Stands and banners everywhere. Throngs of throngers, attending to booths advertising an A-Z display of goods and services. Most of which you never knew you needed, until now.

At one booth was a middle aged lady in a pinafore. She had a mixing bowl on her stand, and was holding a complicated plastic mixing device.

'And as you can see. With the Magimix tool selection, and on a variety of easy adjust settings, you can achieve the magic mix. For cakes, preserves, breads. Magic, every time.'

Behind her was a screen shouting 'Ideal Home Exhibition'.

On the next patch along was another stand. It had

# SHOW

*Sex-x-x* emblazoned in a banner across the top. It was packed with stock from the love boutique.

Ben had his head in his hands, staring sadly into space.

Pauly was entranced by the Magimix display. 'I could do with one of those. '

Julia walked up, suited and booted: well, heeled.. 'I bet you could sweetie. To whisk Ben away from here. So how's your grand exhibition going?'

Ben sighed. With genuine, heart-plummeting despair. 'As you know Julia, the art of successful executive management is delegation. The slight hitch in that technique is when you find you've delegated to someone with less savvy than a squeeze of toothpaste.'

'Hey it's nice 'ere. Big crowd,' Pauly protested, throwing his arms wide.

'Yes. I'll give you that. Only instead of an erotica crazed seething mass of pvc toting sex addicts, we have twenty four coachloads of cardigan clad women's institute veterans.'

'They might be interested,' Pauly sulked.

Sure enough, a little old lady wandered up to the stand. She was actually wearing a cardigan. And orthopaedic shoes. 'Excuse me.'

'See?' Pauly prided.

Julia sniggered. Ben hid his eyes in shame.

The pensioner pointed to a magic wand massager. 'Is that just for feet. Or will it do for your back as well?'

Pauly sales pitched: 'This premium deluxe model,

madam, will provide you with pleasure on any part of your body. Or your partner's.' Pauly whispered aside to Ben: 'See? I said it all right.'

Julia was clutching her sides, in stitches. Ben waved Pauly way.

'No. Just for me, love,' the pensioner replied. 'He prefers his allotment.'

'Oh right. Well we've got a special exhibition price on it. And it comes with a free blow-up,' Pauly said.

'Go for it Pauly,' Julia encouraged.

Ben mimed razor blading his wrist. 'Is it up the vein, or across?'

Pauly handed over an inflatable massage cushion.

'Oh that's lovely,' the pensioner cooed. 'Perfect for out and about.'

'I know. Bar stools can get so hard after a while can't they?'

'Well, more the bus to the Scope shop. But yes.'

'Special exhibition gift wrapping?' Pauly asked.

'Well, it's just for myself. But... is it extra?'

'No madam,' Pauly big smiled. 'All part of the exhibiti-on service.'

'Lovely.'

The pensioner lady handed over some money. Pauly handed over a pre-gift wrapped box with *Sex-x-x* emblazoned on it.

The lady twisted the package to get a better look at it. 'Hmmm. It's just...'

'Here goes...' Ben stepped forward. 'Yes madam.

You're probably wondering why that package, the labelling, in fact this whole bumpin' booth is splattered with *Sex-x-x* right across it. Yes?'

'No not really. I mean, it's all sex these days isn't it? No, it's just - I'm surprised you don't have your email address on there. You know, for repeat orders.'

'Oh!' Pauly slapped his forehead. 'I knew there was something! Oh I'm that sorry Ben. Look, I'll start writing it on some cards here.'

'It's alright dear,' the pensioner comforted. 'I'll look you up on the interweb. Thanks.'

She wandered off with package, into the ideal homes throng.

Pauly started scribbling.

Ben surrendered to utter depression. He leant over to Julia. 'Look, Julia. It hasn't all worked out quite like I... I mean, Pauly... Look, you won't let this change your opinion of me: will you?'

'Oh of course it won't Ben. I promise.'

'See?' Pauly chorused. 'That's like what I always say Sex-x-x is about. Bringin people together. In a nice way. Yeh.'

Night has fallen, again, on the micro world of Sex-x-x.

Katia is doing her accountancy homework. With textbook, exercise pad, pencil and calculator

Toby is balancing a 'realistic cock dildo' on his head, as if he were playing with a football. 'Hey, catch this Kats! Up the Villa !'

'Doh. Boys and dere toys.'

He nods it down, catches it with his foot, and jerks his leg up. All in one smooth Premier League move.

The cock goes flying. A moment later, there is a horrible smashing and breaking sound.

Toby stands embarrassed and speechless.

'Oh no Toby. Dat is expensive stuffs, even if it is de pervy rubbish.'

'Oh. Roight. Well fortunately, oi *am*_store security, roight?'

'Yiss…So?'

'Blame it on burglars in the mornin.'

Toby gets out a packet of crisps from under counter. He opens and offers to Katia.

At first she refuses. Toby nudges with his head. She accepts and takes one.

'It's alroight. I know where they've been.'

The Soho night strolled on. Perhaps, somewhere, some carnal connection was occurring. Bringing people together through the joy of Sex-x-x.

In a nice way. That was Pauly's idea.

## CHAPTER 7

## *GROTTO*

### Part 1: Eggs

The festive season takes people in many different ways. It had proved difficult to agree on how to sex up a the Sex-x-x shop window in a way appropriate both for yuletide and elementary ground rules of decency.

A compromise had been reached, by dressing some of the mannequins in festive lingerie. The rest of Pauly's suggestions had been vetoed. Not on grounds of taste, but because they – mysteriously – involved Easter eggs and bunnies.

Inside, shop had been turned into an xmas grotto An xmas tree, a life size plastic reindeer with sleigh. Baubles, banners and tinsel, all showered with fake snow. A wonderland of festive Sex-x-xing.

Katia was wearing a red dress, with white fur trimming. Toby was wearing a Santa hat, with his usual security uniform. They were playing an xmas themed chess game.

Ben walked in, dressed as Father Xmas. 'Merry sexxxmas! Ho Ho Ho. Ho Ho Ho!'

'Oi loike it boss,' Toby smiled. 'Only thing is, saying that last bit round 'ere, might be misunderstood.'

'Oh I don't care,' Santa Ben grabbed a handful of snow and scattered it into the store air. 'Christmas spirit all round and half price on the inflatables.'

Pauly entered, dressed as an elf. 'Oh dear, I've lost them again,' he muttered.

'Oh Pauly. You looks lovely,' Katia said.

'Lost what?' Ben asked.

'My eggs,' Pauly complained.

Ben scratched his head. With some obstruction from the white beard prosthetic. 'What eggs?'

'Well you know. For the bunny and the egg hunt.'

Toby chipped in. 'Er... Pauly mate. Oi fink that's easter loike.'

Ben motioned at his own outfit. 'And this is christmas.'

Pauly looked around, in a panic. 'Already?'

'Well,' Ben urged. 'Christmas comes but once a year.' He sidled towards lovely xmas Katia. 'Some of us on the other hand...'

'No,' Katia rebuffed firmly.

A customer entered. An average male, with a warm coat.

'Oh! Happy christmas,' Pauly greeted. Adding: 'Apparently.'

'Yes, well just the thing. Now what do you have in the way of christmas toys?' asked the customer.

'Well, there's eggs. But no I don't think you want them.' Pauly said gloomily.

'Sorry?'

Ben took a hand. 'Allow Santa Sexxxmas to ride in on his love sleigh.'

Behind his back, Katia made puking motions to Toby, with her finger and mouth.

'Riiight. Hello. Christmas toys please,' the customer said.

'The finest range that erotic toyland can provide,' Ben boasted. He got out a red dildo. 'A festive vibrator that plays 'god bless ye merry gentlemen' when used vigorously.'

'Anything else?'

'Mince pie flavoured condoms.'

'Why mince pie?,' the customer asked.

'Assurance of a good filling.'

'Are you havin a laugh?'

'Dressed like this?'. Ben motioned to his red and white ensemble.

'Fair point. OK. Anything *normal*?'

Pauly jumped in, elf to the ready. 'Ooh! Our christmas panto DVD range!'

'Go on.'

'Pussy in Boots?' Ben offered.

'Jack and the very big beanstalk?' Toby ventured.

Pauly chipped in: 'Snow white and the seven...'

'Yes yes. I'll try one of those,' the customer snapped.

'Yaay. Comes with a free cracker,' Pauly said.

'OK thanks. But how's that sexy?' puzzled the customer.

'Depends what you use to pull it. Hur Hur.' Ben said.

'Alright. Go on then. But don't think I'll be comin back for new year.'

Katia rang up the festive sale. The customer walked out, muttering: 'Mince pies...'

Raven entered, dressed beautifully. In black.

'Hey Raven' Pauly went to greet the gothic princess. 'That's a brilliant christmas costume, that is.

'No it's not,' Toby objected.

'What's wrong with it?' Pauly and Raven spoke together. Princess and elf in perfect unison.

Ben motioned around the shop. 'The traditional christmas colour is ...white.'

'Well, I'm dreaming of a black christmas,' Raven insisted.

Miss Kitty entered winter wonderland. Holding a lead. Attached to the other end was a leather collar. Wrapped around the neck of a smallish man, clad in pvc top, shorts and boots, his identity obscured by a latex face mask. More traditionally, Kitty was dressed in red pvc latex, with white boots.

'Sounds good to me,' Kitty said. 'Happy black-mas babe!'

Kitty and Raven hugged. Her dog Slave growled. Kitty whipped him. 'Oh. Doggy does get so jealous.'

Ben sighed. 'Another one for the circus.'

'Don't you start, Worzel Gummidge. You got your reindeer. I got my slave-puppy.'

Pauly stepped in. 'Ah - but can you fly him around town giving out presents to all the good girls and boys?

Kitty stepped over to the sleigh-bound animal. She

flourished her whip. Then gave the plastic reindeer a good whack. An antler half fell off. Now it drooped sadly.

'Well,' Kitty placed her dominatrix hands on her hips. 'Can you?

'No,' Pauly shook his head. 'Not really.' Then, brightening up, Pauly pointed to Santa Ben: 'That's *his* job!'

Former feminist activist Nadine entered, with Jessie in tow. Nadine was seasonally dressed, wearing a white fur cape, white jeans and boots and a white top. Jessie was wearing a red tartan miniskirt, red boots and a red tshirt.

Although petite, Jessie wearing a tshirt was guaranteed to attract male attention. This one had "Xmas Appeal" wording and a picture of a polar bear on it. Both girls were carrying collection tins.

Nadine and Jessie rattled their tins and shouted together: 'Happy christmas everyone!

Jessie skittled over to give a hug to her favourite. 'Happy christmas Pauly!'

Nadine eyed up Ben. 'Mildly-pleasant-yuletide-season. Santa Perv.'

'Thank for those few kind words, Ben nodded. 'And yo ho blow to you too.'

'Ooh are you Scottish now Jess?' Pauly asked, looking at her skirt.

'No silly!' Jessie smiled. 'Tartan's traditional at christmas.'

'Oh - I get it. But it's a Scottish bear right? I know it does get cold there. So it's nice you're collecting winter woollies for them,' Pauly said.

'Well yes,' Ben said. 'I was wondering why former feminist campaigner Nadine now looks like a snowy version of Cruella de Ville. Where's your spotless Dalmatians love?

Nadine narrowed her eyes. 'Well actually, I am working to protect a beautiful endangered species...'

'Sex shop proprietors?' Ben shot back.

'Polar bears.' Nadine pointed to Jessie's tshirt.

'Oh! That's what it is.' Pauly said.

Nadine rattled her tin. 'Yes Pauly. So anything you can give?'

Council Inspector Albert Bonsor chose that moment to walk in. With his ever-present clipboard. 'Collectin. Hmmm. Do you possess a valid licence for that Miss?'

'I most certainly do,' replied Nadine at her snootiest. 'And who are you to ask anyway?'

'You've heard of King Herod?' Ben offered.

'Mmm,' Miss Kitty licked her lips. 'He ordered all the infants of Bethlehem to be slain.'

'Never!' Pauly reacted in shock. 'I've not seen that on the news!'

Ben graced Pauly with a sideways glance of irritation. 'Well this is Council inspector Albert Bonsor, killjoy of this parish. Who makes Herod look like a Tellytubby.'

'Well, be that as it may,' Bonsor rallied. 'You can't have christmas decorations in here.

'What? Why not?' asked Katia.

'Do we need a reindeer licence?' wondered Pauly.

'Because it may be offensive,' stated Bonsor, firmly.

That set Ben going. 'Offence!!! Just a minute! On an average day, this place is filled with clit rings, cock rings, furry handcuffs, inflatables of obscene descriptions, bondage packs, flavoured prophylactics, jack mags, whirlers, stuffers, muffers...'

'And a partridge in a pear tree,' Pauly interrupted, joyfully. 'That's how it goes in't it Jess?'

Ben swatted Pauly's interference away. 'How in the name of Judas Iscariot is a bit of tinsel and snow sexxxmas 'offensive'?'

'Werl, to minority ethnic groupings.' Bonsor tapped his clipboard. 'Council equality policy see?'

Nadine stepped in. 'Excuse me, Mr Inspector person. One sees that you have formed an inappropriate and indeed species-ist perception of this carefully crafted environment.'

'Come again Miss?'

'*Ms*. Look around and what do you see?'

'Well, er... Snow? Decorations? Tree?'

'Exactly. And that is the natural - and very endangered habitat of... ?' Nadine pointed to Jessie's tshirt

'Ooh I know!' Pauly cried. 'Robin Redbreast.'

'Sometimes, Pauly, you speak for both of us,' Ben commented.

'Polar Bears! Save the bear!' Jessie shook her tin.

'Er... do you get reindeers with polar bears?' queried Bonsor.

'Well my good man,' Nadine rolled over him like a blonde Tiger tank, 'you really should study your polar ecology more carefully before seeking to ban that which you obviously do not understand.'

'So... nothing to do with christmas then?' Bonsor scratched his head.

'Well, I'm an easter elf,' Pauly put in. 'See told ya!'

'And...' Bonsor pointed at Ben. 'Him?'

'Traditional arctic clothing. Just like Ms here.'

'Beard for warmth,' Toby suggested.

'Red for warning - like me!' Jessie smiled.

'Warning against...?', Bonsor asked, now sinking like an arctic ice floe under global warming.

'Weren't you listening to *anything*?' Nadine sneered. 'Polar bear attack.'

'Or aggressive reindeers,' suggested Pauly.

Ben stepped forward. 'Right then. So where's it say you can ban arctic charity events?'

'Well no. Not…' Bonsor fiddled unhappily with his clipboard.

'Off you go then, irritating little man.' Nadine waved Bonsor away, regally.

Pauly tapped Bonsor's clipboard. 'Ooh I know where you can ban some christmases.'

'Yes?' Bonsor brightened up.

'Churches!' Pauly explained. 'There's loads round here. Although one of them's a gay disco now.'

'Right,' Bonsor nodded, approving his disapproval. 'Well I shall look into that. Right!' Bonsor exited, his clipboard in a hurry..

'Pwuff!' Ben exhaled. 'Quick thinking Nadine. I could almost like you after that.

'Thank you. Wish I could return the compliment.'

Paige made her way in. She was wearing a tight and deeply low cut Santa girl outfit. 'Hellooo everybody! Happy christmas massaging! Although - just had a strange guy asking me if there's a gay disco at St Botolph's.'

'Oh Pauly!' Jessie said.

'Never mind,' Ben muttered. 'Must be a bit quiet for your relaxation services, this time of year Paigy?'

'You're kidding right? This is the stressiest date on the calendar.'

'Yeh deffo,' Pauly confirmed. 'Cos people are worryin about polar bears all the time.'

Jessie pointed to her tshirt and rattles her tin. 'Yaay! save the bear.'

'Sorry?' Paige puzzled.

Ben sighed. 'Pauly and Paulier. Never mind.'

'Yeah. See: all that Yuletide tension. Finding the final presents,' Paige exampled.

'Getting tear-free tinsel,' Miss Kitty said. Her slave puppy barked Kitty whipped him. 'Down slave.'

'Finding black wrapping paper,' Raven offered.

'Losing your eggs,' Pauly pouted.

Nadine lit a cigarette, and looked at Ben. 'Trying to resist the temptation to set fire to a Santa.'

'Stoppin people nickin' the baubles,' Toby noted.

'Yep,' Ben sighed. 'Happy stress-mas. Got it: like a hot mince pie in the eye.'

Lisa came in. Her concession to the festive season was to wear a red and white leather jacket, with white jeans and heels. And a red head band.

Ben looked up. 'See: that's the look Michael Jackson was ultimately aiming for.'

Liza marched up to the centre counter and slammed some flavoured condom packets on it. 'I've got a complaint. A serious one.'

'And you know how it is with Liza here,' Ben said. 'A complaint's not just for christmas. It's for all year.'

Katia fingered through the packets. 'Flavoured condoms. Yiss. What's is problem?'

Pauly had a look. 'Mango. Strawberry. Banana whip. All here an proper Liza love.'

'Aww she was probably after her particular favourite flavours. Jealousy, spite and revenge,' Ben commented.

'Nah, Santa sod. It's not about the flavours.' Liza crossed her arms, defiantly. 'I'm complainin' cos they don't work.'

'Er...' Pauly went into his idea of helpful. 'Did you try gettin someone to actually get inside one? Cos they...

Liza interrupted him, with a snort. 'Yes Pauly. I made the mistake of a drunken evening of attempted reconciliation with the appropriately, and sadly named, Father Christmas here.'

'Ooh - does that mean?' Paige cooed.

Liza nodded. 'Yep.' She took a breath. 'I'm pregnant.'

'Jesus Christ in a manger,' Ben muttered.

Pauly went insane with excitement, running (well, moving reasonably fast) around the people, peopling the shop floor. 'Yaay! It's a proper christmas now. With the virgin birth, and doggy and the reindeer can be the sheep, and Nadine can be a angel, all in white.'

'Virgin?' Nadine queried.

'Don't get my hopes up.' Ben shoved his face in his hands.

A reindeer antler, still smarting under Miss Kitty's whiplash, finally sagged and snapped, dropping to the floor.

## Part 2: Jingle Balls

What is it that makes christmas? The warmth of family and friends around a fire. Long loved songs playing on the radio. Gift offerings chosen with dedication and care. Just that extra spark of kindness from the yuletide log. Or, you could spend it in Sex-x-x.

Dom entered, wearing a smart suit, and carrying a small suitcase. 'Yuletide logs on the fire and a bottle of rum for grandma!' He spied Liza. 'Oh hello sis, what you doin' ere?'

'Hopin' for a miracle,' she said.

'Werl, that makes two of us,' Ben muttered.

'Whatever...' Dom shrugged their anti-xmas spirit off. 'Hey Nadine, you look just like a little christmas snowflake.'

'Awww... thanks.'

'Yeah all cold and frosty and makes the back of your neck itch.'

'Oh no Dom,' Pauly objected. 'Peace on earth and goodwill to all men and reindeers.'

'Yeah,' Toby said. 'Nadine just saved our christmas pudding here.'

'Really?' Dom continued. 'Oh well every icicle has a silver lining I s'pose. Anyway, talkin of that, come and pop your winter socks to these!'

Dom opened his case. Inside it were lots of balls - of something - covered with tin foil.

'Ooh what's these?' Jessie asked.

'The very finest in festive puddings,' stated Dom, proudly.

'Not exactly an *original* offering from the super salesman of Soho, is it?' Nadine sniffed.

'You know how it is Nadine. Some things are best served *warm*. And these'll put three bars on anyone's fire.' Dom got a couple of tin foiled items out. 'Red rave puds.'

'Ooh! You mean with naughty sauce?' Paige asked.

'Oh, nothin' Class A. Just your traditional queen's speech dessert, blended with the finest legal highs that clubland has to offer,' Dom boasted.

Kitty's slave dog barked. 'Woof!'

Kitty gave him a mild whip. 'Mistress first. Shush.'

'Are they alright for reindeers?' Pauly asked.

A christmas customer entered. An attractive lady, wearing a long warm coat.

'Happy christmas-ing,' Katia greeted her.

'Thank you. You too. Busy in here,' the customer noted.

'Oh we're all just friends,' Pauly said.

'Not exactly,' Nadine shot back.

'Nope.' Liza folded her arms.

'Oh well,' the customer continued. 'Anyway. Look, I'm after some tree decorations.

'Erotic novelties!' Pauly offered. 'Yeh we're good on them. Tobes... ?'

'Er...' muttered Toby.

'How about a complimentary christmas pudding?'

Pauly handed the customer a tinfoil wrapped pud from Dom's case.

The customer nodded with a smile, unwrapped, and took a bite.

'No!' Ben cried.

'Sorry?' asked the customer, through a mouthful.

Thinking better of his hasty intervention, and how exactly he would explain it, Ben shrugged. 'Er... ho. And ho and ho.'

Pauly whispered to Toby. 'Come on Toby. I did the shop training with you on this one.

'Er...' Toby was still stuck.

The customer was now swaying a little. She peered across the shop. 'That's a r-r-reindeer.'

'Yaay,' Jessie said. 'They live with the endangered polar bears - look!' Jessie showed off her tshirt.

The customer pointed at Nadine. 'An.. An angel.'

'Aww, thanks,' smiled Nadine, politely.

'She's off her face,' muttered Ben.

Next, the customer pointed to slave puppy. 'And a... a... ?'

'Woof.'

'Shhushh,' Kitty disciplined him.

With another sway, the customer managed: 'I... think I'll... come back later.' She left, carrying the remains of her pud with her.

Julia entered, in smart suit and blouse, showing lots of christmas cleavage. 'Just passed a customer leaving with no sales bag and clutching her stomach. No wonder my warehouse gets so many return items.'

'Yes, well if Pauly wouldn't go handing out my puddings to all and sundry,' Dom complained, mildly. 'How's things with the sexiest executive in Soho then?'

'Fine thanks. Only don't think you'll be lacing *my* puddings with that stuff.'

Dom cleavage gazed. 'Why spoil a perfect dessert?'

'Ooh, did you bring a spoon then?' asked Julia cheekily.

'Aah. Looks more like finger food,' Dom played along.

'Ugh,' Liza muttered. 'You're not fallin for his rabbit are ya love?'

'Hey babe. After a year like I've had, pretty much anything's better than the worn out one left in my bedroom drawer.'

Brightening the mood, three stunning models entered. Each was wearing a sexy xmas outfit.

'The catty-logue girls yaay!' Pauly said. 'Glad you could come for easter.'

'Happy christmas Sexxx shoppers!' said one.

'The party starts here! Yippee!' said another.

'Yeah. We just left the last one,' said the third.

The first through the door said 'Ooh come on - let's have a go in the sledge!'

They all piled in, with a riot of white stocking tops and almost costume-escaping boobs.

'Cowah!' Ben went pop eyed. 'All them christmas stockings - and nowhere to hang 'em.'

'Round your neck?' offered Liza, sourly.

'Oh come on Lize,' Ben protested. 'Can't we at least try to have some seasonal good will?'

'Yeh,' Pauly said. 'Remember what it were like with me mum this time of year.'

Pauly and Ben's eyes lifted to the ceiling, in shared recollection. In their minds eyes, they saw Pauly's mum, in a red basque and stockings, with a Santa hat on, handing round a pint glass wrapped in tinsel, with suited pub gentlemen pouring shot drinks into it.

Liza sighed. 'Pauly's mum in pub panto. That image really helps. Thanks.'

'Look, how about it? I mean, under this ridiculous costume,' Ben motioned to his Santa suit, 'I'm just an ordinary...'

'Pervert?' Nadine offered.

'Lecher?' was Paige's go.

'Kareoke singer?' Pauly put in.

'Yaay I love karaoke!' Jessie said.

'...Bloke!' Ben continued. 'With a heart. An I'll try to open it again for you and...' Ben motioned towards Liza's tummy.

'Aww, that's so nice. Then Jess won't have to get another tshirt made up,' Pauly went misty eyed.

'What?' Ben asked.

'So Nadine dun't have to collect for another endangered species,' Pauly explained.

## GROTTO

Nadine put her hand over the opening. 'I'd rather seal my tin hole up.'

Hard man Jez and bent Inspector Trent entered together.

'Oh look - it's cops and robbers. Which one's which today then?' Ben poked at them.

'Do you get this monkey off of him an all?' Trent asked Jez.

'Depends whether he's bein' hung upside down out of a window or not,' Jez answered.

'Hello misters,' Pauly greeted them. 'Look we've got christmas treats for all our visitors today.

Pauly picked up two of the dangerously stimulating xmas puddings.

Dom took a step forward. 'Uh... just a minute.'

'Let the elf go with this one, bro,' Ben whispered.

'What's special about these then? quizzed Trent.

'Well,' huffed Jez. 'If there's a shillin' in one of 'em, it'll be more than I've got off this lot all year. Go on then.'

The pair unwrapped, and bit into their puddings. The rest of the gathering watched them, in a suspended moment of fascination.

'So, gentlemen,' Ben smoothed. 'You're here about the collection then?'

'In a word, son,' Trent nodded.

'About time,' Jez said, through a mouthful of pud.

'Lovely,' Ben stepped aside. 'Meet Nadine.'

'And Jess,' Pauly ushered Jessie forward.

Nadine and Jess stepped forward in front of Trent

and Jez, rattling their tins aggressively.

'Come on, forces of law and disorder. Give generously,' Nadine insisted.

Jessie thrust her tshirt bosom forward at Jez's face. 'For the polar bears.'

Trent and Jez were swaying now.

'Robin redbreast?' Jez murmured.

'That's what I said,' Paul confirmed.

Everyone clapped and cheered. 'Give! Give! Give! Give!'

Trent groggily reached in his pockets and handed over some notes and change, to Nadine.

Jez, even groggier, handed over a roll of notes to Jess. 'Ugh. It's all I got.'

Everyone cheered.

Toby handed them two more puddings. 'Go on, take another couple wiv ya on your way out.'

By now, desperately stoned, Trent and Jez accepted the puddings, and weaved their unsteady way out.

Nadine stared at the £50 notes half-stuffed into her tin. 'Yaay! Jess. Look at all this! Jamaica here we come.'

'Yaay!' Jessie replied.

'Jamaica? Hang on,' Ben objected. 'Wotcha gonna be protecting: Rastafarian polar bears?'

Nadine hesitated. Briefly. 'Oh - uh. Ah well I was considering branching out. You know. Dolphins.'

'Parakeets,' suggested Jessie.

'Oh! If you go to Easter Island, can I come?' asked Pauly, with excitement.

'Yaay babe.' Jessie took his arm.

'You know what I admire about you Nadine?' Ben muttered. 'You're a woman who really likes principles.'

'Yes? Oh – thanks,' Nadine replied, with some surprise.

'Yeah,' Ben gave Nadine a stare. 'Let me know when you find some.'

The slave puppy rustled around floor of sleigh, making doggy growling noises.

'Oi what you doin' down there?' one of the xmas model girls asked.

'Oww!' said another.

'Hello boy,' said the third.

He came up with 2 red and silver balls. He gave them a shake. They jingled.

'Good puppy,' patted Miss Kitty. 'And what have you found?'

'Oh! My eggs!' Pauly cried.

'No Pauly.' Ben took them off doggy. 'They're that erotic novelty item. Jingle Balls.' Ben gave them a shake. 'Puts me in mind of a song actually.'

'Hey, well music is really good for de-stressing,' Paige said.

'And torture,' Kitty added.

'Oh - you heard 'im before 'ave ya?' said Liza.

'Oi!' Ben protested.

'Go on,' Dom encouraged. 'You sing it.'

'We'll dance it,' Julia joined in.

'Yaay, and we can rattle our tins!' Jessie added, giving her and Nadine's tins a shake.

Nadine whispered: 'Jess: we seriously need to have a chat in the new year babe.'

'Go on Toby,' Katia said. 'You have an i-plop. Plug and play!'

'Hey - that's a good name for a toy brand that,' Pauly said. 'You want to remember that one Julia.'

'After one of Dom's puddings I don't reckon I'll be remembering anything much,' Julia giggled.

'Oh. If only amnesia was that easy,' Liza sighed.

Ben stepped over, and placed a Santa arm round Liza's shoulder. 'Oh come on SpongeBob sourpants. If you can't manage a glass of christmas spirit, at least try a drop or two.'

Liza looked up at him. 'Forgive and forget?'

'Well... one out of two's not bad. '

They hugged. Everyone gathered in the store broke out in applause.

'And a 1 2 3 4!' Pauly shouted, remarkably getting the number sequence right.

'More more more hey!' everyone shouted back.

And it was time for *Jingle Balls*.
*Chorus*
Jingle balls, jingle balls jingle all the way
Oh what fun it is to ride
The jingle balls all day. Yaay !

*Pauly*
Comin through the door
*Toby*
With a customer complaint
*Katia*
Sell dem something more
*Ben*
And always count the change

*Paige*
Fun instead of stress
*Kitty*
It's all a point of view
*Liza*
A virgin birth sounds cool
*Raven*
With girls who needs men too?
*All*
Sexxx!

*All*
Jingle balls, jingle balls
*Nadine*
Jingle till you drop
*Jess*
Oh what fun it is to ride
*Dom & Julia*
With either one on top! Yaay !

*All*
Jingle balls, jingle balls
*Ben*
Jingle in the shop
*Pauly*
Get em home,
*Toby*
And find they're broke
*All*
And come back when we're closed!

Snow cascaded from the store ceiling, as Ben took to the centre of the store and cheered: 'Merry Sexxmas everyone!'

'And a happy easter too! Shop early to avoid disappointment!' Pauly added.

\* \* \*

Later that night, after the sexxxmas celebrations, Katia and Toby are playing table football. With xmas decoration and two red dildos.

One last doped up xmas pudding is lying on the counter, surrounded by empty wrappers.

Toby pauses play, for a moment. 'Ey. Do *yow* believe in the virgin birth Katia?'

'Not really.' Katia holds up her vibrator. 'But is nice to keep trying.'

\* \* \*

And the world of Sex-x-x played delightfully into a brand new future, packed with eroticism, stimulation and bringing people together through the joy of sex-x-x. In a nice way. That was Pauly's idea.

In 2020, it also became Pauly's idea to begin selling pink face masks, from a trestle table, outside the covid-shuttered shop. Ben actually approved of that business venture.

He didn't approve so much of Toby scrawling 'don't stand so close to me' on them.

Liza is still complaining about the condoms.

### THE END OF SEX-X-X

*But the gang will be back in*
*Sex-x-x: the Movie*
*Coming to these pages soon.*[16]

---

[16] Actually: really, really soon.

# *SEX-X-X: THE MOVIE*

**A Pauly Production**

**MMXXI**

# *PROLOGUE*

Amsterdam! City of bridges. Also of bicycles, micro cars, tulips, clogs, windmills, and...

A little shop, nestling in the bosom of the famous Red Light District. Because this is Amsterdam, the neighbours were a Halal butchers and a bicycle repair shop.[17]

Now, if you walked into the wrong shop by mistake, you might be very surprised at what you'd encounter in there. Garish loud pop art posters. Blow-ups. Lots of pvc and rubber. Plastics in all sorts of shapes and sizes, for your enjoyment.

Or you could retreat from your error, and pop next door to Bonk's Sex Shop. Where you'd find, to be fair, much the same things. Only in different fitting sizes.[18]

We join Casper Bonk, the middle aged, slightly paunchy proprietor, being confronted by Dirk Blank. Backed up by his two heavies.

Dirk sported a cheek scar, a side parting that Hitler would have bought a new mirror for, and a shiny pinstripe suit. The sort of visage you see reflected in coffin handles.

Dirk tapped the counter with an, as yet, unopened switchblade. 'So dis place is nice. You wanner keep it dat way.'

He received a terrified Bonk nod, in reply.

'You visit der dentist regularly?'

---

[17] see?

[18] or the same, in one interesting case

Another nod.

'That's good. Good.' Dirk smiled, reaching out the ring encrusted fingers of a hand to grab Bonk's lapels. 'You see: den dey can identify der body in der after-fire ashes of dis place. From its dental records. Ha Ha Ha.'

His heavies joined in the crude laughter. It's not absolutely certain that they actually got the joke. But one of the rules of being a Dutch heavy[19] is that: when the Boss laughs, you laugh. When the Boss shouts: you shout. When the Boss goes to take a pee…[20]

Bonk trembled like a lily facing a tsunami, on its otherwise placid pond.

'So you be a good store keeper, make dat call, and take a holiday. Ja?'

Bonk nodded. His trembling fingers dialled a mobile phone.

Dirk watched and nodded.

\*   \*   \*

There follows, over *Carry On* style music, a hilariously funny[21] dayglo style cartoon of a map of Europe. With a telephone line snaking from Euroland, across the English[22] Channel, to London.

Then, buzzing through the clouds in a descending

---

[19] It's there in the Application Form. Really

[20] They do need an extra box on the form for that one.

[21] OK: mildly amusing

[22] Are we still allowed to call it that?

*PROLOGUE*

arial shot, the Soho alley which houses the famous shop of Sex-x-x.

The innards of that love boutique exploding in a riot of colour, as montage cartoons of its usual inhabitants, flutter the cinema screen. Sort of like the Yellow Submarine cartoon, by the Beatles.

And the voiceover song of course: *Sex-x-x – such a wonderful place, full of dvd's, magazines and interesting pvc lace.*

That was Pauly's idea.

## CHAPTER 1

# *BONK KNOCK*

Pulling out, as we come to view the Sex-x-x shop floor. With Katia and Toby on minding duties.

In the first surprise of the day, a customer came in. He wandered over to the leather good stand. Having a good look, then reaching for a finger-tip inspection.

'Not to touch pliss!' Katia called out.

The customer looked over his shoulder, and walked over to her.

'I sorry. Is strange thees shop. I is looks for de map of de London please?'

'Oh, I is not sure if has diss. Is more from de tourist office.'

'Oh no. That's alroight. We can sort ya,' offered Toby at his most helpful.

'Please?' queried the customer.

Toby handed over "Sex Guide to London" booklet. 'There ya go mate. Everything a Lodon tourist really needs to see.'

The customer looked at the booklet. Proudly displaying London bridge, with its split roads in the erect position. 'Oh! Thenking yo. Goodbyes.'

The customer exited with apparent satisfaction.

Katia turned on his tormentor. 'Toby!'

'It's alroight. We get 15 per cent on each one of these. Plus free entry to La Cabana Strip Club.'

'Oh yiss. And how is dat helping him?'
'It's a sales strategy. Oi never said it was perfect.'

Ben entered, fresh from some erotic business enterprise, guaranteed to expand the horizons of Sex-x-x unto the stratosphere of British commerce. Or from an early round at the pub.

'Oi you two. Why have I just had to explain to a gentleman of foreign extraction, that the Big Ben in his guidebook is *not* in fact the classicly known pinnacle of Victorian engineering for which London is justly famous?'

'15% commission,' Toby answered.

'And "free entry to La Cabana",' Katia added.

'Oh fair enough. I'll take my commission and spend it there later.'

Ben sidled up to Katia and placed a less than endearing hand on her svelte shoulder. 'Unless you'd care to join me.'

Toby raised his hand to object.

'Not to touch pliss!' Katia said, like an Iphone ringtone on repeat play.

'Oh alright,' Ben acknowledged. 'Yes Toby. You instead then.' Ben sighed, running his eyes up and down the no-go area of Katia's incredibly inviting personal space. ' But it's not really a substitute.'

'Yes Boss,' Toby acknowledged. 'But I don't actually moind you touching me.'

'Well thank you for those few kind words, Tobes. Except I don't have an irresistable urge in that direction, in your case.'

Ben picked up one of the tourist guides, and sighed.

'Oh, is this what it's come down to? Here in our field of dreams, our little slice of erotic Soho heaven. All we've got to fill the day is foisting dodgy guidebooks onto unsuspecting punters, and arguin' over the proceeds.'

Ben tossed the tome aside. 'You know, maybe we need to just get away from here for a bit and taste another side of life.'

'See? That's why you're my business partner,' Pauly said, as he came in through the side door.

'Cos I'm having a mid-Thursday depression?' Ben queried.

'No! 'Cos you knew we was goin' away. Just like my plan. And that was my idea.'

'Pauly. The last time you planned an "away day", we ended up at the Little Chef on the Basingstoke bypass.'

'The Little Chef's nice. I mean, the adventure playground's not as big as the Happy Eater, is it Kats?'

Katia rolled her eyes.

Pauly, in full culinary flow, continued. 'But they do do them pancakes with the little bits in. And the toilets are dead hygeni-ky.'

'So where we goin' this toime Pauly?' Toby asked, with genuine interest.

'Am-ster-dam! Yes yaay ! Am-ster-dam. You know with the windmills and the canals and the cuckoo clocks.'

'No, Pauly I tink dat is der Switzerland,' Katia replied, with geographical strictness.

'Camels in Switzerland?' Pauly puzzled. 'But wun't all the water run out of 'em like down the mountainy slopes?'

'Yes Pauly.' Ben grabbed his shoulders gently, to enable some calm and focus. 'Could you connect two, or possibly three of your remaining brain cells to your mouth, and explain how exactly we are all going to Amsterdam?'

'Oh, its me old mum's Dutch uncle, Casper Bonk.'

'Oh yes. Another "friend" of your dear departed mum.' Ben used finger quote marks.

'Yeh. And he runs a sexy shop in Am-ster-dam. A nice one. With counters. And racks. And...'

Ben interrupted the interior décor rendition. 'Yes. Erotic Boutique. Got the picture already. So... ?'

'Well, Uncle Casper...'

Toby was by now snuffling with giggles. 'Bonk.'

'What is de funny?' asked Katty.

Ben waved them quiet.

'Yeh. He's phoned me. On the phone. I've got a phone now.'

'Oh really Pauly? Dat is der nice,' Katia commented.

Pauly brought out his mobile phone. It was the kind you give to your average four year old. With large buttons. And a unicorn emblem.[23]

'Yeh. Paigy gave it me as a present. She said as her little cousin din't want it I could have it. It's got numbers

---

[23] No. Nobody knows why

on look!'

Pauly handed the phone over to Katia.

'Pauly. Yiss.' Katia inspected the sophisticated telecommunications instrument. 'Dis only have der Paige number on it.'

'But there's lots of other ones. Look: one, two, three, four et ceteras,' Pauly pointed.

Toby took a ahnd. 'Roight mate. But you actually have to put them together to ring somebody.'

'Oh.' Pauly held up the phone, seeking inspiration. 'Paigy never explained that. Oh well. I suppose I can just try a few and see what happens.'

'Remind me to get you a job interview with covid Test and Trace. You'll fit right in. Look:' Ben crossed his arms and leant forward. 'Disinterring the bones of your information from the ashes of your communication skills, Pauly. What you're saying is that your Uncle Casper...'

'Bonk !'

'Yes, thank you Toby… Has asked you to ask us to look after his shop for a while. In Amsterdam.'

'Yeh. That was *his* idea.'

'Well, sounds just the job! Alright Pauly, you're on!'

Pauly grabbed Ben by the shoulder and walked him into the middle of the store. 'Just think. If my old mum could see us. Journeyin over the seas, abroad, to a foreigny place, to spread the joy of sex-x-x.'

'Yes my old son. Let's get some Euro price tags flyin across the Netherlands counter.'

Pauly turned his megawatt, although still dim, smile

to Toby and Katia. 'How about it? Yaay! Am-ster-dam. Yaay ! Am-ster-dam here we come. Bringing the joy of sex-x-x to the Am-ster-dam-ese people. In a nice way.'

Katia considered. 'Pauly. You do know where Amsterdam *ees*, yiss?'

There was a pause, as Pauly struggled with that one. 'It's... yeh... where the windmills are.'

Ben took command of the situation. 'Right. For god's sake everyone, don't let him book the tickets.'

Paige and Bentley entered.

'Aww Paigy,' Pauly greeted. 'I'm goin' away for a bit.'

'Aww, no. They've not caught you again have they?' Paige worried about these things.

'No! We're off to the Amsterdam canals. But I'm not sure about the cuckoos.'

'Yeah, know the feeling. Anyway Pauly, I know you're going. That's why I gave you the phone.'

'Ooh yeh! Can we have a go?'

'Alright, but only if you talk dirty. He he.'

'Who to?'

Ben poked an oar of sanity into the whirlpool of their dialogue. 'Look another time, maybe. Bentley, good to see ya.'

They shake hands.

'Now come on, you're the Ansterdam expert. Even if it is the wrong side of the canal.'

Bentley was the king of the European adult trade,

gay division. 'The continental trade. Well it's been doing alright at your end of the Eurotunnel hasn't it?'

'Our "Pink" section of the shop. Yeh!' Pauly enthused. 'That was my idea.'

'No, Pauly,' Ben objected. '*Your* idea was to get glued to an oversize pair of pink angel wings in the shop window. Taking Toby and Katia three hours to rescue you.'

'Oh Pauly,' Paige consoled.

'But we did get a lot of interest from passers by,' Pauly pointed out.

'Yeh,' Toby confirmed. 'I went round with a hat after. We got nearly a tenner in small change.'

'Which went some mild part of the way in mitigating the bill from the costume company, for damaged hire stock,' Ben pointed back.

'Oh well teething troubles, eh,' Bentley calmed. 'Still none of that where you're going.'

'Well, yeah,' Ben nodded. 'What do you reckon to this place, what's the name again Pauly?'

'Bonk,' Pauly supplied.

Toby started sniggering again.

'Toby!' Ben finger-wagged. 'No not your uncle. The shop.'

'I don't know what it's called in Am-ster-dam-ese. "Shoppy" or something.'

'"Shop" is "Vinkel" in Dutch,' Bentley noted politely.

'OK, but how does that help?' Pauly puzzled.

'Pauly!' Katia put in. 'Dutch is de language dey is

talk in Holland.'

'Right...' Pauly considered, hesitantly.

'Which is where Amsterdam is,' Paige pointed out.

'Ohhh! That's where. Gosh it's complicated over in abroad in't it?' Pauly summed up. 'Oh no though, just thought! '

'What mate?' asked Toby.

'How we going to sell magaz-ines and DVD's and anal lubricanty when we don't talk Amster-Dutch?'

'Hey relax, Euro entrepreneur,' Bentley said. 'Everyone in Holland speaks perfect English. Better than us.'

'Yes, well in Pauly's case, that wouldn't exactly be...' Ben started. 'Oh never mind. So, Bentley: any low down on this Bonk emporium?'

Toby was still sniggering uncontrollably. 'Maybe they call it a bonk shop! He he.'

'Shutup Toby.' Ben turned for an injection of rationality. 'Bentley?'

'Oh Casper's place is famous. Right on the best street. I mean, his dolls - own brand- are some of the best you can get.'

Ben nodded. 'OK. Sounds good.'

'Does he sell windmills?' asked the enthusiast.

'Not everybody in Holland sells windmills, Pauly.'

'Oh,' the enthusiast disappointed.

'Aww,' Paige tried some cheering. 'What do you want a windmill for sweetie?'

'In case I ever get a garden. Although I could put it

on top my DVD player for now.'

'See Toby,' Ben said. 'That's what ambition looks like.'

Toby looked blankly around.

Paige changed gear into her fake sexy smoochy thing, with Ben. 'So... Benny, darling.'

'Er... yes?'

'No problem if I bring my little massage table round and help look after the business while you're all gone? Hmmm?'

'Do as much of your electro convulsive therapy as you like, Paige.'

'Yaay, thanks sweetie, mwah.'

'You never know, might finally get you a gig at Broadmoor.'

Liza entered. Having been estranged from Ben, then somwhat togethered, then re-estranged, then...[24]

'Awww, hello Bentley.'

Liza and Bentley hugged and smooched.

'Hi sexy. I'm still glad to be gay, but you're still a prime reason not to be.'

'Oh knock it off,' Ben muttered.

'Oh no it's good that,' Pauly piped up. 'Bringing people together through the joy of sexxx: in a nice way.'

'Yeah, but not with *her*. She's my wife!' Ben

---

[24] You get the picture. Like being on a whirling carnival ride, that makes you wish you hadn't eaten all that candyfloss

remonstrated.

'Ex...' Toby reminded.

'Sort of...' Ben countered.

'Former?' Katia clarified.

'Nearly,' Pauly edged.

'Well are you guys terminally separated, or what?' Bentley put the question squarely.

'We're... working things out,' Ben muttered.

'Ooh Pauly that reminds me,' Paige said.

'Yeh Paigy?'

'If you go to an Amsterdam swingers party, you must let me know. And get some photos.'

'Have they got them there then?' Toby asked.

'Are you kidding?' Bentley laughed. 'The best swings in Euroland.'

'Oh yeh I will do then,' Pauly confirmed. 'Except. I've not got a camera.'

'There's one on your phone babe,' Paige pointed out.

'Oh. Which number is that?' Pauly puzzled.

'Oh god don't start that again,' Ben bad tempered. 'It's like a thalidomide child with a new rattle.'

Katia hit Ben. 'Oi! Dat is not der nice.'

Ben mutely held his hands up in a 'sorry: what can you do' gesture.

'Oh Amsterdam eh?' commented Liza. 'Well it's no surprise that of all the eurozone you'd be goin' there.'

'Why ees dat Liza?' asked Katia

'He's been goin' bloody Dutch all his life!'

'Sorry?'

'Never mind,' Ben shok his head. 'Look, my little doe eyed vixen, I was meaning to invite you. Right? So we could have some time together. You know, just you and me. Romantic. On the canals.'

'And by the windmills,' Pauly added. 'Yeh. Lovely you two!'

'Aww. Really?' Liza looked warmly at Ben.

'Although I think there might be a problem with the cuckoo clocks.'

Everyone's unspoken inner thoughts prompted their heards to turn, staringly, at Pauly.

Hard man Jez, protector of this parish, was sitting having a drink in the pub. His hard thoughts turned back to a conversation, some time ago.

'So that's basically it Jez. I ain't got two sardines to rub together.' That's what Liza had said. Straining forward in an inappropriately sized leopard skin dress.

'Nor even the tin to keep 'em in. Yeah I get it.'

'So, like, I mean. There must be something you can help with,' Liza had suggested with a wheelbarrow load of seduction hinting.

'Alright doll. Leave it with me. I'll give ya a bell, alright?'

'Aah, you're a diamond babe,' Liza had smiled behind lipfulls of lipsticked filler.

'Nar. When it comes to diamonds, I'm more of a transport facility. Cash and carry, know what I mean? Cheers.'

They had clinked glasses.

Jez returned from timewarp, as Ben entered, and sat down opposite.

'Alright Jez.'

'Dover.'

'So what's this bit of business you want me to do for ya? My knuckle duster is a bit worn down these days y'know.'

'Look Dover. I'm the wise guy. You're just a comedian.'

'I thenk yo.'

'Din't say you was funny. Right. Listen 'ere.' Jes leaned in to get confidential. 'You're off to A-Dam right?'

'Yeah. And?'

'So I'll be askin' you nicely to bring back a little holiday souvenir.' Jez leaned back and surveyed Ben, like a tiger regarding a tethered goat.

'Oh god. Right look it's not sniffy stuff is it? Cos whichever of my limbs you wanna confiscate I am *not* gettin' into that caper. Alright?'

'Oh relax. Gawd, you do get like a spastic in a three-legged race sometimes doncha?'

'Well, I'm just sayin...'

'Anyway. Round 'ere, that'd be like bringin a g string to a lap club wunnit?'

'Yeah. Spose. So what highly dubious merchandise are you expecting me to Eurostar then?'

'Bit of Shirley Bassey. Easy enough,' Jez shrugged.

'Come again? Feather boas and high heels? You takin a new turn in your modelling career Jez?'

'Diamond's are forever, you little smut twat.'

'Oh right. I see. And what am I supposed to do: stick 'em in the battery compartment of a gross of duty free dildos?'

'You don't have to worry about none of that. Just go to a address when you're told, collect a package, and stick it at the back of your smut shop. Fink you can manage that?'

'So what's in it for me?'

'Debt forgiveness.'

'Oh! All me debts written off. That's something I suppose.'

'Who said anyfin about "all"?'Jez wagged a meaty finger.

'Gawd. Dealin with you's like tryin to get your arm back off of a hungry crocodile.'

'Just do it right Dover. Then we'll see exactly how much I can spit out.'

'Charmin. You know, I don't really feel like a drink now.'

'That's alright. Just get *me* one on your way out.'

'Alright. See ya later alligator.'

Jez did a crocodile impression with his jaw. Ben rolled his eyes and wandered over to the bar.

Back in the shop, Pauly was demonstrating his Amsterdammed excitement to the gang.

'And there's this model vill-iage. It's the biggest one in the wide world, it is.'

'But if it's, loike, big ones. Then isn't it the same as normal size?' Toby objected.

'Oh no. It never said that in the brochury. Anyway I've seen pictures. And it's the most beautifully thing what I have ever seen. What do you reckon Kats?'

Kats was dazing off into space. 'Huh. Sorry?'

'Oh, she's thinking about them Dutchy swingers parties Paige was talkin about,' Toby said.

Katia snapped back out of her day dream. 'I was not! Just 'cos I had a little accident - wid de curtains - once, it not mean I swing obsessed. My life is fine widout de swing, thank yo.'

Gothic princess Raven entered. 'Quite right honey. Who needs sex when you've got... energy?'

Pauly gave Raven a hug.

'You know Raven,' Ben commented. 'That you can actually ask a question like that, wearing a skirt like that, really makes me wonder what they teach young people these days.'

'Well, to be nice to the elderly, for a start.'

Ben sidled up, to get smoochy. 'Hmm, well that's something...'

'Not *all* of them, though,' Raven said, turning her back. 'So you're off to the Netherlands Pauly, yaay!'

'Are we?' Pauly asked.

'Yes!' Chorused Ben, Toby, Katia, together.

'They do make it confusing don't they?' sighed Pauly.

'Well, to be fair to our European neighbours Pauly,' Ben countered, 'you do still get confused about dealing with a toilet seat in the down position.'

'Aww!' Pauly scowled. ' You said you weren't gonna mention... Anyway. Maybe they've not got them in Amsterland.'

'Or in your little model village. Anyway Raven, what brings you here?' Ben asked.

'Hasn't Pauly told you?'

'No. And why do those words fill me with sudden dread and suspicion?'

'Oh ho!' Katia chortled. 'De same as "Yes you can take me out to de dinner, but is you are de paying."

'Yes, thank you, Poland's answer to Michael McIntyre. I am *not* a skinflint. I'm just careful with my hard earned.'

'And to be fair,' Pauly put in. 'Ben always gives a nice tip to the girls at the Thai Cabin on Brewer Street.'

Ben mimed 'I'm gonna kill him gestures at Pauly. Katia sniggered.

'Tsunami relief fund. Isn't-that-right-Pauly?' Ben clarified.

'Yeh. Su-nar-marie. And you say you love payin them extra 'cos they get so wet.'

Ben turned his back on Pauly. 'So why are you here, little Miss Rocky Horror?'

'Cos I agreed with Pauly that I'd look after his shop while you're all gone.'

'Look, Dracula's daughter, this is a sex boutique. Not the London Dungeons.'

'But Ben!' Pauly said. 'Raven knows everything there is to know about fetish fashions and plastic home alones.

All her friend's 'll come. And she dunt even want payin for the week.' Pauly puffed his pigeon chest out in pride. 'That was all my idea.'

'Oh well why dint you say?' Ben relieved. 'I mean, yeah. That puts a whole different lid on the coffin, that.'

'See what's I mean?' Katia observed.

'Look knock it off!' Ben hit back. 'You're the one studyin your accountancy night and day. What's that make you?'

'Someone in dis shop who can actually add up widout using dere fingers,' Katia shot back.

'Money obsessive. That's what. And yeah, it's me being careful with the treasure dug up from our field of dreams here that means I can pay *your* wages.'

'Sometimes,' Toby clarified.

'Alright, alright! I promise everyone, when we get there, I'll take us *all* out for a slap up Dutch pancake treat and no Euro's spared.'

'That'll be *after* you've lost all sense of your normal reality at a dope cafe, roight boss?' Toby enquired.

'Ooh what's one of them?' asked Pauly, with interest.

'You not heard of dose cafes Pauly?' Katia said.

'Like... Starbucks. I don't like them,' Pauly shook his head.

'Oh why, love?' asked Raven, sympathetically.

Ben explained. 'He had an accident with the lid of a Frauppucino. Had to get him a new pair of trousers.'

'Them places is not friendly,' Pauly agreed.

'Aww. Poor love,' Raven sympathised.

'Oh but it's different at the dope caffs, see,' Toby enthused. 'You just get to smoke all different kinds of mari-juana all day.'

'No plastic tops?' asked Pauly, hopefully.

'No. They loike do little cups of really really strong coffee,' Toby answered.

Pauly nodded in relief. 'Sounds nice.' Pauly paused for a think. 'Do you have to inhale?'

All heads again turned for a Pauly stare.

Ben clapped his hands. 'Let's all just go get packed shall we.'

'Yeah! Let's go get the Bonk!' Toby cheered.

'Yaay! Oh Raven, you'll be alright won't you love.' Pauly went into his being helpful mode. 'You know where eveything is, and I put special extra black toilet paper in the loo, and...'

'Ooh stop de fussing Pauly,' Katia butted in. 'Raven will be de fine.'

'Black toilet... ?' Ben half-asked.

'And if you need to know anythin, anythin at all, you can just call me on my phone. Cos Paigy got me a phone...'

Pauly got his phone out. 'So I've got a phone now. And you can call me. Even in Amster-land!'

'Aww. Sweet. Alright my lovely. What's your number?'

'My...?' Pauly looked around helplessly.

'Right.' Ben sighed. 'Outta here.'

'Yep,' Katia agreed.

Toby concurred. 'Me too.'

They all took a last sorrowful look at Pauly, and filed out.

Raven cuddled Pauly's head to her shoulder. 'Aww. Maybe it's better if you ring *me*, lover'

'Yeh.'

## CHAPTER 2

## *LOVE CANALS*

Amsterdam! City of bridges. Also of… well, you know. And now, temporary home to our valiant Sex-x-x ers.

'Wow, it's lots of smashin kit in here, in't it?' Pauly nodded his head enthusiastically at the stimulating provisions of Bonks Sex Shop.

Ben shuffled a couple of dildo packs in his hand. One was blue. 'Definitely a cut above, Pauly. Yes indeed. Katia, everything OK with the cash register?'

'Oh yiss. I is used to do Euros. Is same my country.'

'Really?' Ben went for a wind-up opportunity. 'I thought they just did barter. You know, lump of coal for a bag of potatoes sort of thing.'

Katia stuck her tongue out, in eloquent Euro reply.

Pauly had got hold of a double ended dildo. 'What's this for then?'

'Maybe they just take turns loike?' Toby contributed

'Oh Tobeeee!' Katia sighed.

A male middle aged customer entered.

'Ey up. Shop !' Ben encouraged.

'Goedemiddag,' the customer said politely.

'Come again,' Pauly asked.

'Heb je rolprent van meisjes met grote borsten op de fiets?'

The gang looked blank.

'I thought Betley said everyone here talks perfect

English?' Ben wondered.

'Maybe he's from the Switzerland part,' Pauly offered. 'Kati - can you help?'

'I am de Polish, Pauly! I not his language!'

'Isn't it all the same in Euro-ey-land?'

'Neem me niet kwalijk?' the customer insisted.

'You can see why we never put Pauly up for the diplomatic service.' Ben stepped into the language barrier. 'Sorry Sir... er...'

Ben mimed being deaf and not understanding.

The cutomer relaxed. 'Oh... de retards... ja. OK.'

Ben forced a smile. He gestured around shop, with his hands open.

The customer nodded. Then, pointed to Katia. He smiled and touched his hair. Then mimed riding a bike.

'He wants to put you on his bike I think, Kats,' Pauly suggested.

'I no going,' Katia insisted.

'Hang on,' Ben said.

The customer mimed 'film'.

Ben tried to follow him. 'You want... Film...'

The customer nodded.

'Of...' Ben mimed big boobs: 'Big boobs...'

The customer nodded, adding a smile.

'Riding a bike!' Toby finished up. Toby mimed bike riding.

The customer was smiling and nodding now.

'I don't get the teeth bit,' Pauly puzzled.

'Me neither,' Toby affirmed.

Ben re-mimed the teeth and hair bit.

The customer ponted at Katia's hair and shook his head.

'Skin head!' Toby suggested.

'Not angry?' Pauly tried.

'Blonde! He wanting blonde hair girl!' Katia provided the solution.

'Blonde haar, ya!' enthused the customer.

Ben summed up the conclusions of the Bonk brains trust: 'You want a film of a big boobed blonde riding a bicycle.'

Katia shuffled through a catalogue.

'Ya! Bijzonder!'

'Any luck there Katia?' Pauly asked.

'Nope.'

'No,' Pauly addressed the customer.

'We could always make one!' Toby suggested.

'That would be,' Ben noted, 'without the bike, the blonde, or...'

Pauly piped up. 'You're always saying how Katia...'

'No,' she pushed in.

'Blaue dildo?' the customer pointed to Ben's hand.

'That we *can* do sir.'

'Ah volmaakt.'

Ben handed the prize it over to Katia, who did a quick wrap and money exchange.

'Tenk yo. Sorry about de film.'

The customer stood back , with this package. 'That is quite alright Miss. It is nice how our liberal government finds work for you retarded people. Good day.'

The customer smiled politely, and walked out.

Across the store arose a haunting, embarassed silence.

Except for Pauly. 'How did he know?'

Alittle later, in Dutch time anyway, a svelte young blonde lady pushed through the shop door. She was wearing a smart business suit, and holding a clipboard and pen.

'Good morning, everyone. Welcome to Amsterdam.'

Ben did a double take. 'Ah now *that's* what I call a welcome. And how can we intrepid travellers on the world of Eurosmut be of assistance Miss.. ?'

'Roos. Annika Roos.' She held out a polite hand for Ben for shake. Which did make him shake, rather.

'I am your representative from the local Chamber of Commerce,' Ms Roos continued. 'And I am here to help with any questions you may have about doing business in our lovely city.'

'Oh.' Ben was, for once, in pleasantly surprised territory. 'Well I *was* worried when I saw the clipboard, Miss.'

'Sorry?'

'Ah you see. In our fair home city, that is usually the instrument of interference in business, the trampling under beaurocratic jackboot of another few flowers in our field of dreams.'

'You want to sell flowers? Sure I can help you with the licence for that. Easy.'

'Ooh are we gonna sell flowers?' Pauly got keen quickly. 'That's very Dutchy. I love roses.'

'Aww, is romantic Pauly, yiss?' Katia smiled.

'Er... I dunno. It's just that you can buy them one at a time,' Pauly clarified his floral stance. 'I tried that with a daffodil and got mean looks.'

'No, no. Stop!' Ben held his hands up, warding off the steamroller of Paulyness. 'It was just a homily on the trials of urban life back home.'

'That's fine.' Ms Roos nodded and smiled. 'I am here to assist with any commercial problems and opportunities.' She offered Ben the clipboard and pen. 'Could you all please just write your names and contact details on here for me. Thank you.'

The gang got to scribbling.

'Yes,' Ms Roos continued. 'And there is much to see in our lovely city. If you wish I can arrange for a tour guide to explain to you the best sights while you are here.'

The clipboard made its inevitable way to Pauly. 'Does it have to be in joined up writing?'

Ben thwacked Pauly over the head with it. Then handed it back to Ms Roos, with a rueful smile.

'Excuse my colleague. The strain of working out which end of the pen to use, gets to him sometimes. I've filled it all in for him.'

'Thank you so much.' Ms Roos gave a warm smile. 'I shall return again to see if there is anything I can be helping you with. Goede dag. That means "good day" in Dutch. Bye.' With a final smile, the lovely Ms Roos walked out.

'Ben! I am de impressed!' Katia exclaimed.

'Well, thank you. Er...why?'

'Well you did not to do de usual speaking about executive cum slut wid de touch of arsy class.'

'And she was all blue haired and blonde eyed,' Pauly observed. 'Very.'

'And in a suit. I know how you loikes that, boss,' Toby put in.

Ben climbed on his horse of moderate height. 'Look you lot. Contrary to what you seem to think I am not constantly driven by an insatiable urge to talk filthy innuendos to every shapely, classy blonde I encounter.'

'Oh. Is good,' Katia nodded.

'Very disciplined example boss. Oi loike it,' Toby commended.

'Right then,' Ben nodded. 'Mind you, should of seen what I wrote on her form. He he he.'

Katia threw a reasonably bulky packet of cut-price condoms in the general direction of Ben's head.

Back in London, Jez was reclining on a steel and leather chair in his office. A vintage pair of boxing gloves hung from a hook on the wall. They still sported a fleck of dried blood from whoever had been the opponent that fight night.

Jez was on the phone: 'Oh, so the muppets are on stage.'

'Ha ha ha. You're tellin' me.'

'All sorted. The second their little feet touch the ground 'ere, my bent copper 'll have their collars good and proper.'

'Yeah. So smarmy Dover an' his gang get their comeuppance. We get the merchandise. And I inherit a nice little shop in Soho.'

'I know! And they say crime doesn't pay. It's the gift that keeps on givin'.

Jez looked over at his old sparring gloves, and gave a nasty wink of triumph.

Back in Bonkland, Ben was organising the gang. 'Right! Well, now we're all settled, and we've done some cultural exchanges, how about seeing some of Amsterdam's bright lights? Any ideas?'

'There's the model vill-iage. It's only a short trip out of town. At Mad-uro-dam,' was Pauly's offering.

'Yes, well,' Ben considered. 'The name kind of gives that one away doesn't it. Look, we didn't just come half way across euroland to visit a soddin' model village.'

'I did,' Pauly sulked.

'Is not half de way across,' Katia objected. 'Is more like, well, a little de bit. 'Cos halfway is more like Vienna or...'

'I was exaggerating to emphasise,' Ben stold the conversation back. 'Thank you very much, madame geography teacher. Alright. So... ideas. Apart from a dismal trip to Pauly's land of the little people.'

'Pancakes,' Toby offered.

'Yes?' Ben queried.

'Pancakes is traditional in Holland, loike.'

'I know that Toby,' Ben rubbed his brow. 'There's a stand right outside this shop.'

'Is there? Oh well I'll go there then.'

'Not exactly a tourist trip through is it?' Ben objected.

'Yeh it is! Unless they do deliveries, loike.'

Ben gave up on that one. 'Katia?'

'Well, dis is de home of European art, Breughel, Van Gogh, Franz Hals. And dere is many museum here, so...'

'Oh give it a break, culture vulture,' Ben butted in. 'Is that our collective best? Boldly going where we have not gone before: for pancakes and dull portraits?'

'I know!' Pauly piped up.

'I doubt that, but anyway...'

'A live show. A show that is *live*,' Pauly glittered his fingertips in the air. 'That was my idea.'

'Yes, your explanation hasn't got too technical for us all to grasp yet.'

'So, I've looked at a brochury. And it says - from memory mind - that "this show will take you to places you have not never experienced. It will illuminer-ate your mind about possibilities."'

'The sales pitch sounds a bit overblown, but yes my son. I get the jolly gist.' Ben clapped his hands with satisfaction. 'Right! You're on! That's more like it. Katia: you can hide your eyes on my chest if you need to.'

'I rader watch - whatever it is - tenk yo.'

'Fair enough. Tobes, you don't mind mindin the shop

do ya? Not with pancake express round the corner.'

'Suits me boss. Banana and pineapple filling here I come!'

'Yeh. I can see the banana filling part heading in our "live show" direction too Tobes. He he he. And, just let me know if you get too shocked, Katia love.'

'Dat happen every time you comes *my* side of de counter. So I is used. Anyway, I sits next to Pauly.'

'OK lovely! Then we can share the popcorn.'

'Pauly!' Ben objected. 'It's a live sex show. Not an afternoon screening at the cinema.'

'Oh I get it! So it's more of a hot dog thing. Fair enough.'

'We'll sort out the food and beverage options when we get there, OK? Now let's go get a *real* Amsterdam experience. Whay haay !'

Ben, Pauly and Katia went off for some Amsterdamming.

Toby, left alone, whirled his own wildest Dam fantasies. 'Or banana and chutney maybe.'

CHAPTER 3

## *CLOG COPS*

A modern modest office building flew the Netherlands flag. Inside, Inspector Vandergriff was seated behind his desk. Slightly balding, but tough looking, like Bruce Willis in a tight but inexpensive suit. He was reading a typed report in a manilla folder.

Miss Roos – Annika - was standing at attention.

'Sho you have shuccessh-fully made your way into their operation Shergeant Roosh.'

'Yes sir. It's all in my report.'

'Sho I shee. Our tip off wash obvioushly right. Thish man, Toby Jackshon, hash a long criminal record in England.'

'And Miss Radek?'

'I shushpect she hash linksh to de Polish mafia. Would be typical, dey working together in a matter like deesh.'

'And Paul Perkins?'

'Der mosht dangeroush of the lot. Shee, he hash no Polishe file at all. Very clever. And you shay he wash de only one not to shign your form?'

'That's right sir.'

'Yesh. Typical of dat criminal cunning. He would not give you hish shignature becaushe he knowsh we could then do a handwriting match through Interpol.'

'Excuse me sir,' Annika hesitated. 'But he did seem,

well, …*achterlijk.*'

'Aha! Yesh. He playsh de role of de reatard well. Too well, Shergeant Roosh. Nobody could be dat sthupid.'

Vandergriff got up and waved the Report at Annika. 'Wid-out doubt, he ish der ringleader. And dish Ben Dover, well, he ish obvioushly de enforcher.' He thrust a page at Annika: 'You shee what de devil wrote on your form?'

Annika read out the words enscribed: "Now that we're acquainted, you should show me a lovely Dutch alley so you can get a bit of Ben Dover. Heart. Kiss"

Annika shuddered and shoved the page back to Vandergriff, as if she were warding off a rattlesnake.

Inspector Vamdergiff paused, and gave a level gaze at Annika. 'I admire your courage, Shergeant Roosh. Already threatsh to your shafety to keep you in line wid der plansh. If you want to be re-ashigned, I will undershtand.'

Annika saluted. 'No sir. Thank you. I will pursue this case to the very end. They will not escape Netherlands justice!'

Vandergriff stood. 'Very good Shergeant. Or ash I might shoon be shaying, Leftenant. Keep the reports coming. And be careful.'

Annika saluted again. 'Yes sir! Thank you sir.'

Annika left, closing the Inspector's door carefully.

Vandergriff took a pen and wrote on the Report "*Zeer gevaarlijk*".

He tapped the pen on his desk. 'Very dangeroush. Ja.

But we will frushtrate your plansh.'

In a darkened auditorium, populated with pin-pricks of electric light, Pauly was on the edge of his seat, taking it all in, with delight. Possibly, a bead of sweat was breaking out upon his brow.

Katia too, was watching. Although looking pretty bored.

Ben had his head in his hands.

A voice whispered through the sound system. 'And so, the little elves found they could restore the princess to life. But only with magic drops from the fountain of dreams.

Puppet elves, on strings, jerkily manifested themselves towards a wooden wishing well. Golden star paper issued from it.

Pauly dared a glance away from his captivated view. 'If you're a bit scared Ben, maybe you can hide your eyes on Katia's chest.'

From either side of Paul's head, they urgently whispered: 'No!'

A kindergarten kid in the row behind, looked at them strangely.

Later, amidst the trams and bustle of bikes, Ben took Pauly to task. 'Well, thank you for that afternoon treat Pauly.'

'Yeh! Told you it'd be good. "Live show". They don't have them back home, do they?'

Ben sighed. His mobile buzzed a text message.

'Well, much as I'd love to accompany you to the Bicycle Museum, or wherever you're off next, I've got a bit of business to attend to. So see you at the shop later OK?'

'Which one?'

'The-Dutch-one-in-Amsterdam, Pauly.'

'Right just checkin. "It is important to make your meeting arrangements precise-er-ley." I read that.'

'Really Pauly, where?' Katia asked.

'In the "Idiot's Guide to Travel". It's packed full of useful information.'

'You really should get a t-shirt made up, you know,' Ben advised.

'Yeh? Of what?'

'That book. A..' Ben described a line across his chest: "Travelling Idiot" logo.' Ben did a creditably nasty smile. 'Save the trouble of talking to you. Bye.'

Ben stalked off.

'Ooh Kats. Do you think they could make us one round here somewhere?'

'Maybe Pauly. Look, if you is into seeing a real life show, why don't I take you some special shops you might to like?'

'Yaay! Is any of them on a little bridge? 'Cos that'd be brilliant!'

Katia considered. 'Uh, well maybe. We go sees OK?'

In London, Raven wakes from a strange slumber. Looking around the love boutique, the gothic princess sees nothing out of place.

But then she stops, and listens… to silence. She steps to the door and pulls it open. Poking her now nervous head into the alley, she sees… nothing. No people. She hears… nothing.

Her nerves jangling like, violin strings slashed at with a bottle, she swallows. Takes some steps. Hesitatant. Then faster. Breaking into a run. Out into Soho Square.

Deserted. Plastic bags, cans, newspapers blown by urban wind. Cars abandoned, some crashed into each other and into walls. A bus, listing against a broken shop frontage. In the last 28 days, something, some cataclysm has occurred.

And then…

Sorry. Uh, really sorry about that. Wrong movie. Must have got a bit mixed up on the cutting room floor. Please don't blame the poor writer. All the editor's fault. Really

Actually, Raven was in the shop, moving bits around, nice and happy. No zombies apocalysing. OK, some odd customers from time to time, but that's life in the erotic trade.

Paige walked in with her massage bed carrier.

'Hello Paige my lovely!'

They hugged.

'Hello sexy.'

Paige put her carrier down. 'Hmm, bit quiet in here is it?'

'Well, what with Pauly and the gang being away…'

'No silly, I mean customers!'

'Aww yeah. Maybe they've gone on holiday as well.'

Paige waved a pink fingernail. 'And I've got just the thing to bring 'em back!' Paige started unzipping her carrier bag.

Now here was the real Amsterdam deal. The infamously famous red light district. Full of red lights. And the delights being illuminated by them.

'Well, what you think Pauly?' Katia asked her travelling companion.

Pauly looked round. 'Where's the bridge with the little shops on?'

'Oh Pauly! Is the windows is special here - look !' Katia turned Pauly by the shoulders to interrupt his line of vision, with something red light illuminated.

Back in the zombie-free zone of the shop, Paige had got the massage bed up.

She had also propped up a life-size cardboard cut-out of her in a sexy nurse's uniform. 'So: how about sex-x-x-ing up that window with this?'

'Oh wow that is awesome!' Raven raved.

'Aww. Sweetie.'

'Yeah. I mean. How did *you* fit in that costume?'

'Oi! I am not oversize!' Paige pouted.

'No no, lover. No.' Raven allowed her gothic gaze to linger over Paige's lollipop figure. 'Well. Not from the waist down.'

'Yeh well anyway. Loud mouth Dover is always sayin' that I've got a bigger frontage than his shop window. So now we'll find out!'

'OK. So how will that bring customers in?'

Paige pointed to cut-out, then table: 'Nurse...' (point) 'Massage...' (point) 'Sweetie, even the punters around here should be able to get that one.'

'Oh yeah. Definitely lover. For sure.' Raven had a quick think. 'Better stick a message on your frontage though. Just in case.'

'Shall I?'

'Yeah. There's plenty of room, lover.'


Back in red light land, Katia and Pauly were looking at a girl in a shop window.

'You see Pauly? Dat is what we comes to look at!'

'Oh my goodness. We don't have this back home. It's... it's like a sweetie box with a see through lid!'

'Yeh. You could to say dat.'

'So what now?' Pauly frowned with the mental processing effort.

'Well... when you sees a sweetie dat you like de look of, you just goes inside and... take her wrapper off.'

'So...' Pauly's eyes raised skywards, as he summoned thoughts into actual words. 'Is this like... a girlfriend?'

'Yes Pauly! Only you don't have to go home wid her, you don't get no arguments and she don't make you buy her shoes.'

'Ohhh. *That's* what they do. Right then. Let's go to

euro disney ! Yaay!'

'Er... dat is OK Pauly. You go ahead. I will get back to Toby.'

'Uh - you not comin Kats?'

'No darlink. Some sweets it is better you eat in your own. Have fun!'

Katia walked off.

To the less kind of heart, Pauly would have seemed to look after her like a lost little Dutch dog.

Then he turned his attention to the shop window, and took a deep breath. He brought some Euros out of his pocket, and began to count the notes carefully.

CHAPTER 4

## *STILL WATERS*

A black canal boat floated quietly, in a canal.[25] Inside was Kees Muff, a well-built build forty-something, with half a growth of beard stubble. He was wearing a traditional Dutch flat cap and clogs.

The scene might have appeared serenely charming, were it not for the silenced Walther PPK lying menacingly next to a bowl of tulips. On a table with a cute crochet cover.

Ben entered nervously. They shook hands.

'Kees Muff. You are on time. This is good.'

'Kees... ?'

'Muff.'

Ben looked around. 'We're not on candid camera or something?'

'We are not on any camera, no. This is secure location. Of course.'

'No, but I mean. It's just. Your name...'

'It is traditional Nederlands name.'

'Yeah but, you know what it means in English?'

'Kees? Yes, is what go in door.'

'No! The other one.' Ben detected a sudden pause. Perhaps an iciness creeping into the barge. He swallowed.

---

[25] Yes, well. Obviously not in the middle lane of the main trans-Netherlands motorway.

'Is kind of scarf. You wears on your face, yes?'

'Well. I suppose. Yeh you *can* do.'

'Anyways dis is nothings. You are here to collect de shipment. So...'

Keys handed over a cardboard box, with the lid off. The box had a lateral red line around it. Nestled inside was a twelve inch high blue ceramic windmill.

Ben wrinkled in genuine puzzlement. 'This is a lot of trouble to go to for a fireplace ornament innit?'

'*Dis* is your cargo.' Muff shushed Ben. He checked the empty view through the barge windows. Then removed the top of the windmill.

Ben stared at what he saw inside, with open mouthed fascination: a glittering pile of diamonds. 'Holy mother mary, jesus christ, and a bag of smarties. There must be... well... how much in there?'

'Enough to make sure you keep de quiet and hand over to contact in London when you get the call.' Muff snapped the windmill top back in place. 'Meantime you keep at shop dere, yes?'

'Yeh. Uh. No problem.'

'Just remember: people will be watching you. So no funny ideas.'

'No, that's alright. Just hope Lize never finds 'em.'

'What?'

'Oh. Just a little joke. Nothin' to worry about.' Ben looked around him. 'So - what - you live here?'

'Is transport. Nobody asks de questions about canal boat. Can go anywhere.'

'Oh. Shame you can't just pop across the channel then innit? Ha ha.'

'No. Is canal only dis barge works.'

'Yeah I know. I know. Was just tryin' to lighten the mood a bit.'

'Dere is no needs. De windmolen get to its safe place. You also get to stay safe and het geld.'

'Geld?' Ben did a quick mental translation. 'Oh money. Yeah, right.'

'Ja. In other case...' Muff moved his eyes to the silenced gun, and mimed pulling a gun trigger 'you is dood.'

'Yeah. Goddit. No mime necessary, Muff. Alright, better get me clogs on then.'

Muff looked at his feet, puzzled. Ben followed his look.

'Is not de necessary. Just take de box and go now.'

Ben picked up box. 'Right Captain Birdseye. On my way. Don't wanna end up a dood dude, do I? Ha ha.'

Muff looked at him flatly. 'Nee.'

Ben backed away slowly, and stepped up the steps, into the Amsterdam skies, holding his suddenly headache-inducing souvenir.

In an Amsterdam street, Pauly was preparing for his big moment. A possibly life-changing experience. He was staring into a shop window. Lights glittered.

A curious passer-by could have noticed one of his hands clenching into a fist, and unclenching and... While his other held tight, a wad of Euro notes.

Pauly licked his lips. He counted his Euros again. He has a last look, drawing all the supportive oxygen he could, into his pigeon chest. Then, like a guardsman marching into battle, he headed into the shop.

Pedestrians passed by randomly, going about their business. More than a few bicycles pedalled down their lanes. A micro car parked up and got attached to an electricity pump.

The lady micro-driver looked up. To see Pauly being thrown out of the shop by a uniformed Security Guard. With a push to his shoulders, Pauly was propelled back out into the street.

The ecologically friendly lady furrowed her elegant eyebrows in puzzlement. Seeing the glitzy lit frontage of an intimate apparel shop, with a range of lingerie clad female mannequins prominently posed in the window.

She watched Pauly shake his mop head, shrug, recount his Euro notes, and wander off.

Back in Bonk's, Katia and Toby had just seen a happy cutomer out. No language barrier problem, shopper satisfaction, and even the right amount of change.

'So Ben dint think much of Pauly's live show then?' Toby asked.

'He he. Was not de performance he was expecting.' Ben entered, carrying a barge-originating box.

'Hello boss,' Toby greeted him. 'Hey what's that? Bought your own puppet theatre now? '

'Oh, thank you for that. No Toby. This is in fact just a little present... er... for Liza.' Ben patted the box guardedly. 'So hands off OK?'

Pauly entered and spied the prize. 'Oh is that one of them puppet theatres in a box. I saw them. They're brilliant.'

'No!' Ben remonstrated.

'Ooh Pauly,' Katia enquired. 'How did your shopping trip go?'

'Oh well I did ask. But they said she wasn't for sale.'

'Katia…' Ben wondered. 'Did you take Pauly to see the window girls?'

'Yes. I thought he might like.'

'Hmm. I had a look,' Pauly confirmed. 'But them windows was all so small. Then I saw a brilliant huge window. Like double size. All the way across and to the top. So I counted me Euros and went in,' Pauly paused, in remembrance. 'But they din't seem interested.'

'Right. Wonderful successful day so far. Toby: how was your pancake?'

'Brilliant! They even added raisins.'

'Well, there's a lesson,' Ben nodded sagely. 'Limit your ambitions in life to alternative pancake fillings, and you're not likely to be disappointed.'

Ben took a sideways look. 'Although Pauly'd still probably drop his in the canal.'

CHAPTER 5

## *THE FANTASTIC LIGHT*

It's a small world. Yes, it does go all the way from one end to the other, and everything. Some still obsess that it is, in fact, flat. Which, of course it is. Until you fall off the end.

So, for those who enjoyed, or endured, sitcomming with Sex-x-x, it doesn't come as much surprise that former feminist vigilante, Nadine Moss entered Bonks, dressed in traditional Dutch girl outfit.

She held a bundle of cards for a Coffee Shop: "*Light Café - light up your life*".

'Khoyde-dagh everyone! Come enjoy a warm welcome at the Light Cafe!'

'Nadine!' Ben exclaimed. 'What are you doin' here?'

'Ooh! Is Jess with you?' Pauly asked, literally tripping over himself with eagernes.

Ignoring him, Nadine responded to Ben: 'Well I could ask you lot the same question. Haven't they got enough perverts in this city without importing them? Where's Mr Bonk?'

'Oh we is looking after his shop for a while,' Katia explained.

'Really? I heard he was a sensible sort of person.'

'Yeh! He's Pauly's Dutch uncle,' Toby put in.

'OK, yes,' Nadine sighed. 'That would explain a lot.'

Paul began trying to get Nadine's attention. She began trying to ignore him.

'Erm... is Jess...' Pauly said, quietly.

Ben rose to the challenge. 'So what brings the former feminist agitator to the city of bicycles and tulips then? Still collecting for Jamaican polar bears?'

'Erm... is Jess...' Pauly tried agin.

'Why would I bother explaining anything to you?' said Nadine with narrowed eyes. 'It's like pouring sludge down a sewer.'

'Erm... is Jess...'

Nadine at last turned to her information-seeking tormentor. 'Yes Pauly! Jess *is* here.'

Pauly looked round. 'Where?'

'At the cafe.'

'What cafe?'

Nadine handed Pauly a card. 'As I was *trying* to communicate, when I entered what's now the Amsterdam branch of retards-are-us, the Light Cafe.'

'You mean you only do snacks?' Pauly quizzed.

'No Pauly,' Katia corrected. 'Is hash cafe yes Nadine?'

'Oooh…' Pauly raised a finger in the air. 'With the strong coffee that you have to inhale.'

'He's nearly got the picture,' Ben sighed. 'We just didn't finish explaining.'

'The Light Bar,' Nadine promoted proudly, 'is an oasis of calm and pleasure. Right here in the heart of Amsterdam. With - yes Pauly - coffee. And snacks. And the best range of stimulating smoke-ables in the Netherlands.'

Pauly tugged her sleeve gently. 'Do we all have to

dress Dutch traditional? I don't mind, but I'll have to find some clogs.'

'If Katia's gonna wear that, I'll get clogs for everyone,' Ben smarmed.

'I is not.'

'No Pauly,' Nadine explained. 'It's just us at the cafe that wears the outfits. But you can if you want.'

'Yaay! Ooh I'm comin, I'm comin!' Pauly did his little jig of excitement.

'He always says that when he gets a new playstation game,' Ben noted.

'I thought it was Wii?' Toby asked.

'Too dangerous,' Ben shook his head. 'He put a baton through a lampshade last time.'

'Katia. Will you come with me please?' Pauly asked. 'I don't want to go into the wrong shop again.'

'Yes OK Pauly.'

'Although maybe. Nadine?' Pauly tugged her peasant costume sleeve again.

'Yes, what now? Jess is there, I told you.'

'Yeh. But you know the Light Cafe.'

'Yes?' Nadine sighed.

'Do you do lampshades?'

The atmosphere in Bonks suddenly seemed a little pressured, as everyone made a stare at Pauly.

Soho has alleyways. Lots of them. Some twist and turn, bringing you to illicit intersections. Some billow with neon-lit smoke from erotic establishments.

Then, there are others, more mysterious. With a little noticed entrance and no exit. Where secret intoxicated lovers might snatch furtive moments.

Or a bent cop and a straight gangster, standing back to back, while practicing the art of ventriloquism.

'Alright copper?'

'Alright blagger?'

There was a pause. Some drops of Soho rain dripped off guttering. A door slam in the far distance gave assurance that here, was safe.

'You square on the plan then?' Jez's muscled voice emerged from the gloom.

'The Dover monkey and his gang come back on the Eurostar. I nick em 'em once they're back at the shop. I take the merchanidise...'

'A box *containin'* the merchandise,' Jez interrupted, forcefully.

'Fine, fine. And deliver it to you. Less my cut.'

'No,' Jess delivered the syllable with hard voiced steel. 'You deliver it to me, *then* you get your cut.'

'What about honour amongst thieves,' Trent protested.

'You're a bloody rozzer!'

'Fair point.' Trent sniffed, and turned up his jacket collar. 'An I suppose you're gonna tell me that I don't need to know what's in the box.'

'Nah, I'm not gonna say that,' Jez said, edging the words out from between his narrowed teeth.

'Oh really?'

'Yeah. I'm just gonna suggest that you *do* need your kneecaps.'

'Huh,' Trent snorted. 'You don't scare me you know.'

'Maybe not.' Jez paused. A few more drops of rain dripped. '*He* does.'

A sombre silence filled the dank alley. Moments stretched.

'Right,' Trent nodded. 'Pleasure not meetin ya.' He turned on his heel. 'Bye underworld scum.'

'Bye bent plod.'

Their footsteps echoed off, in opposite directions.

The city licensed Amsterdamian Coffee shop is regarded by its own burghers as about as exciting, as a cream tea and scones corner shop is, to the Brits.

The Light Bar looked about as intixicatingly menacing as an antiques shop in a sleepy English villiage. Full of rustic Dutch ornaments, exposed wooden ceiling beams, and little round windows.

Jess was wearing a similar traditional costume to Nadine, while wiping down some round placemats, decorated with the café logo.

Pauly and Katia came in.

'Wow! What a place! And they have got lampshades - see Katia?'

'Er... Yiss. Is nice ones.'

Jess ran up to Pauly. They hugged.

'Pauleeeeee!' Jess excalimed with delight. 'Hello! What are you doing in Amsterdam?'

'Oh didn't I tell you?' Nadine tutted. 'Mr Bonk has taken leave of his senses and allowed your retarded porn peddler and his friends to run his shop.'

'Well actually no. Nadine. So there,' Pauly pronouned, firmly.

'You tell her Pauly. Is good sticking up for your selfs,' Katia encouraged.

'Sorry?' Nadine was nonplussed by Pauly's sudden verbal belligerance.

'I said "No Nadine. So there."'

'Yes I heard you. What do you mean?'

'Your just wrong about what you said. I looked it up.'

'Did you Pauly? Aww,' Jess snuggled into Paul's chest.[26]

'Yes. I went to a library. With books. And the librarian lady helped me.'

'Yes, well. And?' Nadine snapped. 'What is it I'm 'wrong' about?'

'A "peddler" is...' Pauly closed his eyes for lexigraphical focus. 'An itiner-ant sales person, or person-ette, who travels from door to door in search of busin-ess.'

'Yeah... so?'

'I don't travel. They come to my shop! Or Mr Bonks. I mean obviously I travelled from Soho to the Riks Canal Markt, but not itinerant-ly. So I am fixed premises. That was my idea.'

---

[26] OK, onto. Alright! – placed her head on – ish. Can we get on now please?

Nadine rolled her eyes. 'Does he always go on like this?'

'Yeah! It's fascinating isn't it,' Jess smiled up at the new Stephen Fry of Soho. 'I could listen to Pauly all day.'

'Well I desire to spend not one more precious moment of my life doing that so: Pauly: what-is-your-point?'

'Oh, well you know when you say that I am a retarded porn peddler.'

'Yessss.'

'I'm not a peddler. So there.'

'Oh Pauly...' Katia sighed.

'See? I told her. Anyway, Jess! You look lovely in that outfit!'

'Aww. Thank you babe.'

'Yeah.' Pauly considered for a moment. 'Do you stand in the window in it. Or just in here?'

'Sorry babe?'

'Do not to worry. I explain,' Katia said. 'Is time for coffee maybe? She paused. 'A lot.'

'Yaay,' Pauly excited himself. 'And I'll inhale if Jess will.'

Ben and Toby were minding the land of Bonk.

'Well, now that Pauly's scarpered off to his puff-me-senseless paradise, we can get on with the noble task of retailing Euro smut. Oh yes, Toby. Our field of dreams.'

'Covered with tulips.'

'Golden tulips, why not?'

'Er... I think that's more loike daffodils, boss. Well

yellow anyway.'

'Toby! The common sense quotient in this place should go *up* when Pauly leaves.'

'Well Oi'm doin the best Oi can.'

You know how it's a small world... Alright, let's come straight out with it. See, there was a limited casting budget for this novelisation. And some of the old series regulars had a clause in their contract which stipulated repeat appearance fees should any film adaptation be made, which recapitulated their character.

So, that's why Dom entered with a suitcase. 'Words to live by old son!'

'Dom mate! What are you doin' here? No: don't tell me.' Ben paused to think back on some of Dom's more absurd business venture suggestions. 'Lapdancing canal boat? Strippers on bicycles? Topless pancake stands?'

'Actually, that's a good one boss,' Toby offered.

'Just like you, I'm euro-enterprising.' Dom opened the suitcase. 'Have a rattle at these.'

Ben looked in Dom's suitcase. He saw clogs. He sighed. 'Riiight brother in law.'

'Former.'

'Nearly. Anyway. Don't want to piddle on your parade like.'

'Yeah?'

'But have you maybe considered that this is like bringing mutton to a kebab shop?'

'How so?' Dom scratched his head.

'We're in Holland.'

'Yep.'

'Where they already-wear-clogs.' Ben spelt it out.

'Not like these bro. These... are Shhh-Shoes.'

'Bless you,' Toby said politely.

'Is the stammer really necessary for retail purposes?' Ben asked.

Dom put his index finger to his lip. 'No! Shhh-Shoes!'

'Bless you,' again from Toby.

Ben looked wildly around in confusion. 'Where's that crack den Pauly's gone to again?'

'No look!' Dom took a clog and twisted the heel. To reveal a chewing gum packet.

'Ey... ey...' Toby chortled. 'You've got gum on your heel. Hey hey!'

Ben picked the clog up. 'Hold on! Yeah you might have something here. Feel the weight. Difficult to identify from the bruise marks. Yes, a first class offensive street weapon.' Ben slapped his hand on the offending object. 'And one that might prove useful in knocking your head back to sense!'

Dom took the clog back off Ben. 'I don't think you grasp the concept, bro. The chewing gum's just an example. You can put *anything* in here. Just imagine. Night out: money, keys. A little something for if you get lucky. And all, literally, at your very feet.'

'Roight! Smart!' Toby enthused.

'So…' Dom contunued. 'It's a secret in a shoe. A Shhh-Shoe.'

'Bless you,' Toby started... 'Oh! Oi see now. Yeah.'

'Well it's definitely Shhh-something,' Ben muttered. He snapped his fingers. 'Oh hey you know what! You really might have something there, Dom mate.'

'Yeah?'

'Yeah bro. If I were you I'd pop down Nadine's new 'Light Bar' and flog a few clogs to some dope donkeys. Looks, here's her card with the address.'

Dom looked at the card. 'Nadine huh? From feminist campaigner to Euro dope dealer.'

'Busy place I bet. And full of potential clog connoisseurs no doubt.'

'Yo bro, good to go! Thanks !' Dom snapped shut his suitcase, and trotted out.

Toby sidled up to Ben's shoulder. 'You really think them cafe customers 'll buy their toes into Dom's clogs then?'

'He might get lucky,' Ben rolled his eyes to the ceiling. 'Somewhere between the third coffee and the tenth joint.'

In that very establishment, a dozen customers were enjoying its high-life delights.

Pauly and Katia were sat down at a table, drinking coffee and puffing weed. Pauly was simultaneously munching a brownie. 'Hey they's lovely these, Kats,' Pauly said between mouthfuls. 'Just like at home, only more chocolat-ery'.

'What do you think to our finest Moroccan, Katia?' Nadine enquired.

'It is de nice and relaxing. Yiss.'

'Pauly?' Jess asked, gently.

'Oh, I don't know. I'm not sure I've got the right end.'

'You just needs to make sure you inhales it properly Pauly,' Katia advised.

'Oh yeh. Sorry.' Pauly grabbed a cup of coffee and sniffed at it long, and deeply. 'Oooo-uuugh! It's happenin'! Oh! Oh!'

'Is he...?' Nadine asked Jess.

Jess shrugged.

Pauly started swaying, then stood up, unsteadily. 'My mind's inna purple haze.'

'No change there then,' Nadine sniffed.

'You alright Pauly babe?' Jess took hold of Paul's spasming arm.

In Pauly's psychedelic vision, Jess's dress had disappeared, leaving her standing in the Light Café, dressed only in bra, knickers and stockings. With dayglo tops.

'Uh noooo! Jess,' Pauly urged. 'You're gonna get cold! Drink some coffee quick!'

In Pauly vision, Nadine now turned into a Chinese dragon, snapping at Jess. 'Dragon! Drag-on! Thhhhere! On your shoulder!'

Jess pointed to her thigh tatoo. 'No silly! It's a skull here, look.'

'Flamin fire. Burnin bright in ecstasy!' Pauly raved.

'Maybe he *was* smokin' the wrong end,' Nadine muttered.

Pauly pointed back at Nadine. 'Hu-ooh! A talkin' dragon!'

'Slap him!' Nadine commanded Jess.

'Noo!'

Katia stepped in and got hold of Pauly's shoulders, shaking him gently, but firmly. 'Pauly. Is you OK?'

Pauly groggily stared at her. 'How come you've got clothes on? Cos Jess is all undressy. An Nadine's a dragon.'

Pauly swayed. Forward. Backward. Sideways. Then backward again. 'I think I need a windmill.'

Pauly fell over. Thankfully, onto an orange banquette leather seat, decorated with a Dutch flag.

Jess and Katia crouched around him.

'Babe, babe. Are you alright? Talk to me!' Jess cried urgently.

'I wanna a tat-aroo like yours,' Pauly dribbled. Only on *my* thigh. That was my...' He relapsed into silent dribbling, then: 'I feel sleepily. Night...'

'Pauly!' Jess cried.

'Oh he's fine,' Nadine nodded at the prone Pauly. 'Just let him sleep it off.'

'You know Nadine,' Katia said sternly, 'you maybe shoulds to be de more careful what you is puttings in de smoking.'

Nadine defensively folded her arms over her peasant dress. 'Look you. I can only warrant the purity of the product that I am supplying. I cannot give customers the mental apparatus to appreciate it.'

Pauly murmured in his sleep. 'Dragons...'

Nadine jutted her chin out, at her somnolent café customer. 'See?'

Back in the safety of Bonks, Ben's phone warbled.

'Hello my little rampant rabbit. How's life in leafy London?'

'Alright. So when am I comin'?' Liza's Liverpudlian tones filled the speaker.

'Well, whenever I do that little wiggle, you know, and...'

'To Amsterdam? I can be on the Eurostar tomorrow.' Liza made that sound sweet and threatening: simultaneously.

'Have they got special soundproof carriages now?'

'Does your therapist know you're still tryin' to be funny?' she retorted.

'Maybe we can find you a sense of humour when you get here.' Ben rolled his eyes at Toby. 'Gimme a text when you're on board. And I'll come pick you up at the station.'

'OK. What's the weather like over there?

'Well it was sunny skies. But there seems to be a cold front coming in over the channel.'

'It'll be a bloody iceberg if you're not there at the station. Oh! Don't go to the zoo before I get there.' There was an unusual pause from Liza land. 'They might keep you as an exhibit.'

Ben put the phone down.

'So, Liza's comin over,' Toby observed, observantly.

'Yow don't look pleased, boss.'

'Yeah. Well. Upsides and downsides aren't there?'

'But yow invoited her.'

'Yeah... in the sense that a swimmer's dangling legs invite a shark to 'ave a jawful.'

'So, what's the upside?' Toby probed.

'Company at dinner.'

'And the downside.'

'It's *her* at the table.'

## CHAPTER 6

# *MASSAGE MESSAGING*

In the wet and windy wilderness of Soho,[27] [28] Paige and Raven were minding the shop.

The massage table was up, and Paige had her stimulating electrodes ready. Now, there was a big cardboard cut out of Paige, in her sexy nurse outfit, in front of the latex rack.

Raven approached with a little bottle of liquid in her hand. 'Hey Paigey my love.'

'Yeah sweetie?'

'I thought maybe's you'd like to try some of this stuff.'

Paige took the popper bottle. She had a look around to check the shop's empty. 'Well, OK. But I thought you weren't into sex.'

'No silly! Not for you and me. I mean, it might help your massage customers get more relaxed.' Raven shook the little potion bottle.

'Hmmm. Could be a bit strong you know.' Paige took it off Raven and held the bottle up to the light. 'Depends how it reacts with the electro-stimulation.'

'Well, what's the worst that can happen?' Raven wondered.

---

[27] OK: not exactly. But nice alliteration.

[28] and the budget on this movie novelisation won't run to special effects. So there.

'Having to give this massage table a good clean down.' Paige considered. 'Oh well. Go on then.'

Inspector Trent entered. 'Mornin my lovelies.'

'Oh good morning Inspector,' Paige smiled politely. 'Hey, you know. Special rates for officers of the law.'

'Really?' Trent said, looking pleasantly self-satisfied.

'Yeah,' Paige smiled, coldly. 'I add ten per cent.'

'Oh right. You're havin a laugh. Very funny. Well anyway, I've had a bit of back trouble. So since your apparatus is here, I thought I might as well have a go.'

'Fair enough Inspector.' Paige waved to the mobile massage table. ' Just jump up, and leave your wallet on the side.'

'Come off it, love. It's my back that's aching. Not my wits.'

Trent got onto the table. He shuffled a bit, trying to get comfortable.

Raven nudged Paige. 'Ooh yes. Before we start, there's a new relaxing potion that we'd like you to try. So you really feel the relaxation experience.'

'Is it extra?'

'I'll include it in your ten percent.'

'Ha ha. Go on then.'

Raven held Trent's head. Paige took the top off the bottle and wafted it under Trent's nose.

'Ohhhh-aaah. That's really quite... Yeahhhhhh...'

Paige got the electro pads. 'Flame on...' She handed the potion to Raven, then started applying her electro apparatus to Trent's chest.

'Ohhhh-aaah...'

Raven looked at Paige, and nodded, as she wafted more joy scent into Trent's twitching nostrils.

'Ohhhh-aaah. Yeah...'

Trent's vision blurred. The sexy nurse cut-out Paige and the real Paige merged, with electro-aphrodisiac bliss, into each other. 'Oh my goddddd... Ohhhh-aaah....'

Paige kept applying electro stimulation, while Raven wafted her psychadelic genie, from the little popper bottle.

'Nursey... nursey... Ohhhh-aaah. Yeah...'

'Is he alright?', Raven whispered to Paige.

'Ssshhh...'

'I'll have me own nurse,' Trent murmered. 'With a stethoso... a stethoso... stocking tops...'

Trent paused, with a blissful sigh. 'When them glitters comes back... from Amsterdam.' Another deep sigh of satisfaction. 'Nick the whole lot. Ha ha ha.'

Paige and Raven looked at each other in shock.

'Officer Trent,' Paige commanded. ' Whom will you be arresting?'

Trent smirked, and lolled his head. 'Bloody Dover. Pathetic Pauly. Shoplifter Toby. That Polish... boobs... with the girl.'

'Oh my god!' Raven whispered.

'Sshhhh!' Paige held up a pad in warning. She moved the pads on Trent's chest, with a calming circular sweep. 'There... and you can just forget...'

'Nick... Nick 'em all...'

Paige motioned to Raven, who urgently wafted more potion under Trent's nose.

'There... And relax... and forget...'

'Nursey....'

'Oh for god's sake...' Page muttered.

In the Light Bar, Pauly was sitting up now, the worse for wear. Katia, Nadine and Jess were gathered around.

It's just not fair is it? The state of Pauly now. Just when he could have handily done a cameo as a zombie in the *28 Days Later* pastiche, a few film scenes ago. No consideration, your modern star of stage and screen, that's the problem. Russell Crowe would have doubled up, no problem. Anyway…

'See Nadine? It was just Pauly's first time is all,' Jess murmered kindly.

'Yeh. See I'm all virginy,' Pauly confirmed.

'That I can believe,' Nadine noted nastily.

A middle-aged balding gentleman entered. With an ill-sitting suit and a clipboard, sporting an EU Flag lapel badge.

He strutted over to the group. 'Now then, I am officially conducting an offical inspection of these premises.'

'Hello Albert,' Pauly said, in recognition.

'Albert Bonsor!' Nadine exclaimed. 'Of Soho district council. And what in all the bridges of Amsterdam do you think gives you the right to inspect anything in my cafe?'

Albert tapped his badge. 'Because I have now officially moved to become an official Euro Inspector, having passed the extremely onerous Euro exams. ' Albert paused for thought. 'And because I very much appreciate Gouda cheese.'

'Yes well, one smell could have told us that. Yuk!' Nadine wrinkled her nostrils.

'But what are you inspecting?' Jess asked. 'All we have is happy customers.'

'And drag-ons.' Pauly added.

'Yeah,' Jess nodded. 'Some customers are more happier than others'

'Be that as it may. I have no interest in happiness.' Bonsor tapped his clipboard with pride. 'I am an Euro-Inspector.'

'Alright,' Nadine sighed. 'Well what do you wish to inspect, inspector?'

'Well I hardly know where to begin. Placement of place mats: regulation 3b. Size and density of place mats. Sub-regulation 7 square brackets sub-paragraphs 3 and 5 of the revised amended regulations. Lampshade opacity. Well there's actually a whole sub-code on that one. Oh yes. And...'

Nadine had already had enough. 'But this could go on all day!'

'No need to worry Miss.'

'*Ms.*'

'I have set aside 3 entire inspection days for the

purpose. So there is no need to miss any corners. A ha ha ha.'

'Sorry?' Jess said, not getting Bonsor's witticism.

'Placemats. With corners. A little Euro joke.'

Pauly held up a place mat. 'These ones is roundy.'

An average looking Nederlander man walked in to Bonks with a large cardboard box.[29]

'Hey up boss. Shop,' Toby helped out.

'A good day sir,' Ben politely greeted. 'And how may we be of assistance?'

'Oh, ja. Hello. I am Henrjk Delf. Where iss Heer Bonk?'

'Oh we're just looking after matters for him. For a few days you know,' Ben nodded.

'Ja. OK. De usual den.'

'Sorry? What's "de usual?'

Henrjk tapped his head. 'Oh. Ja. Now I rememberss. I wash told dat dere would be a retard looking after de shop. Ya. Nice to met you.'

'Hang on! I am not a retard! Whatever in the name of mother Mary gave you that idea?'

'Oh ja. Goesh on about hish mooder and how it was hish idea.'

'Scuse me mate,' Toby helped out. 'I think you mean Pauly.'

'Oh. Ja. Well hello Heer Pauly.'

---

[29] sounds like the opening line for an alternative comedy joke

'No! I'm not Pauly. I am Ben Dover. Erotic euro entrepreneur.'

'Oh. Ja. Well now we has dat shorted out den.' Henryk rattled the box. 'De usual.'

'But I still don't know what you want?'

'Doh. Shall we get dat Pauly here. Might be quicker.'

'First time I've ever heard that one,' Toby sniggered.

'Yes, thank you Toby.'

'Oh Ja. Look. Ish easy.' Henrjk rattled the box again. 'I givesh you dish box of shtuff and you givesh me de geld.'

'Alright, well what have you got?'

'Oh. Ja, well it ish de...'

'Usual,' Ben interrupted. 'Yes. Got that. So - you wanna show us?

Henrjk opened the box.' 'Ja. OK.' He gots some DVDs out, and laid them on the counter. 'Ja.' He tapped one. 'Dere is de new volumesh of de *Animal Farm*.'

Toby and Ben had a look. Ben stood back from the counter display in horror. 'Whoa! Just a minute! I can't sell these!'

'Ja you can. What ish its problem?'

'But this is... it's... I mean...'

Toby did a creditable sheep sound 'Baaaaa.'

'It's disgusting! Filth! Perverted!' Ben waved his hands in disgust.

'Oh ja. Dey ish getting better each volume.'

'Is there, like, a star sheep,' Toby enquired. 'Or do they all just loike, take turns?'

Ben slid him a nasty glance. 'Look. I am not going to Dutch prison, even if they do have colour tellys, ping pong and weekends out. Not for selling hoof porn!'

'Oh ja? What ish de prison wid dish? Everyone shell in Nederland.' Henrjk tapped a DVD. ' Not ash good as deshe of courshesh.'

'And look at the prices, boss,' Toby commented.

Ben snatched a DVD off Toby. 'Fifty euros! For one DVD!'

'Oh ja. Of courshesh de rentalsh ish cheaper.'

'Rentals?' Ben's voice became strangulated. 'Who in the name of perverted hell and damnation is gonna come in here and register for a rental?'

Toby went behind the counter, and came out with a printed list. 'Well it says here boss: "*Farmyard Friends*: Adolf Schmeers. Arnold de Groot. Astrid Elvers...'

'Alright alright. Cultural differences. I get it. So Henrjk. What else have you got in there?' Ben placed his hands on the counter, in an effort to regain some stability. 'Alien abduction sex? Dwarf dogging parties? King Kong's jungle parade?'

'Oh ja. I is shocked!'

'Yer, right. So now it's your turn.' Ben folded his arms.

'Oh ja. I did not know you knowsh sho much about de Nederlandsh porn.'

Ben stared back, open mouthed.

'Oh ja. But I do also have dish.' Henrjk got out a DVD with a spliff taped to it.

Ben read the title: "*Come and Get High*".

'Oh Oi geddit boss,' Toby enthused. 'So what yow do is put the DVD in and smoke the joint and...'

'Yes alright Toby. I really don't need an instruction manual for this one.' Ben sighed. 'Alright Henrjk. How much?'

'Ish one toush-and Euro de whole box.'

'Oi! Toby and me may have just arrived on the banana barge...' Ben waggled the spliff DVD. 'But you're not supposed to get high on your own supply *before* enterin' commercial negotiations.'

'Oh. Ja. Sho what ish you shuggesht?'

'Well, lets find something that'll make us both happy baccy.'

'Baaaaaaa.' Toby grinned.

Ben sighed again.

CHAPTER 7

## *HIGH HEELED CAVALRY*

In the Soho bosom of Sex-x-x, Raven was in something of a panic. 'Oh my god Paige! You heard what that evil Trent said?'

'Yes babe I heard.'

'He's gonna arrest Pauly. When he gets back!'

'Yes I heard.'

'With some illegal supplies of something. And send him to Pauly prison!'

'Raven! Yes! I heard! These boobs make me eye-catching, not deaf, you know.'

'Aww. Sorry my love. It's just... what are we gonna do?' Raven grabbed her goth hair extensions and twisted them, in high anxiety.

'Well we just ring him, right?' Paige said, sensibly.

'Oh yeah. Course! You gave him that Pauly phone. Yaay!'

Paige got her phone out. 'Right. And he's got your number, so...' Paige waggled the phone.

'Yeah...?'

'We ring him up and tell him!' Paige held out her hands, in the manner of a primary school teacher, having shown the class how to put their mits on.

There was an awkward pause.

'No my love,' Raven shook her head. 'I've not got Pauly's number. Have you not got it?'

'Well of course! It's on the phone I gave him.'
They both looked at Paiges phone. They looked at each other. A cloud of despair hovered into the shop.

They spoke, desperately, as one: 'Pauly... !'

Darkness had also descended over the Light Café. New Euro-Inspector Bonsor was measuring a rounded place mat with a ruler, and making notes on his clipboard.

A few feet away, Pauly was furiously puffing and blowing, with a rather large toke.

'Hmm. Radius. Three point two centimetres,' Bonsor proclaimed. 'Well Miss…'

'*Ms*,' Nadine corrected.

'I am not entirely sure that this satisfies the ambit of the revised, amended regulations,' Bonsor smirked, in beaurocratic triumph.

'What!' Nadine shouted.

'An unsatisfactory radius. A very clear hazard to public Euro health, let me tell you, *Ms*. Oh yes.'

'But I am de Polish and I worked in bars in Warsaw,' Katia interjected. 'I never heard de dis.'

'Ah well you see, Miss. Er Ms, er...'

'Katia Louisa Radek.'

'Miss. There may be an opt out under a subsidiarity ruling.'

'Sorry, what does dat means?'

Nadine narrowly eyedly translated. 'Albert can't get his hands on your place mats in Poland.'

'Is goods to know.'

'But why's it matter Albert?' Jess asked, gently. 'I mean, most customers just put their drinks down on the table anyway.'

Nadine tried to shushh Jess.

Bonsor thumped his clipboard in triumph. 'Yes! Game on!'

'Sorry?' Jess said.

'Thank you for that confirmation of what I suspected, Miss. A clear, nay indeed tantamount to criminal violation, of so many public health ordinances, you could build a windmill out of them. A ha ha.'

Pauly leaned in, puffing wildly. 'Did you say windmill? I like them. Hic.'

Bonsor tried to wave Pauly's smoke cloud away. He pointed to the table. 'Look! Look there! See!'

'Drag-ons? I know,' Pauly mused. 'They get in here somehow.'

'Table! With coffee receptacle upon it. *And no mat!*'

Nadine interjected herself between Bonsor and the offending furniture. 'Now see here my good man, obviously you, as usual, have generated a false conclusion from a shaky premise.'

'How so?'

Nadine lifted up coffee cup. 'Item one. A cup.'

'Yes indeed.'

Nadine rapped the table top. 'Item two. A table.'

'It's good this,' Pauly said. 'Nadine have you thought of bein' Sherlockina Holmes? Hic.'

'You draw the two together to reach the conclusion

that this is an un-matted drinking environment, yes?'

'Most certainly,' Bonsor nodded.

Nadine grabbed Albert's hand, which was holding the rounded coffee mat. 'When the regulated object in question is, in point of fact, one extracted - by you - from that environment, in the first place.'

'But I... Ah... Well you see...'

Pauly waved his mega-spliff at Albert. 'Just have a bit of this Albert and you'll find all your worries slipping away.'

'Aww babe,' Jess asked. 'What are you worried about?'

Pauly took a drag and an exhale. Probably in that order. 'Can't remember.'

Panic was still wrapping its icy fingers around Paige and Raven. In Paige's case, it was having a bit of a linger.[30]

'Paigey! What are we gonna do? We gotta warn Pauly!'

'Well, we know where he's gone, right?'

'Bonk's sex shop,' Raven nodded.

'Yeah. So we better just get our bums on the Eurostar and get over there.'

'But who's gonna look after the shop while we're gone?' Raven asked.

'That's OK. I'll give Bentley a ring. He knows all the tricks in this circus.'

---

[30] and would need to go off later, for a hot shower

'Fair enough. Amsterdam here we come then!' Raven said.

'Yaay. We might even get to a Dutch swingers party.'

'Oh no. I don't do sex. You know that Paigy.'

'That's OK, you can look after my dress for me,' she replied.

'Er...Do you wear a dress at a swinger's party?'

'Not for long. He he. Come on! Quick pack and taxi to the Eurostar station.'

Paige grabbed Raven's hand, and they hurried out of the store.

Bonsor was, by now, drowsily high, sharing a Light Café spliff with Pauly.

'Y'see Albert. It's nice here. It's all warm and Jess goes all nakedy.'

Bonsor peered around, through drug hooded eyes. 'Really?'

Jess and Nadine put Bonsor straight, together: 'No.'

'But then there's drag-ons,' Pauly continued. 'Scary ones.' He nudged the table with his spliff hand. 'That's worse than place mats.'

'I'll say,' Bonsor nodded, unsteadily. 'The keeping of mythological amina-erals must clearly be contrar-ady to any number of regu... regla...'

'Don' worry 'bout it Albert. They only comes out when you inhale the coffee.'

Annika Roos entered. Wearing a suit, with a clip board. 'Hallo Nadine. How is your lovely cafe doing?'

'Oh hi Annika. Yes, very well thank you.' Nadine paused to look at Bonsor. Now sprawled untidly against the yellow banquette's Dutch flag. 'Apart from a jumped up Euro inspector over there, who seems to think that my place mats are a public health hazard.'

'Oh OK. Well I will have a word on behalf of the tourist board.' Annika went over to Bonsor and Pauly. 'Excuse me Heer Bonsor. Annika Roos from de Amsterdam Chamber of Commerce.'

'Yes?' Bonsor raised halff a doped out eyelid.

'Hello Annika,' Pauly greeted.

Aannika fixed Bonsor with a stern stare. 'Have you paid for what you are consuming?'

Bonsor was starled into semi-sobriety. 'Well, no. Not as such. Not in fact.'

'Hmmm. Are you - a public Euro official - aware of the penalties for extortion of small businesses?'

'How dare you? I was just, well, sharing this intoxible, when...'

'While making threats about unregulated place mats, hmmm?' Annika interrupted forcibly. 'I think you should consider your position.'

Pauly waved the spliff. 'About half way down. If you include the tip.'

Bonsor rose to his feet. Like a puppet struggling against the fact that its strings had been cut. 'Well, I would rather not involve a hostile exchange between the civil authorities. So I shall exit these premises, and make my report in due course.'

'And you can give me my place mat back, thank you very much,' Nadine added.

'Yeah,' Pauly contributed. 'Jessy might need to sit down later.'

Bonsor handed the mat over, as if it were made of gelignite. 'Right well. Good day. Yes.'

'Told ya about the drag-on,' Pauly said to Bonsor's slowly retreating back.

'Yaay! Thanks for that Annika!' Jess cheered.

'Yeah babe,' Nadine agreed. 'Let's get you a nice cup of coffee.'

Annika moved over and sat next to Pauly.

'So, Mr Pauly. You are enjoying our lovely city?'

'Well, some of the windows need a bit of adjustin'. But comin' here, yeah. That was my idea. And it is very nice in Dutch-land.'

'So you are meeting people. Doing deals I suppose?' Annika's voice had an edge to it, which Pauly didn't notice.

'Oh yeh.'

'Really? Hmmm.'

'Well, I'm gonna to arrange something special with a windmill later. But shhh... it's a secrety.'

'Oh, shhh. Yes. I understand.' Annika leaned over a little closer. 'And you leave Mr Dover at the shop?'

'Well yeh. I mean this is not really his sort of place. His breathin is heavy enough as it is, I reckon.'

'Yes, he is de heavy. Hmmm.' Annika made a mental

note, for the file.

'Anyway. I'm gunna see if we can get more Dutchy costumes to wear.'

'Aah... for disguises,' Annika nodded.

'Well, between you and me and... me, Ben really likes his girls in uniform. So it'd be a bit like the same.'

'What sort of uniform?' Annika prodded, her undercover antennae bristling.

'Oh, maid. Nursey. Police Officer-ette, sort of thing.'

'Police person...?' Annika prompted.

'Yeh. But I like what Jess is wearing.'

Annika looked at Jess, splendid in her traditional Dutch dress.

'Ja. Very nice. But might be a bit hot in that?'

'He he he. I shouldn't think so!' Pauly chuckled.

Annika stared at Pauly and turned her head, in revulsion.

In his cool, custom office, the very model of a modern Euro-gangster, Dirk was on the phone:

'You are watching. Good.'

He played with his favourite flick-knife on the desk top.

'Just don't allow that windmill man out of your sight.' He stabbed a packet of post it notes. 'Or I will hang you from a real one.'

Pauly was in his element. Staring, wide-eyed at history, brought almost to life. 'Ey it's all just amazin' in't it Kats?'

Despite herself, Katia managed to nod. 'Yiss, is very de interesting, Pauly.'

Pauly brought himself to a stop at another display case. 'You know what this is Kats?'

'Er, yiss Pauly, it says on de label.'

'Yeh. This is proper culture, this is.' Pauly opened his arms in the joy of civilisation. 'This is like, grand masters of the art. The accumulater-ered artifacts of a thousand years of Europeany culture. Curated-ed together by the bestest experts in antiquey things.'

'Really Pauly?'

'Yeh. Read it in the brochury.'

Katia took the pamphlet out of Pauly's hands. It read, in bold letters across the top *"Amsterdam Sex Museum."*

Staring with utter fixation at a glass case containing "Dildos through the ages", Pauly breathed, as if he were witnessing the Mona Lisa being originally painted.

Then he turned to Katia. With the look that puppies have long practiced, when their owners are eating at the dinner table. 'Kats...'

'Yiss Pauly?'

'Can we go to the modelly village now please?'

CHAPTER 8

## *DAM AND BUST*

The Eurostar station was packed, as always. Business visitors and tourists thronging, amidst balloon and waffle stands. With a traditional Dutch jazz trio, in waistcoats and bowler hats, playing welcoming songs.

Ben was standing at the end of a platform, peering down its length. He looked at his watch. 'How the hell can she manage to be late?' he asked himself. 'Probably had an argument with the driver,' he muttered, glumly.

'No, it's just you'se standin on the wrong platform'. Liza announced her arrival with a tap on his shoulder and those few kind words.

Ben turned to greet his semi-estranged wife, ex, sort-of. 'Don't tell me. They all got off, an' made you push the last ten miles into town.'

'Ha bloody hah' Liza retorted. 'Is it my fault that the great Mr Dover can't find the right platform with both hands on his timetable?'

'Oh go on'. Ben gave Liza a welcome hug. 'Lemme take that for ya.' Ben reached an arm out for Liza's suitcase, nearly dislocating it as he went for a lift.

'Mother Mary on a donkey! What 'ave you got in there? The complete weight-lifting kit for the energetic over-forties?'

Liza shot Ben a look of malice, mixed with pity. 'I'm on 'oliday, right?' That means dresses, and heels, and make up, and walking shoes, and sunglasses, and hats. And stuff.'

'Yeah, well it's the stuff what's causing the problem. Hold on.' Ben looked around. 'Have they got any porters in this god-forsaken Euro terminal?'

Liza snorted. 'Wel lof course they 'ave!' How'd you think I gorr all this kit over here?'

Ben gritted his teeth. 'Right... I'll go grab a trolley monkey. You hang tight here.'

'But...' Liza started.

'Oh you'll be alright.' Ben nodded at the suitcase equivalent of heavy metal.

'Not like any Euro tealeaf 'll be making off with that in a hurry. Not without a slipped disc and easy arrest.' Ben wandered off into the throng.

Just beyond Liza's line of sight, Paige and Raven ran down another platform, carrying overnight bags: one pink, one black.

The black matched Raven's traditional goth attire, which, with black spiderweb tights and shiny black Doc Martens, was actually ideally suited to running.

Paige's ensemble, of ultra sheer pink teddy, matching tennis style skirt, and heels, wasn't. But her marathon training was running her in good stead.

'Paige,' an out of breath Raven panted. 'Do you know where Bonk's shop is?'

Still running, Paige replied over her shoulder. 'Look. Amsterdam city centre's a pretty small place. Been here before, in the old filming days.'

'Oh really?'

'Yes, another time for that Raven curiosity OK?' Paige came to a stop. 'So any taxi driver will know.'

Raven stopped as well, although her gothic bustier was heaving under the pressure of her strained breaths. 'God, Paigy, you can't half run. An' you're not even out of… breath,' she gasped.

'It's filming in Hungary babe. You learn a lot of tricks there.' Paige put a calming hand on Raven's still heaving shoulder. 'Or, you don't get to come back with all your anatomy in the right places.'

Raven looked at Paige, in puzzlement. Paige gave a sly wink. They set off for the cab stand, at a slower pace.

In Inspector Vandergriff's office, Sergeant Roos was giving her latest report. 'Dey are de most disgusting, verachtelijk, frightening criminals in Amsterdam.'

'Ja Shergeant. Please continue.'

Annika referred back to the long roll of notes, on her Iphone. 'Dis Pauly. He is der leader.' Annika sighed. 'You know, Inspector, dat mijn vater was a Captain in de Netherlands Korps Commandotroepen.'

'A decorated hero to hish country, ja Shergeant.' The Inspector rapped his knuckles in his desk in approval. 'He would be proud to shee you follow in hish footshtepsh.'

'Bedankt, Heer Inspector. But I do not think he face an enemy more dangerous than these Soho mafia.'

'I shee…'

'Dis Pauly. He treat respectable café owner like a hond. He make wid drugs and the café girls like some Hughie Heffner.'

'Excushe me Shergeant?'

'Oh, sorry. That awful man wid his Playboy mansion and bunnies. So anti-women.'

'Ja, I shee.'

'But this is their weak spot, sir. The Achilles heel of their horrible organisation.'

'How sho?'

'It is simple, sir. I can infiltrate their wicked organisation: through sex.'

'Nee nee Shergeant,' Inspector Vandergriff shook his head, stiffly. 'I... thish department could not ashk you...'

'Oh of course sir. I could not to be having sex with these repulsive animals. Nee. I just play their creepy games.'

'I shee?'

'Ja. The enforcer, Dover, he is even more the perverted, with dressing up.'

'Like for the opera?' Inspector Vandergriff's brow puzzled.

'Nee nee, sir.' Annika leant forward and placed hand hands on the Inspector's desk. She lowered her voice to a disgusted whisper. 'That evil man. He likes... uniforms.'

Inspector Vandergriff sat back in his chair. He wordlessly gestured his hand, first to himself, then to Annika's starched, ironed and creased Police blues. He raised an enquiring eyebrow.

Annika shook her head. 'Nee nee sir. We are supposed to wear these. So that the citizens of this city know they can turn to us for help.'

She clenched her fists tight. 'These sick people – like this Dover – they want women to wear uniforms sir: for sexual purposes of sex.'

Inspector Vandergriff took a long breath, and rolled his eyes to the ceiling. 'Sho what ish your plan Shergeant?'

'Sir. I shall get into the trust of this corrupt monster Dover, by giving him what he wants. And then…' Annika put her hand on the flap of her service revolver. 'Once I have the information on their plans, this gun and my badge, will throw them in Netherlands jail, for a very long time.'

Inspector Vandergriff stood, and placed a paternal hand on Annika's shoulder. 'Even braver than her father. Your plan is approved Shergeant. Jusht, be careful.'

'Ja Herr Inspector.' Annika snapped to attention, and threw a parade ground salute.

On the delightful main canal of the city, a tourist barge serenely floated. The helpful tourist guide announced sights being passed, as spring sunshine dappled on the waters.

Less serenely, Liza was indulging what Ben liked to call her three hobbies: complaining, nagging and repetition. 'Well why couldn't one of your overpaid employees take my bag to the hotel.'

Ben sighed. Staring at the canal waters, he tried to

remember whether it's that witches float, or sink.

'I mean,' Liza continued (or repeated), 'I've come all this way, and wouldn't of hurt one of them to give us a hand, would it?'

Ben took the question mark as an opportunity to get something approaching half a word in. 'Lize love. Like I said. Pauly's taken them off on a fact-finding expedition.'

'Yeah right.'

'Look, turtle dove. There are endless erotic commerce opportunities in Euroland. And no harm done. Your precious belongings are stored safely in a station locker.'

'Hmm, good thing you had a few handy. How come?' she wondered.

'Oh, just some kit for coming back home with, love. Amazin' what you can pick up on the barge sales round here.'

'Huh?'

'Well, like a car boot sale,' Ben felt himself digging deeper, with a bent paddle. 'Only more aquatic, you know.'

'Right...' Liza's short attention span[31] had already wandered.

Ben did his best big smile. 'An' here we are, out in the Amsterdam sunshine...'

'Looks a bit cloudy to me.'

'I think you're just makin' the weather a bit shy, love. I mean, how can rays of canal sunshine compare to you?'

---

[31] dwarfish, really

Liza stared at Ben for a moment. Then her face softened. Which was dangerous, given the amount of ready mixed pancake scaffolding it.

She reached out a crimson fingernailed hand. 'Aww. Why can't you be that lovely always Benny?'

Ben thought of half a dozen immediate answers, each of penetrating accuracy. He settled for: 'I guess because your eternal beauty just makes me nervous, sometimes, sweetheart.'

Liza actually smiled.

Unsteadied for a moment by the thought that this rictus was directed at her, the canal boat guide faltered for a moment. Then continued: 'End yo can see de dom of de Dom Kirk, which is de tallest building structure in de whole of Amsterdam.'

Having exited from the station, Paige and Raven had found some difficulty in actually locating a cab.

'Paigey,' Raven suggested. 'You know how's you said the city part's a small place?'

'Yes love?'

'So how's about we asks someone if they know where Bonks is, or at least maybe the general area.'

'Good thinking batgirl! OK – let's try him.'

Paige spotted a solid looking townsperson, wheeling his obligatory bicycle somewhere. 'Excuse sir, do you speak English?'

'Ya, of courshe young ladies.'

'Aah great. Well, me and my fiend here are looking

for an adult video store. It's called Bonks. Any chance you could direct us?'

'Oh ya, you are wanting me to direct you?'

'Yes please, if it's not too much trouble.'

The cyclist stared at the pneumatic fillings of Paige's pink teddy top. 'Nee, nee ish goed. Zeer besonders!'

'Uh...?

'Good, ya. Ish very good.'

'Oh right. Yaay. So...er...'

'Ja. I finish de afternoon works at vijf uur, sho I can be directing you den.'

'Sorry? We have to wait till five o' clock for directions?'

'Uh ja. I cannot do it now. In de straat ish OK, if you likesh de public porn, but I needsh to arrange de camera.'

'Just a minute,' Paige wagged an instantly cross finger. 'Are you thinking of filming us?'

'Well ja. You are de famoush Paige Ashley. Everyone who watch de erotic videosh in Hollands know you. And in de real lifesh - wow! - you ish even bigger dan in de moviesh. Verbazend!'

'Now look you...' Paige began winding up the crossbow of her outrage.

Raven stepped in. 'Sorry Mr Dutch. As her manager, I will need to make proper arrangements for filming. Oh, she's so eager! But, you know, I have to just cool things down.'

'Oh dat is OK, ja. I understandsh.'

'So let me just get to her hotel,' Raven nudged Paige,

and maybe I can give you a call later.'

'Oh ya, ya, wonderful! Wait till I tell me friendss at de *Uber Boobsh Fan Club*.' Mr Dutch held out his phone to bump his contact to Raven's device. 'So so net to meet you Miss Ashley. And groeten to Amshterdam!'

Mr Dutch held out his hand, which Paige reluctantly shook. He walked his two-wheeler off, whistling happily.

'Sorry babe, but…' Raven started.

'Yeah it's OK. You did the right thing. One more comment and he was headed for that bloody canal, bike first.'

Paige sighed. 'You know, Raven, being an ex pornstar is like being an ex Prime Minister.'

'Not doing TV interviews any more?'

'Because nobody can bloody forget about what you used to do.' Paige had a thought. 'Look, let's just phone Ben and see where he is, right?'

'Yeah sure love. You got his number?'

'Well seeing as he once scribbled it in bumper pen on my bum, yeah.'

Paige got out her phone and dialled. 'Come on. come on. The one time I actually want to talk to that depraved dongle, and…'

Raven's hand tapped Paige's shoulder: Tap tap. 'Yes, I'm ringing again, maybe it's a problem with European dialling…' Tap tap. 'Yes Raven, what is it?'

Raven turned Paige's gaze towards the waterway which had almost been congested by an over-eager film director, and his transportation.

Paige did a double take. 'Ooh yeah!'

In unspoken communication, the girls began to run along the canal side. Waving and shouting.

At a tourist barge, serenely washing through the waterway, carrying a smiling Liza, a resigned Ben, and a slightly anxious tour guide.

Across the canal, two muscled men, in leather jackets were taking careful note. One had a pair of binoculars, trained on the pleasure barge.

The other nudged him, and pointed.

Mr Binoculars looked back at him, puzzled.

His comrade grabbed an arm and used it as a pointer, across the canal.

Mr Binoculars scanned the far bank. he raised his instrument to eye level. He followed the movement. A brunette girl in black. And a blonde girl, with slim legs, a tiny waist and...

Mr Comrade nudged him, and nodded. He got out his phone and dialled. 'Heer Blank...'

On the far side, Raven finally persuaded Paige to cease the running. 'Uh... come on babe. Give it a rest...Uh... it's no good'.

'Aww Raven,' Page patted her shoulder. 'Don't you ever do any running?'

'It's not really a goth girl thing, you know.'

'Yeah. I supose vampires just fly everywhere. Well, OK, back to Plan B then.'

'Plan B?'

'Bonk shop locating. Although this time, no asking dodgy passers by. We'll just google map it, OK?'

'Sounds plantastic. But Paigey…'

'Yes sweet.'

'Let's just walk there, please.'

## CHAPTER 9

# *SMALL FAVOURS*

Madurodam: home to the largest model village in the world. Pauly was in a place that made seventh heaven look like the bottom of a drain pipe. Scampering about, hand in hand with Jess. Delighting over little people and actual little aeroplanes coming into to land at a mini airport.

'It's actually quite good, innit?' Toby said, having a choc ice with Katia.

'Yiss Toby. I can see why Pauly was so de excited to come here.'

'Er... you don't think maybe two's company and fours a crowd for them?'

Katia watched Paul and Jess crouching on the grass to get a better look at a mini monorail. 'I don't thinks dey even knows we here right now, Toby.'

'Fair enough.'

'Although I is thinking dere is something we should be doing.'

'Another choc ice?' Toby waved his wrapper.

'If you like. Not for me thanks. No, is we should buy that windmill for Pauly.'

'Oh gawd, really? An' a bunch of plastic tulips as well?'

'Toby! Be nice. Is Pauly is always being der nice, and it is simple thing to does for him. Make him so happy.'

'Yeah, sorry, you're right. My bad.'

'Yiss. It only takes a minute. See – over dere dat shop.'

'Yeah. An if we don't we'd never hear the end of it on the trip home.'

They headed off to the souvenir shop. Built in the shape of a windmill.

Ben and Liza snuggled through the door of Bonks, like two teenagers popping round the back of a disco.

'So this is the famous Bonks,' Liza looked around.

'All ours for the duration love,' Ben said. 'Hey,' he grapped Liza's waist, there's a cracking selection of Euro sexy costumes in here. And we've been waiting for the right model to show them off properly.'

Liza giggled. 'You serious?'

'Go on, how about that one?' Ben pointed to a sexy ward sister Euro nurse.

'What, you want me to give you a domestic injury, so I can come and heal it?'

'See? That's the idea.'

'Ooh no I can't,' Liza giggled.

'Go on… there's changing space out the back. I can pop the closed sign up at the door. And we can see if this shop really lives up to its name.'

'I shouldn't have had so many cocktails on the barge. Oh… go on then.'

Ben reached the outfit down from the shelf, and passed it to Liza, with a squeeze. 'Your Euro patient's ready and waiting. And I've got a terrible hard problem that only those Euro nursey hands can salve.'

'You bad lad,' Liza giggled. 'Alright Mr D. You just sit yourself here and wait for a minute.'

Liza grabbed the outfit, and swished through the beaded curtains, out into the back.

Ben sat on a stool and whistled. 'The joys of married life eh? Not so bad after all, my old son.'

The door pushed open.

'Oh gawd, what?' Ben muttered.

'Hallo Mr Dover' Annika said, as she walked in. She was wearing high heels and a beige mac.

'Oh sweet mother of milk and alcohol, not now,' Ben muttered under his breath.

'Sorry?' Annika said.

'Oh nothing. It's just I wasn't expecting…'

'Oh I am sorry. It is just dat I thought you might be wanting something nice. Being de hard and dangerous man you are.'

'Uh… really?'

'Oh ja. So…' Annika whipped off the mac to reveal an incredibly sexy police woman uniform. A bust busting top, complete with Europol badge, shorts so skimpy that an anorexic would have complained. Topped by fishnet stockings in matching navy blue.

'How do you like, Mr Hard Man?' Annika winked.

Ben stood up, knocking his stool over. 'Well I… da… I mean… phoowa… no… I mean…'

'So, is patient D ready for some sexy surgery,' Liza

trilled as she stepped through the beaded curtains.

Ben froze, like a rabbit trapped between the headlights of a Porsche going well in excess of the speed limit, and the bumper of an aggressive articulated lorry.

Liza looked at Annika. She took a sharp intake of breath. She looked down at her medical apparel, what little there was of it. Her eyes narrowed. Her cheeks flushed. Her temper, always simmering around the edge of the pot, burst over like a psychotic volcano.

'You rotten cheatin' bastard!'

'Liza love! No! It's not how it looks. Annika's just helpin' out from the Chamber of Commerce. Bein' friendly.'

'Friendly! I'll give her bloody friendly! You lyin' cheatin' slimin'… just gettin' me outta the way so's you can stroke your Euro sausage!'

Liza catapulted forward and rended Ben's cheek with a slap so hard, it shook the bridge over the nearest canal. Ben went down.

Liza aimed a crimson fingernail at Annika. 'He's all yours love. Though what you're gonna do with that worthless, stinkin' pile of Euro dog pooh is up to youse.'

Liza stalked past a bemused Annika, grapped her coat from behind the door, and marched out.

Ben, on his knees, sobbed with the ironic tragedy. 'Trouble and strife life on one side, Euro crumpet gaggin' for it on the other.' Ben put his face in his hands. He looked up, his eyes bleary with grief.

'Look, I'm sorry about all the body bashin' Annika.'

Ben suffled on his knees towards a horror-stricken undercover Sergeant. 'Maybe another time, eh, when it's all died down a bit.'

All Annika could see, was a demented, middle-aged pervert, shuffling towards her, while muttering about dead bodies, after an argument with some transvestite-type person, probably over drugs.

Her right fingers scrabbled instinctively for her side-arm, with the chilling realisation that she was basically naked, apart from navy blue fishnet stockings, and a fake Europol badge.

In threatened desperation, she pulled a rack of Bonk's finest erotic candy assortments, and shoved it with all her strength, at the psychopathic nightmare creeping towards her. Then she turned and ran, as fast as her unusually high heels would allow.

Ben sat, slightly glazed, after the edge of Bonk's erotic shelving had caught the side of his head. A small rain of sexy confectionary scattered around him.

Ben miserably picked up a pink candy pair of boobs, and a blue love heart. He stared at one each, in the palm of his hands.

'Riight then.' Ben sighed, and scrunched his palms. 'Sod this for a game of Euro soldiers. Home it is. And not soon enough.'

Ben stood. He looked round the shop. He sniffed. 'Euro porn, huh. I'm votin' Leave.'

Ben dusted himself down. He took a firm and determined step on his road back to the safety of Soho.

Then slipped on a candy cock, and skidded back onto his bum.

Paige and Raven were at last making progress along Amsterdam streets.

'Yeah, this is definitely the sex shop district, babe,' Raven said.

'A funeral partner, bike stand, and a specialist delicatessen?' Paige looked at the nearest shops.

'Other side of the street.' Raven tapped her shoulder.

Paige looked again. 'Oh yeah…'

Raven tapped Paige's shoulder again.

'Yeah babe, I got it. Just follow the pervy breadcrumbs.'

'No Paige – look,' Raven said, urgently.
Two burly men in dark leather coat jackets had suddenly appeared. Mr Binoculars and his mate.

'We needsh you to come wid ush, now,' Mr Binoculars said.

'Well, that's very flattering,' Paige said. 'But I don't have my massage equipment with me right now.' Paige whispered out of the corner of her mouth to Raven: 'Run…'

Paige took a step towards Mr Binoculars, then staggered. 'Oh dear! These cute cobbled streets.' Paige straightened up, knowing that her former pornstar pneumatics had escaped from their pink spandex confinement.

'Gentlemen, sorry you were saying?' All four

assailant eyes were transfixed.

Paige gave Raven a nudge with her elbow. Raven started backing away. The beef boys' brains had no access to peripheral vision, at that point.

'Uh...,' Mr Binoculars muttered. 'You ish... your... er...'

Raven ran for the bike stand. She grabbed a machine, jumped on and was halfway down the street, before either beefy brain lurched back to reality.

Paige looked down in mock shock and covered her frontage with her hands: well a bit. 'Oh no, the elastic's gone!' Paige made a song and dance of pulling the unwilling fabric back over pinky and perky. 'Now, what was it you were saying, gentlemen?'

'Uh... you needsh to come wid ush,' Mr Binoculars said again.

'Oh OK!' Paige replied, brightly.

'What do you mean, OK?' Mr Mate said.

'Well, I do like a couple of hunky leather jacket guys on a warm afternoon. My favourite ice cream is strawberry, in a cone, with an extra ninety nine. And I only do DP after kissing, OK?'

The heavies looked at each other, in utter bemusement. Mr Binoculars shrugged.

His mate offered: 'OK ja you is come wid ush.' he looked at Mr Binoculars for support, who nodded, severely. 'But only for de ische cream, ja.'

Raven looked over her shoulder. 'Never underestimate the power of plastic.' She pedaled on.

Just for variety, this time their carefully chosen meeting place was in an even tineir alley, round the side of the Cock Hen pub.

'So it's on then?' Trent said, using the side of his mouth.

'Yeah rozzer,' Jez confirmed. 'The whole rotten gang should be arriving back in Blighty, later today.'

'To a very warm welcome, hur hur,' chortled Trent.

'Ere,' Jez nudged him. 'You sure you got enough pairs of 'andcuffs for the lot of 'em?'

'No worries son,' Trent nodded. 'Special police van on standby.'

'Right,' Jez nodded.

'Right,' Trent nodded.

There was an awkward pause.

'Well who's sidlin' out of 'ere first then?' Jez muttered. 'Law or order?'

'I'll go,' Trent sniffed. He stepped to the edge of the alley, peered out both ways, then walked off.

Jez looked out into the empty alley space. He blew a slow breath out. Then rubbed his hands, and sauntered out.

To the totally tone deaf, he might have been whistling a tune about diamonds being forever.

Raven's bike skidded to a stop outside Bonk's. The front wheel still spinning, Raven pushed through the door and hurried into the shop. 'Pauly! Where's Pauly?'

Jess looked up. Now wearing more street sensible pair of jeans and a top. 'Hey Raven. What's up?' Jess appeared to be tidying a mess of candies from the floor, with a dustpan and brush.

'Pauly! I need to find Pauly! And Ben and that lot as well.'

Jess paused in her labours. 'Aww, he's gone home dear.'

'Whatttt!'

'Yes,' Jess nodded, very seriously for her. 'I was worried about him finding his way to the train station. But Katia was with him, and she said it'd be OK, and…'

Raven grabbed her arm. 'He's gone to the station?'

'Yes babe. With Katia and Toby, and the weirdy one.'

'You mean Ben?' Raven clarified.

'Yeah. It's like he's always looking at my clothes.' Jess shuddered.

'Uh…babe. That's what clothes are for, isn't it?'

'Not when I'm wearing them. Like,' Jess gestured to her outfit, 'I've got nothing on under these, you know. Well, apart from a g-string with a little unicorn and a rainbow.'

'Riggght.' Raven shook her head, slightly. Despite her head mostly living in a land of vampires, werewolves and witches, Raven had a stubborn streak of Somerset-born reality. 'So, love, if I get to the train station I can still catch them?'

'Oh no babe,' Jess shook her curls, 'they'll be long gone by now. I just volunteered to tidy the place up a bit for Herr Bonk.' Jess picked up some erotic candy pieces. 'Looks like they had a bit of a party – look!'

'Right, yeah, lovely.' Raven gently took Jess' hands. She forced a patience in her voice, remembered from her days on the farm. Of training a new puppy to pee on the mat. 'So: they-have-gone-back? Yeah?'

Jessy looked around the shop, puzzled. 'Who?'

Raven stood back. 'OK, got it. Thanks Jessy love.'

'Yaay OK sure.' Jess gave her big, beautiful pixie smile.

'You know Jess, I can really see why you and Pauly get on so well.'

'Aww I know. I'm going to dust down some of these erotic candies, and do a gift for bag when I see him.'

'Uh, that's really – uh - thoughtful. OK babe, I'll head on out.'

'Yaay, OK Raven. But, please don't tell Pauly about the present: it's gonna be a surprise.'

'Uh, I really won't. Thank hun. Bye.'

Raven headed back to bridged and cobbled streets, peopled with dangerous men in black leather jackets, over-enthusiastic amateur film directors. And, at least, the cold canal air of sanity.

At a quite pleasant outdoor café, the heavies were keeping Paige company. Or perhaps the other way round.

'Yaay that banana and rum was good.' Paige picked up the multi-coloured plastic menu, packed with ice cream illustrations.

'Now, maybe the toffee and lychee. Very healthy choice, see?'

Mr Mate whispered to Mr Binoculars. 'My colleague want to know where you putsh it all?' he enquired.

'Excuse me. That's hardly a question for a lady is it? Bit better manners expected in Holland-land.'

'But yoush already had tree ische cream, plush waffle and brownie.'

'I like a high-sugar diet. Gives me energy and keeps me sweet. All on the plus side.'

Paige allowed pinky and perky to rest on the table. 'And if you're not actually interested in burning some energy off with me, then I might as well get something out of the afternoon, right?'

Mr Binoculars looked at his mate. The mate shrugged.

Mr Binoculars' phone jangled. He stood up and answered. 'Ja. OK. Ja is sure dey back? And now to let go? OK.'

He turned, looming over Paige. 'OK, you can go now.' Paige shook her head. 'Oh nooo mister. You're not getting away with that one. Sit down. There's another six flavours to try, at least.'

Paige grabbed his leather sleeve and waved him back to his chair. 'Right, call a waiter over.'

Paige sat back. 'Did I ever tell you about the time I was filming in a forest in Hungary and this big Alsatian dog stole my knickers?'

The heavies rolled their eyes and sighed. Mr Mate beckoned for the waiter.

## CHAPTER 10

## *STAIN ON MY NAME*

If filming without budget constraints, we would have experienced a swooping arial shot, passing over Amsterdam central train station.

Then sweeping along the line, until reaching the emerging darkness of the Channel Tunnel.

It's OK: we can still get the voiceovers.

'Pauly! How many soddin' boxes are you bringin' back to our Soho field of dreams?'

'Lots…'

Rattling train carriage sounds.

'It's alright,' Pauly's voice continued. 'They've all got Dutchy stuff in.'

'Er boss. You know yow've got bits of erotic confectionary stuck to your trousers?'

'Yes, thank you very much Toby. Maybe you can do a dust off when we get home Katia.'

'Huh! I is not de cleaning maid.'

'No didn't think so. Worth askin'.

Rattling train carriage sounds.

'Is Liza comin' separately then boss?'

Rattling train carriage sounds, changing as they emerge onto the St George's side of the tunnel.

'Yeah Toby. For a long, long time, it looks.'

Rattling train carriage sounds.

'Are we there yet?'

'Calm yourshelf, Shergeant.' Inspector Vandergriff laid a paternal hand on Annika's shoulder.

Sitting on a chair in front of the Inspector's desk, Annika was still breathing heavily.

Fortunately, she had saved her Inspector from dealing with her previous state of immodest uniform, and had changed back into a whole one.

'Dey desecrate our fair city with their depravity,' she spat. 'Then escape, like the bandits dey are.'

'But only ash far ash England,' Inspector Vandergriff inclined his head.

'You mean…?'

The Inspector sat back behind his desk, and steepled his fingers. 'We are de Shity Polishe. We hash no jurishdiction over de udder shide of de tunnel.' He tapped the side of his generous nose. 'Officially.'

Annika looked up at that last, loaded word.

'But if one of our mosht dedicated offishersh wisht to take a holiday – short leave of abshenshe – in shay, Shoho…'

'That would be her own business, er… vacation,' Annika put in.

'Exshactly. Of courshe, firearmsh ish not permitted dere.'

'But if a toursit was able to obtain any information which might lead to arrest..'

'Yesh.'

'Or even to persuade return of persons we would

very much like to talk to…'

Inspector Vandergriff nodded. 'Dere could be no official problem wid dish.'

Annik stood, and threw a salute that a Marine Sergeant would have been proud of. 'Sir, I respectfully request a week's leave, beginning tonight.'

Inspector Vandergiff nodded, gently. 'After what theshe deshperate criminalsh have put you trough, Shergeant, it ish well desherved.'

Sex-x-x. Still looking the same, to the same old gang. Except for a massage bed in the middle of the room, and a life-size *Nurse Paige* cut-out standing next to it.

'Toby, have you shoved all Pauly's rubbish boxes out of the way?' Ben asked, his temper not noticeably better after half a night's sleep. On the massage bed.

'Yes boss. There's just one loike that he wouldn't let go of.'

'Yeah. Probably got his instruction manual for the loo in it.'

'Aw dat is not der nice,' Katia objected.

'You try standing next to him next time, and see what you have to say then.' Ben took a second look at the box. It had a familiar red line around it.

'Oh dear, nothing like a holiday for creating arguments,' observed Miss Kitty as she slinked in.

'Oh gawd,' Ben muttered. 'At least they have the good sense to keep pvc clad dollies harmless, behind thick panes of shop glass, over there.'

'Hello Kitty. We had a nice times actually,' Katia said.

'Yeah, the pancakes get all in yer mouth and everything,' Toby confirmed.

'Lovely,' Miss Kitty nodded. 'Pauly said he had something for me?'

'Oh I'm sorry,' Ben griped. 'Did we bring any ball gags back from Bonks?'

Just then Paul entered. 'Oh no, we never. Sorry.' Pauly went over to the central counter. 'But we did get you this. A Dutch thing! From Amsterdam-land.'

Ben eyed the box. 'No, Pauly…' then went wide-eyed, and with a facial colour to match the best pink latex, as Inspector Trent strode through the door.

'Right you lot.'

Oblivious as always, Paul popped the top of the box and was holding out to Miss Kitty, a quite towering windmill. With a blue plastic top. 'Here we are Miss Kitty. This'll look right nice in your dungeon. Just next to the spanking paddles and thumbscrews.'

'Oh Pauly,' Kitty said graciously. 'I don't really know what to say.'

'Oh no you don't, catwoman!' Trent darted forward, making a grab for the Amsterdam ornament.

'Oi gerroff!' Kitty protested, hanging on to her end. 'What do you think you're doing, Inspector nutcase.'

'Let go woman,' Trent shouted, as he grabbed the windmill base more fiercely.'

'Is like a tug of war in a hamster cage,' Katia commented to Toby, behind her counter. Toby nodded.

Ben, rooted to the spot, covered his eyes in horror.

Pauly tapped Trent on the shoulder. 'Mr Inspector. You should be careful, you know. There's valuable stuff that's valuable in there.'

'Pauly!' Ben shouted, in panic.

Distracted, Trent momentarily lost his purchase. Miss Kitty, putting her full dominatrix force behind her pull-power, fell backwards onto a pvc clad posterior. Bringing the plastic top with her.

'Oh sweet jesus mary, and all the saints, no!' Ben cried.

The shop went deathly quiet, as a shower of something sparkling dropped to the floor of Sex-x-x.

Pauly bent down to collect them. 'See? It's all the little silvery model people, and they all have something Dutchy. Like this one's a little clog. And this ones a tulippy daffodil. And this one's a tiny bicycle. With little wheels – look!' Pauly held up his elegant souvenirs.

Ben staggered against the centre display counter.

'You silly silly little man,' Miss Kitty spat at Trent. Look what you've done to Pauly's present. What's wrong with you?'

'Yiss, was not der nice to do that,' Katia joined in.

'Look you lot,' Trent protested. 'There's lots of things what come through Customs and shouldn't, right?'

Ben eyed Trent closely. 'Bad information, Trent?'

'Well, I...' Trent muttered.

'Yeah. Wonder how that could have happened...' Ben got hold of Trent by the shoulders and propelled him to the door. 'Time to go and work that out with a large gentleman, eh?'

Ben walked back in. 'Right, happy now everyone?'

'Yeh,' Pauly said from the floor. 'That's the good thing. You can't hurt plastic people.'

Ben bit his lip. He gave Pauly a look.

Allow the film camera to do a big close up of Ben's face.

Then focus in on his bloodshoot, despairing eyes. Filling the screen with an unspoken kaleidoscope of emotions. The slightly cracked windows to his troubled soul. Pathways to the whispered thought, pounding against the lattices of Ben's brain: 'Well if that's not Muff's windmill… then where the bloody hell is it?'

The shower of insanity was brightened by Paige and Raven running in. 'Pauly! You're OK!' Raven shouted, as she rushed over to cuddle him.

'Oh, yeh, I'm fine Raven love. Just sortin' these little Dutch people out.'

Paige strode, with steel backed determination over to Ben, a finger already wagging the air. 'Dover. I want a word with you.'

'Well at least somebody does.'

'Yeah, I…'. Paige stopped, as she took a glance at the bed. She peered more closely. Then she turned to her 3-d self image. 'What is that doing *there*?'

'You put it Paige, for de advertising,' Katia nodded.

'No I didn't.'

'Yeah loike, you did,' Toby nodded.

Ben began shrinking away from the shop floor.

'No: uh-uh,' Paige shook her head. 'I was standing over there.' She pointed to a spot by the leather goods rail.

'Ooh teleport-oration!' Pauly enthused. Seen that on the Mystery Channel. I didn't know you could do that Paigey.'

'Well no I can't. Which means that some perv has spent the night on my massage bed…

'Er dat is der yukkky,' Katia grimaced.

'Ahu…' Paige continued, every syllable grinding at her patience. 'And propped me up next to it, so he could…'

'I think I've fixed her back on the bicycle,' Pauly announced proudly.

'Yeah, something like that.' Paige caught Ben's disappearing act round the corner of the side door.

'Oi Dover! I've had it with you! Come here!' Paige broke into a chase after the elusive massage bed stainer.

'Hey she's got a fair turn of speed, all considerin,' Toby mused.

'You should see her next to a canal, love,' Raven commented.

'But I'm sorry. I think the tulip's still a bit bent,' came from the floor.

'All back to normal then, kids,' Miss Kitty announced.

Darkened, in a dank alley, Jez had Trent up against a wall, by his suit lapels. 'Wotcha mean, they wan't there?'

Trent struggled. 'Look, you wannabe mafia moron. I'm a Inspector. Put me down.'

Jez relented. Trent straightened his jacket. 'Look. I done the bust right? They was all there.' Trent poked Jez in the chest. 'But the sparklers weren't: alright?'

'So how do I know you ain't just wodged them somewhere, makin' it your lucky day?'

'Cos I'm bent and greedy. Not stupid. You'd have to have a death wish to cross Dirk Blank and his heavies.'

Jez's phone ruffled. He showed Trent the number. 'Put him on speaker,' Trent insisted. Jez sighed and thumbed the button. Blank's harsh voice filled the alleyway.

'So, where is my merchandise, little English-man?' Just around the corner, a slim woman, her blonde hair pulled back into a severe pony-tail, held her breath.

She checked the digital recorder was running on her phone.

She slipped a hand in the pocket of her mac, and prssed her palm around a badge, emblazoned with the word 'Polite', and a canal bridge.

The Light Bar was thronging. Good natured conversation rose through the smoke. Incongruously, a brand new yellow Lamborghini was parked outside.

Nadine and Jess appeared to be having an animated conversation, with much smiling.

They had swapped their traditional Dutch costumes, for very smart Chanel skirt suits. Nadine's in white, with gold buttons. Jess, in a pretty pink, with silver decorations.

A sign on the door read "Under New Management." Sitting prettily, in a window alcove, was a foot tall windmill statue. With a blue top.

\*   \*   \*

It is the quiet of night, in Soho.

Having cleared away a massage bed, after a good wipe-down, Pauly is showing Katia and Toby his new erotic venture.

'You see! I had the brainwavy while I were in this other shop.'

'Not one with special lights in the window, Pauly?' Katia checks.

'No, I weren't that keen on them,' Pauly replies. 'But, look, Toby's fetched me box from out back.'

'Yeah, here it is,' Toby confirms, patting a cardboard box on the centre counter.

'Right, so this is it. The big revelatory,' Pauly promises. 'Now, have you heard of Dutch Caps?'

'Of course,' Katia frowns. 'Is to use to stop de babies, yiss. So…?'

'Well then, that's just the thing in here in't it? I mean, we sells all the things to help people get all sexy together – in a nice way – and now we can sell the thing that stops that getting out of hand.'

'Yiss, I supposing,' Katia wonders.

'Right Toby!' Pauly rubb his hands with expectation. 'Get one out and pop it on.'

Toby does as instructed.

'See,' Pauly preened. 'Perfect fit.'

Katia had to admit that the flat headpiece, and brim, did look quite fetching. Especially with the double braid running around it.

Then, with the final loss of her Sex-x-x shop etiquette, she fell off her stool, with chronic, helpless, Katia giggles.

Pauly looked at the temporary Toby mannequin, with pride. While probably thinking about matching clogs.

'See? And that was my idea.'

\* \* \*

We would have run a lovely Credits sequence. With the theme song. Some blooper out-takes.[32] Maybe a bit of sponsorship from the Netherlands Tourist Information Office. And, some unfortunate people actually taking responsibility for the whole career-ending production.

### THAT WAS THE END OF SEX-X-X

### But the gang will return, exclusively, in the next 007 instalment: *Dr No, No No.*

---

[32] Yes, that was always going to be difficult to tell from the actual movie scenes

*SEX-X-X: The Movie*

| | |
|---|---|
| Blofeld | Ben Dover |
| M | Pauly |
| Moneypenny | Katia |
| Q | Toby |

*If you have enjoyed reading this novelisation, then you should definitely seek urgent psychiatric evaluation.*

*If, on the other hand, you didn't, then you'll be glad to know that there probably won't ever be another one.*